HEAD START ON MURDER

It took many seconds for the sight to penetrate my mind, and when it did I turned around in horrible sick blindness.

The room was large and square, and at the end of the room was a large divan. A man had fallen forward on the carpet before the divan in a kneeling position. The fingers of his hand were outspread as if he were about to spring forward.

But the man had no head.

The head stood upright on its neck on the carpet in the center of the room. It showed white eyeballs, and gaped at us with an open mouth. A breeze blew through the open window and ruffled the hair with a slow and lifelike sway. . . .

Mysteries from the
Masters of Suspense

By Sax Rohmer

DAUGHTER OF FU MANCHU	(1818, $3.50)
THE DRUMS OF FU MANCHU	(1617, $3.50)
THE INSIDIOUS DR. FU MANCHU	(1668, $3.50)
THE TRAIL OF FU MANCHU	(1619, $3.50)
SHADOW OF FU MANCHU	(1870, $3.50)

By John Dickson Carr

THE MAN WHO COULD NOT SHUDDER	(1703, $3.50)
THE PROBLEM OF THE WIRE CAGE	(1702, $3.50)
THE EIGHT OF SWORDS	(1881, $3.50)

Available wherever paperbacks are sold, or order direct from the Publisher. Send cover price plus 50¢ per copy for mailing and handling to Zebra Books, Dept. 1931, 475 Park Avenue South, New York, N.Y. 10016. Residents of New York, New Jersey and Pennsylvania must include sales tax. DO NOT SEND CASH.

JOHN DICKSON CARR

IT WALKS BY NIGHT

ZEBRA BOOKS
KENSINGTON PUBLISHING CORP.

ZEBRA BOOKS

are published by

Kensington Publishing Corp.
475 Park Avenue South
New York, NY 10016

First printing: November 1986

Printed in the United States of America

TO
WOODA NICOLAS
AND
JULIA CARR

CONTENTS

I. THE PATRON OF GRAVEDIGGERS—11
II. IT WALKS BY NIGHT—25
III. THE HEAD THAT LAY UNDER THE LAMP—38
IV. WE DETERMINE THE POSITION OF THE PUPPETS—49
V. "ALICE IN WONDERLAND"—64
VI. IN THE BLACK PARLOURS—78
VII. AN APPOINTMENT WITH THE WORMS—89
VIII. "WE TALKED OF POE"—99
IX. THE SHADOW OF THE MURDERER—114
X. BENCOLIN WEAVES—128
XI. SWORDPLAY—140
XII. A HAND IS MOTIONLESS BENEATH THE CYPRESS—153
XIII. DEATH AT VERSAILLES—166
XIV. "THE SILVER MASK"—180
XV. WHEN THE WALL FELL—193
XVI. HOW A MAN SPOKE FROM A COFFIN—205
XVII. WE HEAR THE NAME OF THE KILLER—219
XVIII. THE LAST BATTLE—226
XIX. THE HOUR OF TRIUMPH—239

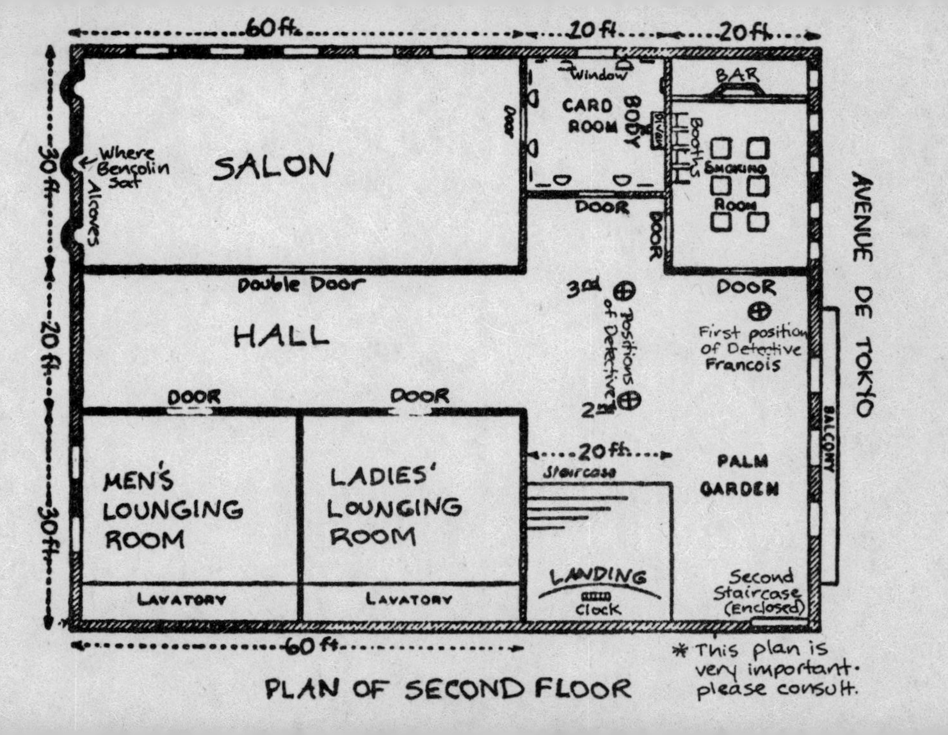

PLAN OF SECOND FLOOR

I. The Patron of Gravediggers

". . . and not least foul among these night-monsters (which may be found even in our pleasant land of France) is a certain shape of evil hue which by day may not be recognized, inasmuch as it may be a man of favoured looks, or a fair and smiling woman; but by night becomes a misshapen beast with blood-bedabbled claws. So I say to you, even you who live in the city of Paris, when your fire burns low by night, and you hear a gentle tapping of fingers at the window-pane, do not open your door to this supposed traveller, who . . ."

The meaning resolved itself out of the queer and crabbed French which Archbishop Batognolles of Rouen had written in the middle of the fifteenth century. Bencolin had sent me the book that afternoon, and it lay open on my bureau while I was dressing for dinner. From among a litter of brushes and collar-studs the eerie words shaped themselves suggestively, for Bencolin had written in the note that accompanied it, "This book was found in Laurent's possession, and this is the sort of man Laurent is."

At eight o'clock of an April evening in Paris on the very stroke of the clock, with the opening of that book, these events began. I had come up from Nice in response to a wire from Bencolin saying merely that there was danger ahead, and was I interested?—to which I wired back, "Yes," without knowing what he meant. As yet I knew nothing about the man who was to murder the Duc de Saligny, and to walk through our dreams with his sly and grisly smile.

But I knew that there were to be ugly things in the future when Bencolin rang my door-bell at nine. Something was behind the constraint in his manner; he sat across the table from me in the drawing-room, and while I listened to his grave, courtly voice I wondered, as one is always tempted to wonder about the man. Your first impression (and others have agreed with me in this) was one of liking and respect. You felt that you could tell him anything, however foolish it sounded, and he would be neither surprised nor inclined to laugh at you. Then you studied the face, turned partly sideways—the droop of the eyelids, at once quizzical and tolerant, under hooked eyebrows, and the dark veiled light of the eyes themselves. The nose was thin and aquiline, with deep lines running down past his mouth. A faint smile was lost in a small moustache and pointed black beard—the black hair, parted in the middle and twirled up like horns, had begun to turn grey. Over the white tie and white shirtfront, it was a head from the renaissance in the low light of the lamps. He rarely gestured when he spoke, except to shrug his shoulders, and he never raised his voice; but whenever you were in this man's company in public you felt uncomfortably conspicuous. This, then, was M. Henri

Bencolin, who at that time was *juge d'instruction*, the adviser of the courts, and the director of the police.

I have known him all my life, for he was my father's best friend when the two were at college in America. When I was very young he used to visit us every year, bringing me toys from the boulevards and telling me the most delightful hair-raising stories. But I never understood his knowledge or his position until I came to live in his own city. In his hands a thousand facets came glittering out of the revolving jewel of Paris—lights and shadows, perfume and danger—the *salon*, the greenroom, the pits—abbey, brothel, and guillotine, a Babylonian carnival through which he walked in the name of the prefecture. The twirled hair, the pointed beard, the wrinkled eyes, and the inscrutable smile were known wherever he chose to go; whatever happened, his expression was always that of one meditating over a glass of wine. He sat alone in his office, with his fingers on all Paris as on a map. A finger moved across lights and grey squares, up streets, and paused at a house; he said a few words into the telephone at his elbow, and on the instant the police trap snapped like a deadfall. Even so, I had never accompanied him on an investigation until this night of April 23, 1927, when we were united in pursuit of the murderer Laurent.

The high lamps were blooming out over Paris as we went down the stairs to my car. He stopped in the doorway to light a cigar, and he stood for a moment looking up and down the blue-shadowed street—a tall figure silhouetted against the light of the tall doorway, cloak flung over his shoulder, leaning on his silver-headed stick. Then he said:

"There is a man in the greatest danger of his life. It is no part of my work to oversee his protection, except that he appealed to me personally. . . .

"Raoul de Saligny!" he muttered, after a pause. "The athlete, the *beau sabreur*, the popular idol!—it is grotesque. A trifle too loud and back-slapping for my taste, Saligny, but a good sort. Well, you shall hear about it later. Let's have dinner now; then we are going to Fenelli's."

During dinner at Les Ambassadeurs, he said no more, except some reference to danger from werewolves. That one word, "werewolves," spoken of as threatening Raoul Jourdain, sixth Duc de Saligny, added to a growing sense that even Bencolin was more than a little disturbed. I could not keep my mind on the meal for trying to place some elusive memory—a newspaper item, or possibly a bit of *salon* gossip—connecting Saligny with some horror. The trouble was that the man's doings were too widely chronicled.

It was always, "The Duc de Saligny is expected to give Lacoste a strong fight in the semi-finals at Wimbledon tomorrow," or how he had knocked out some light-heavyweight in an amateur bout; he shot and rode and fenced with such uniform triumph, he was photographed so much, that he grew to be an almost unbelievable legend. He was a great unlettered aristocrat, of childlike charm, blond and jovial and eager. I did not know the man personally, though I fenced with him once in Maître Terlin's *salle d'armes* off the Étoile. He was a smooth, steel-spring opponent, with eyes as inscrutable as those of an ox, a guard slippery and powerful, and a number of startling tricks from the Italian school. He ran over seven touches in half as many minutes. Then he tossed back his yellow mane, let out a gust of laughter, and strutted round the *salle*, flipping up his foil and catching it like a pleased child.

Bencolin and I had finished our dinner before I remembered. Saligny was to be married, or perhaps had been married; I had paid little attention to the newspapers in Nice for the past few weeks, but some mean little piece of comment in connection with it came back in an ugly echo. "The bride is beautiful," one of my friends had said, "and at least *this* husband knows that razors should be used only for shaving."

It was eleven-ten when we left Les Ambassadeurs to set out for Fenelli's. This Fenelli's, off the Quai de Tokyo, was then the latest tourist restaurant which attempted to carry out the illusion of being exclusive—a combination restaurant and "dancing." Beyond a wall on the hill across the lighted river, it reared three floors of grey stone and shuttered windows at the corner of the rue des Eaux. To further the illusion, M. Fenelli sent out engraved cards as the only means, theoretically, of allowing one to lose money in the roulette-rooms upstairs. The street was full of automobiles when we went through the iron gates in the wall and up the walk to the front door. One entered through a tall marble lobby, on the right of which was a dining-room and on the left an American bar, frequented by a notorious and noisy crowd. The place was all aglitter with skeins of lights, and the throng had the lopsided look of the bright blatant decorations on the walls, with a jazz band from the dining-room blasting through the glare. Bencolin did not stop downstairs. He led the way under the lofty lights of the foyer towards a marble staircase at the back.

Still he had said nothing about our mission. He was looking for somebody in the throng; finally he saw his man, who was sitting on a chair near the door to the bar and looking very bewildered.

He was a huge man, bulging out of seedy clothes. On his vast head, which hung forward between his shoulders, the bronze hair was cropped close to the skull, except where it stood up bristling in a straight line across his forehead. His skin was ruddy, and he wore square spectacles through which pale-blue eyes peered in a naïvely intent stare. When he spoke, his big bronze moustache blew out over a slow-moving jaw buried in his collar. He kept clasping and unclasping his hands, shifting his shoulders, and peering from right to left with near-sighted abstraction. Thus he sat while Bencolin introduced us, the *juge d'instruction* shouting in his ear above the din, and the man nodding with slow emphasis before he raised his pale eyes and grunted.

This was my introduction to Dr. Hugo Grafenstein, head of his own clinic of psychiatry and neurology at the University of Vienna. He spoke French with a strong accent, but very fluently, and as we all started upstairs he was arguing with violence against Bencolin's choice of a meeting-place.—Bencolin turned, and nodded slightly. I saw two men come out of the bar and close in behind us.

At the top of the staircase a uniformed attendant demanded our cards. We were in a long marble hallway, floored with red carpet, and from the double doors of a *salon* facing the rue des Eaux came the sound of many voices. We stopped on the threshold of this room, where Bencolin scanned the occupants. It was a room sixty-odd feet long, panelled in dark wood and lighted by three crystal chandeliers from the tall ceiling. Opposite the double-doors by which we entered, a line of curtained windows overlooked the street. In the far wall to our left were a number of curtained alcoves where drinks were served; and in the fourth wall of the oblong, at our right, a small door. Roulette tables were in play under the three white-glittering chandeliers. The marble floor held echoes of the merest whisper. Voices rose like a mist, mutterings and low laughter, the rattle of a rake among the chips, the scuff of felt-shod chairs. The players hung about the tables, peering over one another's shoulders, bending tense across backs, whispering in each other's ears. The croupier's voice sang shrilly:

"Le jeu est fait, 'sieurs et dames; rien ne va plus."

They became so still that anywhere in the room you could hear the ball ticking about in the wheel; they froze with motionless raised eyebrows and craned necks. The bored voice chanted:

"Vingt-deux, noir, 'sieurs et dames . . ."

A woman laughed. One man got up from the table stiffly, with an impassive face. He made a defiant gesture at lighting a cigarette, but the flames of the briquet wabbled in his hand. He smiled in a sickly way, and his face glistened as he glanced from side to side. I heard the booming of an English voice, swearing triumphantly. For a moment the tension lifted, and all the air of the room flowed back—perfume and cigarette smoke, powder, jingle of bracelets, clacking footfalls, and once more these people burst into talk. . . . It was a gaudy crowd, bright of plumage, excitable, and bold-eyed, as though everybody were slightly tipsy, and when people turned to look they stared at you with great intensity. The harsh light showed worn places on faces and furniture. The harsh band-clatter beat up from downstairs, mixed with a hum as of fans and the clinking of glasses; all the house seemed to be strung on thin wires of hysteria.

"Our point of vantage," said Bencolin, "will be one of those alcoves."

The alcove in which we installed ourselves was a semicircular padded seat with a round table in the centre, partly cut off by curtains from the *salon*. A rose lamp hung above the table, behind which Bencolin sat down facing the long room, with Grafenstein and I on either side of him. Your eye ran out a tremendous distance over that chattering throng, which we saw now from the narrow side of the oblong. Bencolin had taken out a cigar and was turning it over in his fingers, studying the crowd with blank eyes. We were silent while an attendant brought a tray of cocktails. Dr. Grafenstein tasted his drink and made a gesture of repugnance; then he began pushing his glass aimlessly back and forth on the table.

"Pah! That nonsense out there; I hate it!" said the big Austrian, with sudden vigour. "And this cocktail—" The glass was tiny in his hand; his slow eyes blinked at it in contempt, and he seemed to meditate crushing it in his fingers. Presently he looked at Bencolin over his spectacles.

"I came with you because you said something about a case in my line of work. *Hein?*"

Bencolin lighted the cigar and blew out the match thoughtfully.

"Yes. I am bothered by a point very much in your line, and I wanted to take advantage of a visiting specialist, Doctor. I have promised my young friend here that he shall see me in action. I begin by consulting advice."

"Well?"

"The Duc de Saligny, whom you are likely to see here tonight, is wealthy, good-looking, and still young," continued Bencolin. "He was married today to a very charming young woman. There, you would say, is the perfect cinema romance. Both of them are here this evening, I learn."

Grafenstein grunted. "In *my* day," he said, "we went on wedding trips. We were not so casual. That is bad, Bencolin. The effect on the mind—"

"To the modern marriage," mused Bencolin, "there seems to be something slightly indecent about privacy. You must act in public as though you had been married twenty years, and in private as though you had not been married at all. That, however, is not my affair. There is a deeper reason for this casualness. . . . Has either of you ever heard of the bride?"

Grafenstein muttered, "I do not see—" and shifted restlessly.

"She was Madame Louise Laurent. Four years ago she was married to a certain man named Alexandre Laurent. Shortly afterwards, her husband was committed to an asylum for the criminally insane."

"Ach!" cried Grafenstein, striking the table. "You do not mean the Alexandre Laurent *I* examined?"

"Your favourite case, I believe, Doctor. It seems to me that I remember your writing several learned treatises about him."

The doctor eagerly adjusted his spectacles and settled himself to spreading gestures. "M. Laurent, yes! Of course I remember. What did you want to know about him?"

"Just talk, if you don't mind. I am searching for inspiration."

"Well, I thought to myself," said Grafenstein, "here is a pure case of hyperaesthesia; of lust-murder. But I had never known of a case in which the patient attempted lust-murder on his wife. This M. Laurent, shortly after his marriage, had attacked madame—with a razor, I believe. Fortunately, she was possessed of unusual strength; she eluded him and locked him in a room until help could be summoned."

He had drawn some envelopes from his pocket, and a stylo. As he checked off each point he would write down some lengthy word, with a careful period after each. Bencolin was watching the smoke-rings curl out of his mouth.

"It was in Tours, where I happened to be visiting, and they called me in to see him. It was astonishing. His brain was perfectly clear, his mood calm and pleasant. I found no cerebral disease—he seemed slightly amused at this—but there were traces of hereditary epilepsy. No physical defects, except a slight weakness of the eyes, due to overstudy. The man was tall and well formed, with no signs of anatomical degeneration; he evinced disgust at the idea. He wore a short brown beard and eyeglasses; the eyes were brown and mild, but very penetrating. The whole face was of an absolute dead pallor, and the eyes acquired a singularly wide, fixed prominence.

"He was one of the most accomplished linguists I

have ever met. He spoke German perfectly, without any accent. 'I can explain my own case,' he said to me—no emotion at all! 'But if there is an association in my mind with lust and murder, I am unaware of it. I do not think it is due to an inherited taint. Very probably it is my reading.' "

Dr. Grafenstein spoke slowly, groping after each word:

" 'An exaggerated tension of the nervous system,' Laurent said. 'Since I was eleven years old—I was precocious as a child, if that helps you—I have been reading along one line. Scherr, Friedreich, Dessoir, on the licence of the Middle Ages; Suetonius, Friedlander on what they call the "depravity" of Rome (and you know Wiedemeister's *Der Casarenwahsinn*?); particularly the Borgia chronicles, the Marquis de Sade; Upminsing's *La Vie de Gilles de Rais*—' " Grafenstein paused. "I am sorry; I cannot remember offhand all the works he cited. I remember that he had a fondness for the imaginative writers: Baudelaire, De Quincey, Poe, the latter two of whom he read in English with as much ease as he read German.

" 'It comes over me,' he said, 'sometimes as an impulse, often as a slow process of thought, that there would be pleasure in seeing blood—the blood of man, woman, or beast. There are no lustful feelings. It is as though I were starved, and to kill would feed me; or say, rather, the sensation one gets from regarding a work of art. It is very powerful.'

"Ach, you should have seen him! He was sitting with his hands on his knees, on a little white chair under a drop-lamp. He smiled at me. As he talked, his eyes widened tremendously and his smile grew broad. His hands were very soft and white, as white as his face, and his brown beard, though neatly trimmed, was ragged, as though it were moth-eaten.

" 'I often kill,' he said to me. 'This is the first time you have known it. I love my wife very much, so much I wanted to kill her. You know the legend of the *loup-garou*, the werewolf? . . . There were some sheep in a meadow outside Tours not long ago, *Herr Doktor.* I killed one of them, and then I fancied it would be nice to kill the wife of the farmer who lived there. I have a way of getting into houses, *Herr Doktor*, which nobody knows but myself. That night I tapped on the window-pane and beckoned to this woman, but she refused to come out; I think she was frightened by the blood on my mouth. But I was tired, and so I let her alone.'

"Often he would twitch his shoulders, as with some nervous malady, and once he touched my arm. Usually he sat quiet, with that silky brown beard, and the smile, and the wide eyes behind his spectacles.

"Ach, yes! another thing I remember made an impression on me. He said, 'They're going to shut me up, friend. They'd better not, because they can't keep me there. You know that lovely line, "Oh, whistle and I'll come to you, lad!" Tell them to remember that, won't you?' "

The big Austrian, whose precision of detail had created a ghastly picture, completed his notes and sat back.

"He said that, did he?" asked Bencolin, after a pause. "Well, Doctor, I will take up the story, because I think you will be interested.

"I was not present at the trial. My entire information comes from the *Gazette des Tribunaux*, but it is fairly complete. He comes of a good family, and has some relatives now in Tours. He is wealthy in his own right, and so he was sent to a private asylum there. Ten months ago—in August of last year—he escaped.

"Now, when it is too late, we have traced his movements. He went to your own city, Doctor—to Vienna. There he put himself under the care of Doctor Rothswold. . . ."

Grafenstein uttered an exclamation.

"This Doctor Rothswold, I may explain," Bencolin said to me, "was part genius and part quack; but he was known as the criminal's surgeon."

Grafenstein said, very slowly, "Rothswold was murdered nearly a month ago."

"So I hear. It takes the police of Paris to tell you that Laurent killed him."

"Rothswold specialized in plastic surgery," said Grafenstein. "I suppose that's your link?"

"Yes. In what way he was altering himself there we do not know. The Viennese police have the testimony of Rothswold's nurse; this nurse knew that a patient had come there, and that something was being done to his face, but she never saw Laurent. Rothswold administered the anaesthetic himself, and, while the nurse attended to the liquid-feeding in the first stages, the patient's face was swathed in bandages."

Past Bencolin's Satanic countenance drifted the smoke of his motionless cigar. He had never raised his voice, and his eyes were fixed on the crowd. But now there was a thrill in the way he spoke, a clenching of his fingers and a tensity of stare.

"For a man of imagination, what a Grand Guignol picture! Rothswold's home, a cottage in the shadow of the poplars off the Kirchofstrasse, with a low lamp in the surgery window. . . . Laurent left the cottage on the night of the seventh of last March. A policeman saw somebody coming out of Rothswold's gate, carrying two valises, and this man bade the officer good evening as he passed, and continued down the street, whistling cheerfully. . . . Later in the night a neighbour phoned in a complaint that the cats were setting up an infernal yowl in Rothswold's yard.

"There was still a light in the surgery. They found Rothswold's head looking out from one of his own jars of alcohol on a shelf, but there was no trace of the body."

It seemed to me that the voices out there in the *salon* had grown more shrill, gestures more elaborate, the lights hard and cold. Bencolin let his cigar fall into the ash-tray and drained his cocktail glass; he seemed entirely unaware of the tinny beat of noise. With slow nods of his head, Grafenstein was shifting and tapping his fingers tips together. It was, I suppose, nothing new to them.

"Laurent is now in Paris," said the detective, shrugging.

II. It Walks By Night

"I am struck with that statement of his, 'I have ways of getting into houses, which nobody knows but myself,' " Bencolin went on. "I do not think that we of the police are dunderheads, yet how have we contrived to miss him? . . . No, let us get the story in order. We now shift back to a time over two years ago, when Laurent was safe in the asylum. His wife moved to Paris—the marriage, of course, was annulled—and she was living alone, on a small income of her own, and staying away from people. She had been through a tremendous nervous ordeal, that woman, so much so that she had a horror of all men." Again the detective shrugged. "But what will you? Let your psychology explain her attraction to M. le Duc de Saligny, who swaggered past, preened, and conquered."

He was silent a moment, looking thoughtfully at his glass.

"No matter; their engagement was announced in January of last year. In August, as I have said, this Laurent escaped. He must have known of that engagement, for it was widely chronicled.

"She was terrified. The ex-husband had timed his

escape as a gentle warning to remain faithful to his amorousness with a razor. She postponed the wedding until he should be captured. Well, he was not captured!—our swashbuckling Saligny was as patient as possible, but he would not wait forever. Even a fall from a horse could not damp his ardour. The wedding was arranged. . . ."

Bencolin leaned across the table.

"Two days ago Laurent sent a letter to M. le duc. It said, simply, 'It will not be best to marry her. I am watching. I have put myself close to you, but you do not know it.' Messieurs, explain that in any way you like. I am simply stating facts; I reserve my conclusions for my reports to the court.

"The Duc de Saligny brought me this note, when I had just finished tracing Laurent from Doctor Rothswold's, and I was able to tell him that it was no crank letter. The note was actually written by Laurent; we had specimens of his handwriting forwarded from Tours. Saligny is excitable, and I think he was frightened. Yes, he would go through with the marriage immediately, and so would Louise. But you will see that he longs for public places now, until my men can step out and lay their hands on Laurent."

Grafenstein cleared his throat.

"Still, I cannot see that it interests me," he argued, gruffly. "I am not a detective. Crime in the course of being traced is not interesting; love of God, no!" He snapped his big fingers, and moved about with walrus-like motions.

"No?" said Bencolin, frowning. "Well, if a psychiatrist does not see the point that glares out at us, how should I? But it bothers me."

He put his head down in his hands, elbows on the table, and knocked against his temples in irritation. Presently the puckered face was raised again. I said:

"Pleasant honeymoon!—trailed everywhere by the police. How does madame la duchesse take all this?"

"I can fancy only a few ways by which Laurent could have got across the French border. . . ." Bencolin was musing, when he drew himself up and realized my question. "Madame? You shall see for yourself. Here she comes now. . . . You notice? Where's her husband, I wonder? I've been looking for them all evening, and I know they're here."

She was walking slowly towards the alcove. Her hair was very black and glossy, and she wore it parted and drawn low over her ears, so that it contrasted with expressionless eyes. These eyes had a cold shine, dark, unmoving, under thin-arched brows. There was also a contrast between the straight nose and the full sensuality of the lips, which were moist pink in a faint smile against the pallor of the face. As she saw us the eyes widened suddenly, with a glimpse of depths, and then her eyelids drooped in speculative appraisal. . . . Her white shoulders moved above a black silk gown; one hand was vaguely twisting a rope of pearls. There was a little silver anklet under the grey stocking. You sensed a hard shell over this suppleness, like defensive armour.

She came straight up to Bencolin. When he rose to bend across the table over her hand, she was negligent, but, closer, you could see shadows hollowed beneath the eyes. Bencolin introduced us, and added: "Friends of mine. You may speak freely."

She looked at us in turn, slowly, and I had a sense of

veils being drawn away. It was a look of scrutiny, not unmixed with suspicion.

"You are affiliated with the police, messieurs?" she asked. It was a voice well modulated, yet one that ran the scale in shrill unevenness. "You know—?"

With true Teutonic thoroughness, Grafenstein seemed about to assure her that he had made a special study of her first husband, omitting no gory detail; Bencolin interposed: "Of course; they are here to assist me. Won't you sit down?"

She sat down, refused one of my cigarettes, and took her own from a little wrist-bag. Leaning back, she inhaled deeply. Under the red-shaded lamp I could see that her hand was trembling. On her left hand, as she moved it across her forehead brusquely, the wedding ring shone with a sudden lustre.

"Monsieur le duc is here?" Bencolin asked.

"Raoul? Yes. Raoul is getting nerves," she answered, and laughed shrilly. "I don't blame him, though. It's not a pleasant thing, this. I keep thinking I see Laurent. Yes, *I'll* mention the name, if none of you will—!"

Bencolin gently raised his hand. She shivered, looked slowly out across the *salon,* and then said, "There goes Raoul now, into the card-room."

She nodded towards the small door at the far end of the room, through which a broad back was disappearing; then the door closed. I saw no more than that, for I happened to be looking at my wrist-watch. I looked at it twice, absently, before I noted that the hour was eleven-thirty.

"Orange blossoms!" she said, laughing again. "Orange blossoms, lace veils. A lovely wedding, lovely bride, with even the clergyman looking at us and wondering if there were a madman in the church. You know, once when I was looking at him, I thought it was Laurent marrying us; wouldn't *that* have been a joke?—he could have played priest very well. Orange blossoms, 'till death do you part!' Death—very possibly."

This was sheer growing hysteria. The sights and sounds of the casino blended in with it; the jazz band beat tin cymbals, the bawling voice of the croupier sang over noisy crowd and singing wheel. Louise, Duchesse de Saligny, said, abruptly:

"M. Bencolin, I did see Laurent this afternoon."

Nobody said anything, but Grafenstein dropped his stylo. Both the doctor and I glanced at the *juge d'instruction,* who was smoking placidly. He pursed his lips, nodded, and asked:

"You are quite sure, madame?"

"M. Kilard—that is Raoul's lawyer—entertained for us this afternoon. We were to have dinner there later, and then come on here. There were many people in the house. There was noise. I drank, to forget."

She spoke slowly, as though she were turning over in her mind the memory of the afternoon and finding it incredible. The eyes were strained and intent. Studying her sideways, I thought that there was a queer yellowish tinge round the pupils.

"It grew darker in the afternoon, and they said, 'Showers,' but we could hear only the thunder. They danced, and drank, and people would come past and nudge us; it was horrible, that." Her shoulders lifted in disdain. "Now, listen. At seven I went upstairs to dress. It was in Madame Kilard's room, and her maid was helping me. It was very dark outside; I could still hear the thunder. . . .

"There were little rose lamps burning—like that one. (Please, monsieur, understand that I am telling you the simple truth!) I had finished dressing, and I was standing looking into the mirror of the dressing-table, and I wondered to myself . . . It does not matter. Presently there was a knock on the door. There were Raoul and M. Vautrelle—M. Vautrelle is a great friend of Raoul's—to take me downstairs. I had dismissed the maid. I found I had left my wrist-bag on the washstand in the bathroom. . . ."

Her cigarette had gone out; she looked at it in a strange, shuddering fashion, and then dropped it into the ash-tray.

"It was so homelike there, with the lamps, and I could here a piano playing downstairs. But how can I make you"—she gestured—"how can I make you understand that it was terrible? Every once in a while you could see the lightning through the windows.

"I remember just how it happened. Raoul and M. Vautrelle were standing by a table over in the middle of the room, and they were laughing . . . ah yes; that was it! . . . and Raoul was turning over the pages of a magazine. . . . I went over to the bathroom, which opens off the boudoir, to get my wrist-bag. The lights were off there. When I opened the door, all I could see was a blur of white tile, light and gloomy. There was a window with coloured glass. Then I heard the thunder; it frightened me. . . . The lightning flashed through the window, all of a sudden, and I saw Laurent standing there, grinning at me."

She seized Bencolin's arm; she was now all of an

unnatural brightness and quick breathing.

"He was standing there very shadowy, with that queer lightning through the window on one side of him, and his head partly turned to the side, too. I could see him smile. He had one hand hanging in the air, and when he grinned at me he opened his fingers and let something drop with a metallic ring on the tile. . . . Then it was dark."

Louise de Saligny sat back and searched our faces. But when memory went, the masklike expression settled back, in stoicism or cool pride; you became conscious again of the inscrutable black eyes under drooped lids, the faint smile, the languorous warmth of her body reclining with one arm along the cushions. She flipped her fingers and shrugged; an impish gleam came into her look, and her next remark gave one a sudden chill:

"Very artistic of my cracked first husband, *hein*?"

It was like a hard iron clang of gates. Bencolin enquired, calmly:

"What happened then?"

"Oh, I suppose I must have screamed; it was the proper gesture, don't you think? Raoul and M. Vautrelle came at a run. They turned on the lights and searched the bathroom. . . ." She paused. "Well, although you may not believe it, there was nobody there."

"He went out another door, then?"

"There were no other doors except the one by which I entered. I tell you he had gone. The window was locked on the inside."

Grafenstein, who had been listening with elephantine attention, now nodded ponderously and made another note.

"It is easy of explanation, madame," said the Austrian. "Your conscious mind had been forcing to the background the image of this man; but all suggestions which have been made tended to create the image. You mention the lamp and the mirrors. It may even be a case of self-hypnosis, induced by those bright surfaces. The metallic sound, of course, was the result of your association of Laurent with a ra—"

"I have already told you," she snapped, "that it was not an hallucination. I saw him as plainly as I see you now. He was gone. They looked everywhere. I told them, afterwards, that I must have been mistaken; I didn't want to disturb Raoul. But I was not mistaken. Oh, you will not believe me; very well!"

Gathering up his envelopes, the big Austrian blinked paternally over his spectacles and smiled. He sat back in complacence, with his big hands folded.

"Ah, well," said Bencolin, shrugging, "we may easily settle that. What was the object which this caller dropped on the floor?"

"It was a trowel," replied the woman, whimsically. "A gardener's trowel. I remember M. Vautrelle picked it up and said: 'Good Lord! Queer thing to keep in a bathroom.' "

There was a startled silence. Bencolin burst out laughing. Suddenly he checked himself, and said, soberly:

"I beg madame's pardon. I did not consider the matter at all comic, but I usually find that the ridiculous is not very far removed from black fear." He clucked his tongue. "Well, Doctor, does your psychology attribute a phallic significance to a trowel, I wonder?"

"Madame is joking," Grafenstein observed, rather violently. "I do not care for jokes. I do not care to be insulted. She tells us an impossible story, which we in my profession can always explain; husbands—razors, it is perfectly clear. Then she tries to substantiate it by an insult—"

Madame's head was thrown back. The light lay along her white throat and glossy hair. An expression of weariness and pain crept up from her mouth. Sitting up abruptly, she said:

"I have been through much, more than you would understand. Once I loved Laurent. Now I hate him so terribly—" She looked down at her tense and hooked hands, and said, with a fierce clarity: "Has a person no right to happiness? Must your dirty God hound a person even in His own church? Jokes! I do not make jokes; I hate them. . . . You can find the trowel, monsieur, if you care to go to M. Kilard's home. I remember M. Vautrelle inanely putting it away in the medicine-chest."

A new voice said, "Pardon?" and I almost jumped. A man had come up to the alcove. He was looking at us enquiringly, with one hand on the curtain.

"Your pardon if I'm intruding," he observed. "Louise, I don't believe I know—!"

She nodded towards us, quite self-possessed again. "Oh yes! These are gentlemen from the police, Edouard. Allow me to present M. Edouard Vautrelle."

Vautrelle bowed. He was a tall man, with waved blond hair, and an eye aggressively hypnotic. Wide nostrils flared above a narrow moustache. The face was lined in wrinkles, and smelt of astringents; his bow suggested the soldier and the corset. There was a sort of heavy poise about the way he toyed with a monocle on a black ribbon.

"Very happy," he murmured, and hesitated.

Bencolin mentioned the weather. I noticed that in acknowledging the introduction he had not even looked at Vautrelle. He was sitting bolt upright, and ever since he had seen the Duc de Saligny go through that far door into the card-room he had not moved his eyes from the door. He added, still with that gaze of intense speculation on the card-room door:

"Madame, even though you suffered an hallucination, how did you recognize Laurent? Was his appearance changed? We have reason to think so."

"I don't know! It was an impression—I just saw him in that half-light. Certain gestures, the way he opened his eyes. . . . I don't know! *I* could not be deceived if I saw him—"

Vautrelle smiled sourly, and said with deprecating petulance:

"Oh, come! Why encourage this brooding, monsieur? You all act as though you were afraid of this man. I've seen half a dozen minions of the law hanging about this place. Ridiculous, all this fuss! . . . Louise, Raoul's gone to the card-room," he added, abruptly. "He's been drinking too much. I think you'd better see him. Or let's play the wheel awhile, if you prefer. Do something."

"That music—" she snapped; "damn that music! I can't stand it! I won't stand it! Why must they play the same thing for half an hour—the same thing—?"

"Doucement, doucement!" urged Vautrelle, and looked round in a nervous way. For a second the man seemed

frightened; but he smiled at us with inflexible assurance. Then, in easy stages and with many apologetic nods, he began to get madame out of the alcove. She seemed to have forgotten our existence.

Bencolin reached over and picked up the cigarette-stub she had left in the ash-tray, but he did not remove his gaze from that door at the far end of the room. Madame and Vautrelle were in the centre of the *salon,* directly under one of the large chandeliers, and Grafenstein was saying, grimly: "There, you've got it! Now you'll understand why I said what I did," when all our movements were stopped.

We all heard the crash of breaking glass, and saw the white-coated steward leaning against the door of the card-room. He had let fall his tray of cocktails, and he was staring stupidly at the wreckage.

Everyone turned to look. With the cessation of voices, the jazz band had stopped, too. The proprietor, his fat stomach wabbling, was hurrying across the room. But most distinctly emerged the drawn, shiny face of the servant, who had seen something, and was desperately afraid.

Can I make clear a horrible emotion without a name, a sort of cold, sick shock that smote all of us in the alcove? It was momentary, but it stamped every detail into the brain. Voices had died away thinly, so that you heard a roulette counter fall on the floor with a click against the quiet. The heads turned ghoulishly, the surprised faces, the croupier glancing up in irritation, the giggle of some schoolgirl; but in all the *salon* there was no movement.

Bencolin rose very slowly, knocking over his glass with a tiny clatter. I can see him yet standing over the mahogany table, outlined against the back of the alcove under the pink-shaded lamp. His knuckles supported his weight. The light over him turned his face to a devilish and inhuman mask. The black eyebrows slanted and hooked down over gleaming eyes; the thin, cruel lines going down from shadowed cheek-bones past small moustache and pointed beard, the parted hair twirled up like horns. . . . "Don't hurry," he said, mechanically. "Follow me, you two; but don't hurry."

The laughter had started again; they were returning to their tables with a shrug. The three of us moved casually across the room, pushing among them. From the corner of my eye I could see one of the tables with the numbers, silk and broadcloth pressing against it, even the glitter of the silver pivot in the wheel. One blazing chandelier passed over our heads, two, three—then we reached the door of the card-room. Bencolin extended in his hand, for the manager's gaze, the little card with the circle, the eagle, and the three words, "prefecture of police." Grafenstein and I followed him through the door.

It took many seconds for that sight inside to penetrate my mind fully. When it did so, I turned round and bumped into the manager in horrible sick blindness. . . . The room was large and square, with walls of stamped leather in dull red. Old shields and weapons were hung against them, emerging with a poisonous colour of copper in a low reddish light; but the blades of these weapons showed thin bright lines of sharpness. At the end of the room opposite us was a large divan. Beside it was an inlaid table on which burned a lamp of red glass. A man had fallen forward on the red carpet before the divan. The fingers of his hands were outspread, as though he were about to spring forward—he was squashed against the carpet in a kneeling position. But the man had no head. Instead there was a bloody neck stump propped against the floor.

The head itself stood in the centre of the red carpet, upright on its neck; it showed white eyeballs, and gaped at us with open mouth in the low red light. A breeze blew through the open window in the wall at our left, and ruffled the hair with a slow and lifelike sway.

III. The Head That Lay Under the Lamp

With the utmost coolness, Bencolin turned to the manager:

"Two of my men are on guard downstairs. Summon them; all the doors are to be locked, and nobody must leave. Keep the crowd playing, if it is possible. In the meantime, come in yourself and lock that door."

The manager stammered something to the white-faced servant who had dropped the tray, and added: "Sweep up that glass. . . . Don't answer any questions. Do you hear?" He was a fat man, who looked as though he were melting; a monstrous moustache curled up to his eyes, which bulged like a frog's. Tumbling against the door, he stood and pulled idiotically at his moustache. Bencolin, taking out a pen, used it to turn the key in the lock.

There was another door, in the wall to our right, at the left side of the dead man as he lay before the divan. It was ajar, and a startled face peered through.

"François!" Bencolin said, whereat the face edged around the corner of the door. "One of my men. . . . *Peste!* don't look like a damned sheep, François!" He turned to the proprietor. "That is the door to the main hall, monsieur?"

"Yes," said the manager. "It—it—"

Bencolin went over to it and held a short consultation with the operative called François. "Nobody has come out *there*," he observed, closing the door. "François was watching. Now!"

All of us were looking about the room. Grafenstein stood huge and motionless, cropped skull hung forward, blinking down at the head. I tried to keep my eyes off that head, which appeared to be gazing at me sideways; the wind blew on my face, and it felt very cold. Bencolin walked over to the body, where he stood and peered down intently, smoothing his moustache. Beside the neck stump, near the twisted, red-splattered left hand, I could see projecting from the shadow a part of a heavy sword. It had come, apparently, from a group on the wall over the divan (its mate lay diagonally under a green carved shield with a spike in the middle), and, though the edge was mostly dulled with blood, a part near the handle emerged in a sharp glittering line.

"Butcher's work," said Bencolin, twitching his shoulders. "See, it has been recently sharpened." He stepped daintily over the red soaking against the lighter red of the carpet, and went to the window on the left side of the room. "Forty feet from the street . . . inaccessible."

He turned, and stood against the blowing curtains. The black eyes were bright and sunken; in them you could see rage at himself, nervousness, indecision. He beat his hands softly together, made a gesture of incredulity, and returned to the body, where he avoided the blood by kneeling over the divan.

I moved over against the wall where the divan stood, so that I could see them all in a line by that dusky red glow: Bencolin's inclined back, head partly turned;

Grafenstein blinking down at the thing on the floor; and the manager still leaning soggily against the *salon* door, stupid gaze fixed. The red curtains flapped at the window. That scene had the ghastly unreality of a waxworks, all the more terrifying for not being human. Then Grafenstein bent over and deliberately picked up the head by the hair; he adjusted his spectacles and studied it with those mild blue eyes, turning it this way and that for closer inspection, and grunting thoughtfully.

"Put it down," Bencolin ordered, glancing up. "We don't want the place disturbed. Watch out, now; don't get the blood on your trousers. . . . "

To the manager he said: "Come here, monsieur. This sword, it comes from the room here?"

The manager began talking excitedly. His syllables exploded like a string of little firecrackers popping over the room—the almost unintelligible clipped speech of the Midi. Yes, the sword belonged here. It had hung with that other, like itself, crossed under the Frankish shield on the wall over the divan. It was an imitation antique.

"Ah yes," said Bencolin. "Are you in the habit of keeping on your walls heavy two-handed swords sharpened to a razor edge for the mere convenience of your guests in matters of this sort?"

The proprietor struck his chest.

"Me, I am an artist! Everything in my house is perfect. When my patrons come and see swords, they are real swords, and they are sharp." He waggled his lifted arms and slid into a picturesque Italian oath: "Blood of the Madonna! Do you have clocks that do not run? Do you have—"

"A sound reason," said Bencolin, "against having swords that do not kill. I wish your passion for realism had not included those raised brass nailheads on the handle—you see? We shall get no clear fingerprints from it, I fear. . . . Is this room ever used for any purpose other than assassinating guests?"

"Why, certainly, monsieur; it is the card-room! But we haven't used it tonight. See, the card tables are folded against the wall. Nobody wanted to play. It was all that roulette. . . . Do you think it can be hushed up, monsieur? My trade—"

"Do you know this dead man?"

"Yes, monsieur; it is M. le Duc de Saligny."

"He is a constant patron of yours?"

"Ah, for the last few weeks he has been coming here frequently; he liked my place," said the manager with pride.

"Did you see him come in this room tonight?"

"No, monsieur; the last I saw him was early in the evening."

"Where was that?"

The artist reflected, twirling his moustache, one finger set in an elaborate gesture at his temple. "Ah!" he cried, making a discovery. "I remember! I saw his party coming in when I was downstairs. I congratulated him on his mar—" the manager's eyes popped. "*Diable!* his marriage! This is terrible!"

"Who was with him?"

"Madame, and M. Vautrelle, and M. and Mme. Kilard. The Kilards had to leave shortly afterwards. This is terrible!"

"Very good, then. You may go out now and inform madame la duchesse; be as quiet about it as possible—

better take her out in the hall, in case she makes a scene. Tell M. Vautrelle to step in here."

The manager, composing his fat shoulders, walked with a stately motion out the hall door. Bencolin turned to us.

"Well, Doctor, what do you make of it?"

"Hm! . . . Method of killing is not unusual, for this kind of mind," Grafenstein replied, nodding ponderously. "Wandgraf of Munich is an example. In this case, the impulse to kill was present, and the sight of the sharp sword was instantly associated in the murderer's mind with the idea of blood. He yielded to the impulse and attacked Saligny—"

"Please! You are so occupied with what the murderer thought that you are completely forgetting what he did. This was no impulse; it was carefully and deliberately planned beforehand. Look at the position of the body. Does it convey nothing to you?"

"Only that there seems to have been no struggle."

"Obviously not; he was struck from behind, as he stood or knelt with his back to the divan. Can you conceive of an infuriated madman reaching four feet up over the divan —he would probably have to stand on it to reach the shield—pulling down that enormous sword, and beheading Saligny, who obediently bent over and offered his neck for the blow? It would have been necessary for Saligny to have been deaf and blind not to notice it."

"Nevertheless, he *was* beheaded."

"Come over here to the divan," said Bencolin. "You see these pillows? I lift them up—so. You notice that long imprint in the padding of the surface? The sword was there, concealed by the pillows. The murderer had set his stage. Therefore he was here before Saligny came. He was waiting; he knew Saligny would come here. He could talk with Saligny—who feared strangers—without suspicion on the former's part."

Bencolin made a gesture. "Therefore—?"

"Nonsense! You say we must look for Laurent in the guise of one of Saligny's friends?"

"At least as one of his acquaintances, yes. Further, it is somebody who could go and come in these rooms without exciting suspicion; in short, a patron and not an intruder. . . . He could draw that sword from under the pillows while Saligny's back was turned."

"But, my God, friend!—Saligny is bent as though he were awaiting this blow!"

"Ah, that is the point that is likely to tell us who the murderer is. And the murderer is now in these gaming-rooms. Nobody has left, unless my agents are asleep."

"By the hall door?"

"François has been there since eleven-thirty. Do you know what time Saligny came in here?"

"Yes," I interposed. "I recall exactly, because when madame pointed him out I was looking at my watch. It was eleven-thirty."

Bencolin looked at this own watch. "Just twelve. It should be easy to check alibis. . . . " He was rumpling his hair with a nervous hand, and bewilderment sat oddly on the hollows of that face. "I do not understand," he muttered, looking about slowly—"I do not understand. All I am sure of is that it was no sane mind. . . . How do you account for the fact that the head lies at some distance from the body, standing up?"

"The question," observed Grafenstein, brightening

"had entered my head. I feel safe in saying that it could not have rolled to that position."

"Well, stranger things have happened, but it didn't; you can see that there is no direct blood trail between the head and the body. The murderer put it there."

"I understand, A gesture of triumph not unnatural for our man's brain. He wishes to hold it up, to gloat—"

Bencolin was staring at him with blank eyes. He said in a low voice:

"Stretch the imagination, Doctor, and a parallel enters the mind."

"You people," I observed, irritably, "have the most cheerful imaginations. . . ."

"But it is necessary," Bencolin murmured, shrugging. Then he bent down gingerly and started to go through the dead man's pockets. Presently he straightened up to indicate a pile of articles on the divan. There was a queer smile on his face.

"The crowning touch . . . his pockets are filled with pictures of himself. Yes. See?" he ran his hands through clippings and pasteboards. "Newspaper pictures, and a few cabinet photographs. Photographs of himself, of every conceivable sort; pictures where he looks handsome, pictures where he looks ghastly . . . here is one on horseback, another at the golf links. . . . Hm. Nothing else except some banknotes, a watch, and a lighter. Why these photographs at all? and especially why are they carried in evening clothes?"

"Pah!" said the doctor. "You should not be surprised to find conceit in such a person."

Bencolin was squatting by the divan, idly turning over the clippings. He shook his head. "No, my friend, there may be another reason—which is the peak of all this odd business. . . . Do you notice anything missing?"

Grafenstein loosed a few tremendous and terrifying comments in German. Afterwards he said:

"Have I any means of knowing what he carried in his pockets?"

"Yes," answered the detective, imperturbably. "I was referring to keys. It is advisable, in this business, always to conceive of what should be present and yet is not. Keys to his car, his house, his beer-cellar—anything. I am inclined to think that they have been taken." He looked at us searchingly. "The strangest thing that is missing, and most inexplicably missing, as I will show, you two have overlooked altogether. You have overlooked a very solid substance which by every law of sanity should be right here in this room. but nevertheless is missing."

"A clue to the murderer?" hazarded the doctor.

"The murderer himself," said Bencolin.

We were suddenly startled by a tearing, rattling sound. The door to the hall was pushed open despite a protesting officer in plain clothes. There wandered into the room a pudgy, vacant-eyed young man with a paper hat stuck on the back of his head. Even then you noticed irrelevant details: the paper hat was in stars and stripes, and had a pink confetti plume. In a face which resembled squashed clay his eyes had a bleared and smeary stare. He grinned foolishly, his clothes were awry, and the noise was being made by one of those wooden twirlers they give as favours at night clubs. He inclined his head in that sort of drunken leer very popular at weddings, shook the rattler at us, and smirked at the sounds it emitted.

"Party here," he explained in English, " 'scort couple home." Then he suggested that everybody have a drink, and, struck to admiration by the merit of the idea, he demanded interestedly of the plain-clothes man, "Got any liquor?"

"Mais, monsieur, c'est defendu d'entrer—"

"Cutta frog talk. No comprey, Where *I* go, by Jesus, they speak English! Big drink for everybody. Generosity—that's me—set 'em up for a crowd. Got any liquor?"

"Monsieur, je vous ai dit!—"

"N'lissen. You wanna speak frog to me, and I toldja I don't speak frog! I toldja that, didn't I?" He inclined his head as though for an answer, and then admitted in a mollified tone: "A'right; I toldja. Now look here. Gotta see m' friend Raoul. He's married. Ain't *that* a fine thing t'do, now? Ain't it a *fine* thing t'do whena guy goes and gets himself tied in f'lic'tations of connub'l—" He gargled and made spreading gestures indicating oratory.

I hurried over to the stranger, who showed a tendency to hold forth on the theme, and spoke in English.

"Better go out, old top. You'll get to see him—"

The young man pivoted with wabbly dignity and studied me with increasing animation.

"By God! you're m' friend!" he crowed, opening his eyes wide and thrusting out his hand. "Got any liquor?"

"Please! this is necessary. Let's go out."

"I've been drinkin'," he confided in a low tone, "but gotta see Raoul. Did I tellya he's married? Do *you* know Raoul? Let's have a drink."

Suddenly he sat down in a red-plush chair beside the door. For a moment the bell-cord hanging beside him engaged his thoughtful attention; then he fell into a half-stupor, still twirling the rattle. Its sharp rasping sound in that room of death, flimsy and foolish like the paper hat, intensified the horror by contrast.

"Monsieur!" cried the policeman.

"I'm gonna pop *you*," said the newcomer, opening his eyes and pointing a finger at the policeman with a curiously intent look. "Sure as hell I'm gonna pop you 'fyou don't getaway! Now you lemme 'lone in this chair. . . . " He relapsed again.

"Who is this?" I asked Bencolin. The detective was studying him with narrowed eyes.

"I have seen him before, with Saligny," Bencolin replied, shrugging. "His name is Golton, or something of the sort. An American, naturally."

"We had better put him—"

Again there was an interruption. We heard a woman moaning, "I can't stand it! I can't stand it!" and other feminine tones urging her to be quiet. It was Madame Louise's voice. The door to the hall opened, and Edouard Vautrelle entered. His eyes travelled past me, past Bencolin, and down to the floor. He winced with a startled spasm, which seemed to come from inside his locked jaws like the rip of a sore tooth. He was pale, but almost immediately became very calm and very supercilious. Polishing his eyeglass on a handkerchief, he looked round coldly.

"Was this necessary?" he said.

Supported by a little wizened woman attendant, Madame Louise came after him. She glanced at the thing on the floor; then she stood stoically, upright and motionless, with the rouge glaring out on her cheeks. Her eyes were dry and hot. I have seen few things so stately and arrogant as she was then, standing before her dead. She did not cry out, or make any movement, though one of the shoulder-straps of her gown had slid down, and her hair had an uneven look as though frenzied hands had smoothed it. She shook off the arm of the woman attendant and walked slowly across to the shattered body, where she bent her head.

"Poor Raoul!" she said, as one would speak to a child who has hurt its finger. Then she turned about, and her eyes brimmed over.

There as a little space of silence, so that we could hear the red curtains flapping at the window. Abruptly Golton, the American, looked up from his glassy contemplation of the floor and saw her. He emitted a crow of delight. Never noticing the body, he hoisted himself unsteadily to his feet, made a flamboyant bow, and seized madame's hand.

"My heartiest congratulations," he said, "on this, the happiest day of your life—!"

It was a ghastly moment. We all stood there frozen, except Golton, who was wabbling with hand extended in his bow, the paper admiral's hat stuck sideways on his head. It was the only time that drunkenness ever seemed to me to partake of the horrible—here, over the body of the fallen athlete. Golton's eyes moved up to Vautrelle, and he added, waggishly:

"Sorry you got the gate, Eddie; Raoul's got more money'n you, anyhow. . . . "

IV. We Determine the Position of the Puppets

Vautrelle snarled, "Get that drunken dog out of here!" and made a movement that was restrained by the plain-clothes officer.

"Take him out," Bencolin whispered to me, adding under his breath, "Learn what you can."

Golton was more easily led away by one of his own nationality; besides, at that moment he gave signs of becoming unwell. The policeman passed us out into the hall. It was very quiet here, with a subdued noise coming from the smoking-room, a deserted palm garden at the end of the hall, and opposite the card-room door a big curving stairway of marble, with a grandfather clock at the turn of the landing. The inevitable strip of red carpet against the marble floor haunted one again. Some guests were coming up the stairs, laughing, but they gave us only a casual glance as I supported Golton down the corridor to the men's room.

It was a comfortable room, walls set in mirrors, standing lamps beside deep brown-leather chairs, and in the middle a big table piled with magazines; but it had that intense depressed solemnity and quiet which pervades such places everywhere. Golton disappeared into the lavatory for a time, and presently emerged, looking pale but considerably more sober.

"Sorry to be such an inconvenience," he growled, sinking into a chair. "Can't hold it. All right now." After a time of staring at the floor he regarded me morosely and complained: "God! I feel rotten! . . . So you're an American. Nothing but Americans. I s'pose you're another of these tourists. . . ."

His squashy face assumed a tragic look which may be seen in any American bar. He pronounced the word "tourists" with all the fervid sadness and loathing with which Job must have said "boils."

"All the tourists comin' over here 'n spoilin' things. They never know the French, the real French. Ugh!" He grew morbid. . . . "Now, *I* know Paris. I know a *Frenchman*."

"Indeed?"

"Yeah; I know Raoul. He's been married." He began musing, and into his throbbing head penetrated an idea. "Say! What's alla fuss about? Up in that room where I was—they all looked kind of funny—"

We were getting down to business. I disliked this person intensely; under any other circumstances he would have been merely irritating, but now he might be an important if creaky cogwheel in the mechanism of a murder case. His face was assuming normal lines after its squashed-clay appearance, and resolved itself into pudgy reddish features under thin hair plastered flat back like a jazz-band player. His bleary blue eyes came into a focus, stirring now with the vague idea that another drink might not be out of place. So he grew more genial.

"Have you known him long?" I asked.

"Oh no; not very. Only a coupla weeks. Thought it might be a good idea to meet some nice people—you know; gotta meet nice people, *get* you somewhere—?" He looked at me with crafty enquiry, and, though it seemed to me the most unpleasant thing he had said yet, I nodded. Warming to the subject, he continued: "Say, lemme introduce myself. Sid Golton's the name. . . ."

After the amenities, I suggested that he was talking about Saligny.

"Oh yeah. Y'see, he got a fall off a horse out near the place where they shoot pigeons in the Bois—clay ones, I mean. Well, he fell off a horse. Don't think he had his girths tight. I know a lot about horses; used to be a ranger in Yellowstone. As I was saying, he fell off a horse. See?"

"I think I follow you."

"Yeah. Well, y' see, he hadda go see a specialist in Austria about it; it did somepin to his wrist and back—you know, landed sideways. I didn't see it, because I was in Austria then, but they told me it was an awful spill. . . . Well, I met him on the train comin' back. I'd seen his pictures in all the papers—great sportsman; so'm I. I just went up to him and said: 'I'm Sid Golton. I wanta shake your hand. Believe me, Duke, if I'd been with you, you wouldn'ta cracked up like that. . . .' "

"That was very tactful."

"Sure. Well, he spoke English all right. We got to be good friends comin' back. He was kinda laughin'; he liked me. Y'see, it's *not* hard to get acquainted with these big bugs if you know how," he concluded with complacent pride. "Give y' a hand any time. . . . I used to go call on him regularly, but sometimes he wasn't there, and I didn't meet his gang. I will, though. But I know him. Be glad to introduce you.—He invited me to his wedding today, but those damn' high-hats—!" Golton's face darkened venomously; he checked himself with a jovial smile, and continued: "I wasn't feelin' very well, y' see, so I didn't go to this guy Kilard's house for the shindig. . . . Lookit—What'd you say your name was?—Lookit, le's us go up and see Raoul. Why was everybody so steamed up? I seemed to remember—"

He was groping blankly in his mind after a puzzling image.

"Mr. Golton," I said, "I am sorry to tell you that the Duc de Saligny has been murdered—"

Golton's eyes turned as glassy as marbles. He looked at me with a glare of suspicion, as though he said, "Trying to trap me, are you?" nor did he ask for details. It was enough for him that there had been trouble. He was halfway out of his chair when Bencolin entered with Grafenstein and Vautrelle. The ensuing few minutes showed Golton, maudlin and fearful, grotesque with features twisted, insisting that "he didn't know a damn thing about it, and if he wasn't let out of there there'd be trouble, because he was a sick man."

"You are at liberty to go, of course," Bencolin said. "But please leave your address."

Golton blundered out the door, loudly declaring that he was headed for Harry's New York bar. His address he gave as 324 Avenue Henri Martin.

Bencolin, who had taken up his position behind the centre-table, contemplated the closed door. "I am inclined to think," he commented, "that the American

Volstead Act was the worst law in the history of France. . . . No matter; Golton can come later."

Pushing aside the magazines, Bencolin sat down behind the table, leaning back with lowered eyelids. "Sit down, please, M. Vautrelle. I shall have to get most of my information from you. Take chairs, messieurs."

It looked, I thought, rather like the judge's chambers in the Criminal Courts Building at home, with the buff-coloured lights on brown-leather chairs and floor in squares of black and white marble. A business conference, you might have said. Grafenstein stood with his back to the mantelpiece, blinking as he filled a pipe. In a chair before the table, Vautrelle sat bolt upright. Seen sideways in the full lamplight, his face was now a mask of lines hemming the yellow moustache. Those impersonal eyes were now cool and insolent, slightly enquiring; the waved blond hair, you noticed, was grey around the temples. His shirt front did not bulge, he was a model of poise and tailoring, almost like a dummy. But one received the impression of tremendous restlessness and intelligence, with more than a trace of gesture and charlatanism. He would, you felt, strike a great attitude and say immortal fiery words as he led troops to battle, then, when the limelight left him, calculatingly watch his position and use cold caution to see that he was never by any chance in danger. The material of a general, an artist, a side-show barker. . . .

"A few questions, please, monsieur," went on Bencolin. "You understand that this is necessary. . . ." (Vautrelle inclined his head.) "May I ask what time you arrived here tonight?"

"I can't recall the exact hour. It was some time after ten o'clock."

"I wish you would tell us everything that happened afterwards."

"That is not too difficult. I did not care particularly to come"—he looked round with distaste—"but Louise had had an unpleasant experience, and Raoul thought the life of this—rather gaudy place would take it off her mind. We came with the Kilards, who were forced to leave early. Besides"—at this juncture he regarded Bencolin as though he were thinking of some very entertaining joke—"besides, I believe he had an appointment here with somebody. . . ."

"Indeed? You say 'somebody' as though you might possibly be referring to a woman, M. Vautrelle—"

Vautrelle shrugged. Bencolin appeared to be hardly interested in the conversation; but the two were looking at each other warily, like duellists.

"I really don't know. We came upstairs. Louise was immediately surrounded by her feminine friends and carried away. There was a very small crowd; there was nobody in the smoking-room when Raoul and I went in to have a drink. Afterwards he left me there; he was going in for a try at roulette. 'I'm going to play the red, Edouard,' he cried; 'red is my lucky colour tonight. . . .' "

I could have sworn that again the sardonic smile flickered over Vautrelle's face. "Then Raoul turned to me as though with an afterthought. 'By the way,' he said, 'what was that cocktail you were describing to me—the one the man makes in the American bar at the Ambassador?' I told him; it is a particularly devilish concoction called, I believe, a monkey gland.

'Well, then, do me a favour, will you?' he said. 'See the bar steward here and show him how to make them. Get him to mix me a shaker of them. I'm expecting a man on something very important tonight . . . and while you're there, you might tell him to bring it to the cardroom when I ring. I expect the man about eleven-thirty o'clock. Thanks.' I remained in the smoking-room—"

"One moment, please," interposed Bencolin. To Grafenstein he said: "Doctor, would you mind ringing that bell? The cord is beside you."

When the Austrian had complied, we all waited silently until there entered the white-coated servant who had dropped the tray on entering the room of the murder. He was a pale and ineffectual person with an earnest manner, and his watery eyes showed fright. Vautrelle twisted round to look at him.

"Steward," said Bencolin, extending his hand, "you were the person who discovered the dead man?"

"Yes, monsieur. Monsieur there"—he nodded nervously towards Vautrelle—"had told me to expect a ring around eleven-thirty from the card-room. I took in the cocktails monsieur had ordered. I saw . . ." His eyes wrinkled up and he protested: "I could not help breaking those glasses, monsieur! Really, I could not! If you will speak on my behalf to—"

"Never mind the glasses. You heard the bell ring, then? At what time was this?"

"At half-past eleven. I know, because I was watching the clock for it. M. de Saligny always tips—tipped—well."

"Where were you at the time?"

"In the bar, monsieur. The bar opens on the smoking-room, and both of them are next door to the card-room on the side towards the front of the house."

"Where is the bell-cord in the card-room?"

"By the door into the main hallway, monsieur."

"You came immediately when you heard the ring?"

"Not immediately. The bar steward took his time about mixing the cocktails, and insisted that I wash some sherbet glasses. It must have been ten minutes before I answered the ring."

"By which door did you enter the card-room?"

"By the door opening on the main hall, naturally, monsieur. You see, there was a man standing just outside it (he was your detective, monsieur). I knocked, and got no reply. I wondered—you know!—if I had better go in; it might be embarrassing. . . . I knocked again, very loud. No answer! So I said to your detective, I said: 'Is there anyone in there? Do you think I'd better go in?' He said: 'What do you mean? Who is supposed to be in there?' I said 'M. de Saligny.' *Voilà*! he got as white as a candle. 'Go in,' he said; 'go in, or I will.' I entered—"

The man began to speak very fast, and shift his glance from side to side. "*Alors*, I go in. At first I do not perceive that anything is wrong; your man is looking over my shoulder. No, at first I did not see the—I did not notice. *Alors*, I walk across and—*mère de Dieu*!—I almost stumble over the head! I cry out; I reach the door of the main *salon*; I can hold the tray no longer! That is all, monsieur, I swear—!"

He was doing elaborate pantomime, eyes frozen with the memory. Then he backed towards the door, and he was breathing hard.

Bencolin sat back and for an interval he stared up at

a corner of the ceiling, bearded face pinched in thought. Then he motioned the steward to go. With a deep breath, as of one again taking up a burden, he addressed Vautrelle:

"To continue your story, monsieur: Saligny left you in the smoking-room. When was this?"

Vautrelle's amused smile grew broader. "I don't know that I can time every movement I made tonight, my dear man. It was shortly before eleven; perhaps five minutes of the hour." His tone was one of mild expostulation, but the watchful gaze never wavered. "So," he shrugged, "I really can't say. You might trip me up. . . ."

"You stayed in the smoking-room, then?"

"Yes. In one of the booths. Neither Raoul nor I had many friends here. Zut! this clumsy social set," he wrinkled his face disdainfully. "And roulette!—you see, monsieur, a game of mere chance I cannot tolerate. It is no matching of wits. It is not what Poe called 'the measuring of one's antagonist.' . . . No, I stayed there very comfortably. I was reading a book which somebody had left behind in the booth. It was a very amusing book, in English, called *Alice in Wonderland*."

"Good God!" said Bencolin, despairingly, and struck the table. "Messieurs, the fates are intoxicated. They are throwing custard pies. They are splitting their celestial sides with mirth at the spectacle of one man who pays a visit in order to drop trowels on the floor, another who leaves a copy of *Alice in Wonderland* in a gambling-casino, and still a third who placidly reads the book while a murderer prepares a feast of blood in the next room. There must be sanity to the play somewhere; if there is no meaning in any of these incidents, there is no meaning in all the world. . . ." A freezing change came over him: for one instant, as brief as a snapping of your fingers, his face had the terrible triumph of Satan beholding at last the weakness in the armour of Michael, and the dart of his eyes was like the lunge of a conquering spear. Then it was gone. He said, briskly:

"Very well. . . . Now, I must trouble you for time again, M. Vautrelle. I have consulted the clocks in the smoking-room and on the staircase. They agree with my watch that it is now—What hour have you?"

Vautrelle turned a thin silver watch over in his palm. He consulted it with great deliberation, and announced, "Exactly twenty-five minutes past twelve."

"So have I, to the second." He turned to me. "You have—?"

"Twenty-four and a half minutes, to the second."

Bencolin scowled. "Very well. To proceed, M. Vautrelle: Can you tell me your whereabouts at half-past eleven, when M. de Saligny entered the card-room?"

"Within a few seconds, monsieur, I can." Vautrelle hesitated, then, startlingly, he burst into a roar of laughter. "I was speaking to your detective on guard at the end of the hall. I stayed with him for eight minutes or so, when I walked into the main *salon* under his observation and was introduced to you."

Bencolin very nearly lost his temper. After an interval of silence, the bell was rung again. François, the plain-clothes detective, came in with an air of importance, rubbing his large nose.

"Why, yes, monsieur, the gentleman was there with me," he responded. "I had come on duty five minutes before, and I was sitting in a chair before the door of the smoking-room when he came up to me and offered me a cigarette and said: 'Can you by any chance tell me the right time? My watch seems to be slow.' 'I am positive,' said I, 'that my watch is right—eleven-thirty—however, we can consult the clock on the staircase.' "

François refreshed himself with a glance at all of us. He resumed: "We walked to the head of the stairs, right opposite the door of the card-room, and, as I knew, the clock confirmed my watch. He set his own, and we stood there talking—"

"So," interrupted Bencolin, "that you were directly before the hall door to the card-room at the same time that M. de Saligny entered this room from the *salon* side?"

"Yes. He stayed with me—M. Vautrelle, I mean—for over five minutes, and then he walked down the hall and entered the *salon*. I remained at the head of the stairs. . . ."

"All this time you watched this door, did you?"

"Not consciously, monsieur; but I watched it. I was standing with my back to the staircase."

"You are positive, then, that nobody either entered or left that way?"

"Positive, monsieur. . . . I was standing there when the boy came up with the cocktail-tray—he has probably told you about that—and I was behind him when he went into the room. I saw the body when he did. I did not leave that door until you yourself came in from the other side, as you remember; and even then I still had my eyes on it. Nobody!"

"That is all."

Bencolin sat at the table with his chin in his hands.

Throughout this questioning, Vautrelle had become restive; he tapped his monocle on the chair-arm, fidgeted irritably, and those graven lines of his face wrinkled into a sneer around the narrow moustache and wide-set teeth. The long nostrils twitched. Pale malevolence shone in his eyes, as though in a reaction of weariness or relief. He said, softly:

"Of course, you are at liberty to imagine that there has been tampering with the clocks."

"There has been no tampering with the clocks, nor with my friend's watch, nor with mine. I have made certain of that."

"Then I suppose I am free to go? I dare say madame needs attention, and I shall be glad to take her home—"

"Where is madame now?"

"In the ladies' room, I believe, with an attendant."

"I presume," observed Bencolin, with a crooked smile, "that you will not take her to the home of M. de Saligny?"

Vautrelle appeared to take the question seriously. He put the glass in his eye and answered: "No, of course not. I shall take her to the apartments she previously occupied in the Avenue du Bois. In case you want my own address"—he extracted a card-case—"here is my card. I shall be pleased to present you with a duplicate," he added, politely, "at any time in the future you feel called on to be as insulting as you have tonight."

Preening himself, he rose to his great height, lip partly lifted, glass in his eye, and his manner said, There's no reply to *that*! It was as though he had leaned over and calmly flicked a glove into Bencolin's face. I saw a rather dangerous silken film come over Bencolin's eyes. Thoughtfully turning over the card in his fingers, the detective looked up with wrinkled forehead.

"Possibly," he said, very gently, "it might be embarrassing for monsieur. Possibly monsieur's experience does not extend to the knowledge that the duelling code unfairly allows monsieur's adversary to have a sword also—?" The blank, expressionless eyes met Vautrelle's without moving, politely surprised.

They stayed thus for a single tense instant, as though every nerve force of the two men were locked and fighting over that table. I heard the small crash as Grafenstein's pipe dropped and broke on the hearth, and saw his bewildered head-turning between the two of them. And if I remember nothing more of Edouard Vautrelle—though Lord knows I have good reason to remember him—it will be at that moment, smelling faintly of lilac-water, with his handkerchief hanging just so out of his pocket and his sharp-tailored body poised. It was not, I think, any implication of guilt in Bencolin's words that swept the momentary twitch to his wrinkled mouth and the quiver to his eyeglass. It was rather the slow, sick knowledge that some one had again discovered him to be a coward.

He carried it off beautifully, of course; in an instant he was cool and amused and very jaunty; but through all the man from his polished hair to his polished boots was the crushed futility of one who had seen defeat under many flags.

And so Vautrelle laughed, and said, quizzically:

"And so you believe me to be the murderer?"

"No," said Bencolin, "no, at the present time I do not. Any man is conceivably a murderer, but no man is conceivably a wizard. . . . I am merely asking questions." To prove it, he asked a somewhat extraordinary one, "Tell me, M. Vautrelle, did M. de Saligny speak English?"

"Raoul? That is the most amusing question yet. Raoul was essentially a sportsman, and nothing else. He was a swordsman, and a spectacular tennis-player—he had a service that nearly stopped Lacoste—and the best of steeplechase riders. Of course," Vautrelle added smugly, "he *did* sustain a fall that nearly paralysed his wrist and spine, and had to see a foreign specialist about it; it nearly prevented the marriage, you remember. But yes, he was a fine athlete. Books he rarely opened. *Tiens*! Raoul speaking English! The only words he knew were "game, set.' "

A servant had brought in Vautrelle's coat—long and dark, with a great sable collar, and hooked with a silver chain, it was like a piece of stage property. He pulled down on his head a soft black hat, and the monocle gleamed from its shadow. Then he produced a long ivory holder, into which he fitted a cigarette. Standing in the doorway, tall, theatrical, with the holder stuck at an angle in his mouth, he smiled.

"You will not forget my card, M. Bencolin?"

"Since you force me to it," said Bencolin, shrugging, "I must say that I would much prefer to see your identity card, monsieur."

Vautrelle took the holder out of his mouth.

"Which is your way of saying that I am not a Frenchman?"

"You are a Russian, I believe."

"That is quite correct. I came to Paris ten years ago. I have since taken out citizenship papers."

"Oh! And you were?"

"Major, Feydorf battalion, Ninth Cossack cavalry in the army of His Imperial Majesty the Tsar."

Mockingly Vautrelle clicked his heels together, bowed from the hips, and was gone.

V. "Alice in Wonderland"

Bencolin looked over at me and raised his eyebrows.

"Alibi Baby!" I said. "I don't see how you're going to shake it, Bencolin."

"For the present, it is not necessary that I should. Question: Where does this species of fire-eater get the income to go about with a millionaire like Saligny?" He frowned. "The unfortunate part is that there are so few people here tonight who know either of them. . . . François!"

That officer hurried in.

"François, you are seeing to it that these various people are followed when they leave here?"

"Oh yes, monsieur."

"Very well. Put Rotard to work finding people who positively remember seeing Saligny at the roulette table and in the smoking-room. Ask the bar steward if he saw Vautrelle there. When you go to the smoking-room, look in the booths and see if you can find a copy of a book called *Alice in Wonderland.* Find out, if possible, who left it there. That's all. . . . Wait! Send the proprietor in."

When François had gone, Bencolin turned to us.

"I am not sure that I can answer my own question about Vautrelle's income. However, I am inclined to believe that he has been supplying madame la duchesse with drugs."

"Ah!" Grafenstein exclaimed, heavily. "That was it, then. I make no statement till I am sure, but I thought—"

"Yes. When she came over to us this evening, I remarked that she looked as though she were in a drug-fog. That was the literal truth. Did you see me pick up the cigarette she left in the ashtray?" Bencolin fished it out of his vest pocket. "There will be no maker's name on *that.* Come here, Doctor. You notice how loosely packed and thick the tobacco is, with the paper edges folded over the ends? Smell it. You note those brown dried leaves inside the tobacco? Marihuana or hashish, I think; I can't tell until our chemists analyse it. They eat green hashish leaves in Egypt; this is a deadlier variety from Mexico. Whoever supplied her with that is carrying on an extensive and far-reaching trade. . . . Symptoms, Doctor?"

"Contraction of eye pupils; heavy breathing when stirred; pallor; clammy skin; congestion; hallucinations. Didn't I tell you? She told us that mad story—"

"No more mad, Doctor, than the situation we are facing. I'm not sure that it was an hallucination. You're speaking of hemp derivatives in large doses; this was a small one, and it gives no such paradise as the Indian sugar pellets. It was a stimulant. She is a confirmed user, or it would have made her violently ill. There are no languorous dreams in *this* preparation for a confirmed user. It kills, you know, within five years. Somebody is most earnestly trying to do away with her."

He was silent, tapping a pencil against the table. Grafenstein, hands folded behind his back, took a few lumbering steps, removed his spectacles, wiped them, and stared at his companion. The removal of the glasses gave his face a wholly different, rather caved-in expression of bleariness. He growled through the big moustache:

"I was wrong. You don't want a psychoanalyst here. . . . *Donnerwetter!* The place is more unhealthy than my clinic." He shook a huge fist.

The doctor was still stumping about when the proprietor of the house came in. That gentleman came in wild-eyed, his moustache drooping like a dog's ears.

"Monsieur," he cried, before his stomach had preceded him through the door, "I beg of you, you must countermand that order that nobody is to leave! Several have tried to go, and your men stopped them. They are asking all sorts of questions of my patrons. I am telling everybody it was a suicide—"

"Sit down, please; a suicide will enhance the reputation of your establishment. You need not worry."

The other demanded, with a kind of ghoulish hopefulness: "Do you think so, monsieur? The reporters—"

"So it's been given out, then! . . . Is the medical examiner here?"

"He has just arrived."

"Good! Now . . . before coming here this evening, I consulted our files for some information about you—"

"It is a lie, of course!"

"Of course," agreed Bencolin, composedly. "In particular, I want to know if there are any patrons here tonight who are unknown to you."

"None. One must have a card to enter, and I investigate them all; unless, of course, it is the police. I should be grateful if my compliment to you were returned." He was drawn up in offended dignity, rather like a laundry bag attempting to resemble a gold shipment.

Bencolin's pencil clicked regularly against the table.

"Your name, I am informed, is Luigi Fenelli; not a common patronymic in France. Is it true that some years ago the good Signor Mussolini objected to your running an establishment for the purpose of escorting weary people through the Gate of the Hundred Sorrows? Briefly, monsieur, were you ever arrested for selling opium?"

Fenelli lifted his arms to heaven and swore by the blood of the Madonna, the face of Saint Luke, and the bleeding feet of the Apostles that such a charge was infamous.

"You give good authority," said the detective, thoughtfully. "Nevertheless, I am inclined to be curious. Does it require a card, for example, to be admitted to the third floor of this establishment? Or is the soothing poppy dispensed, like the cocktails, by courtesy of the house?"

Fenelli's voice raised to a shout. Bencolin's hand silenced him.

"Please!" said the detective. "The information was mine before I came here. I give you twelve hours to throw into the Seine whatever shipment you have on hand, opium and—hashish. This leeway I grant you on one condition. That you answer me some questions."

"Even the illustrious Garibaldi," said the other, "was sometimes forced to compromise. I deny your charge, but as a good citizen I cannot refuse to assist the police with any information at my command."

"How long has M. le Duc de Saligny been a user of opium? Don't deny it! he has been known to come here."

A peculiar watery flabbiness had begun to overspread the manager's face. For a moment you saw there the triumph of one who has vindicated a theory. He choked, "I was right—!" but again he smiled effusively, and made a deprecating gesture. "Well, then, within the last month, monsieur. To allay pain is a noble thing," he explained, virtuously, "and M. de Saligny suffered much from his hurt. He was downcast. He thought that perhaps he might never ride again. I was shocked and grieved that such a fine young man—"

"No doubt, no doubt. Did the woman who is now his wife contract any charming habits here also?"

"Each," explained the manager, loftily, "was very much concerned about concealing it from the other. I—I think she has been taking it a long time."

"Ah yes. Now—no moralizing, if you please; I want a direct answer—did you supply her with hashish cigarettes tonight?"

Fenelli was sweating profusely. "It—it is possible, monsieur."

"Answer me! *Did you?*"

Before this blast the manager wilted.

"In brief—yes, monsieur. You see, she needed it; I swear to you she needed it, and it is not good for them to stop suddenly. It was a little while after the party had come here. She was with some ladies, and she left them and implored me to get a few cigarettes. I took her up to my—my office on the third floor. She was upset; I gathered she was nervous about her marriage. She kept talking about bathrooms and trowels. . . . Ah, these brides!" He smiled a ghastly, flabby smile.

Bencolin interrupted the questioning long enough to look at Grafenstein.

"You see, Doctor? What you call an 'hallucination' had existed before she took any of the hashish. . . . Now, Fenelli, what time did she leave you?"

"Oh, around eleven o'clock, monsieur. Please I—"

"What did you do afterwards?"

"I stayed upstairs. I was going over my accounts. Just before eleven-thirty I came down. . . . Monsieur, I have answered enough questions! I have helped you, have I not? That is all I will tell if they subject me to torture!"

"Such a contingency is hardly likely. At any rate, I advise you to become busy turning your third floor into a bar or a bagnio or something equally harmless. . . . That is all, Fenelli."

When the manager had gone, I said: "May I ask how much of your information you're concealing, Bencolin? That was the first intimation of this angle—Saligny as a drug-user."

"Ah, but that's another pair of sleeves completely. I was not sure it had any bearing on the case. Now I am morally certain it has."

"How did you learn about Fenelli's private parlour on the third floor?"

"Saligny told me about it."

"*Saligny* told you about it?—You don't mean Saligny, do you?"

"Yes. He volunteered the information when he brought me that note. It is inexplicable—but there it is. Now in a moment we shall be invaded by a whole horde—I hear screamings and protestings out there—but first let us argue the case a bit." He sat back and put his arms behind his head. "What are your impressions, messieurs? Do you notice any leads? Any contradictions, inconsistencies—"

"Personally," said I, "there seemed to be at least one glaring contradiction—"

Grafenstein cut me short with a vast flip of his hand. "Wait! Here is something I want to know. Bencolin, you say that Laurent must be masquerading as somebody we have seen tonight?"

"Oh, not necessarily somebody we have seen, though it might very well be the case. Identification papers are easily forged, even under the prefecture. I said merely that Laurent is masquerading as somebody Saligny knew."

"All right, then. Now"—Grafenstein's face was puckered as though he were trying to hold a dozen things in mind at once—"you are sure, are you, that it was Laurent who killed Saligny?"

Bencolin replied, with a queer twisted smile, "I am positive of it."

The doctor nodded his head doggedly. He checked off the points on his blunt fingers as he went on:

"So! We know Saligny had an appointment at eleven-thirty. Good! He ordered some cocktails. At eleven-thirty he went into the room. Good—"

"Shortly afterwards, the bell was rung. Don't forget that."

"The bell was rung, yes," said Grafenstein, waving

the point aside. Bencolin looked at him as though tempted to swear. Instead he merely grinned sourly, and the doctor resumed: "The murderer, then, was already there. He had prepared the sword under the pillows."

"Yes. Which way did the murderer go into the card-room?"

"By either door. He was there early, remember."

"Yes. Now let me ask you"—Bencolin suddenly leaned across the table—"*which way did he go out?*"

During a long and tense silence a deep red crept up Grafenstein's thick neck, and he had the look of a person at once stung by wasps and hypnotized by a snake: surely a distressing plight. I said, meekly:

"Doctor, I was trying to call it to your attention—"

"Wait. *Wait!*" ordered Grafenstein, loosing his breath like a steam-shovel. With slow tenacity he continued, "The murderer did not go out by the hall door—"

"Because," supplemented Bencolin, "my detective was standing directly before it a few seconds after Saligny entered the room from the *salon* side, and he did not leave it even after the murder was committed."

"And the murderer did not go out by the other door into the *salon*—"

"Because I myself was watching it from the time Saligny entered until the time we ourselves went in! I never lost sight of it for one second, and yet nobody came out. . . . Isn't it possible that you've realized the implications of this situation? I wondered how long it would take you to do so."

Nobody spoke. The *Juge d'instruction* continued patiently, as though he were explaining it to children: "Here were two doors, both guarded, one by me, and one by my most efficient man. We will take our oaths that nobody left by either door, and I trust François as I would trust myself. I examined the window immediately, you remember; it was forty feet above the street, no other windows within yards of it, the walls smooth stone. No man in existence—not even a monkey—could have entered or left that way. Besides, I found dust thick and unbroken over the sill, the frame, and the ledge outside. But there was nobody hiding in the room; I made certain of that. . . . In short, our murderer disappeared as completely as he disappeared from the eyes of Madame de Saligny. Are you so sure now, Doctor, that it was an 'hallucination'?"

"Oh, this is incredible!" snorted Grafenstein. "He must have been somewhere! He must have been hiding—he . . . François must have been mistaken or lying. . . . How about false walls?"

Bencolin shook his head.

"No, the murderer was not hiding; I saw to that. François is neither mistaken nor lying. There is no possibility of false walls, for you can stand in any door and test the entire partition of the next room. Tear open floor or ceiling, and you will find only floor or ceiling of the next room—that should be apparent to anybody who has studied the architecture of this house." He paused, and summed it up wryly: "In short, there are no secret entrances; the murderer was not hiding anywhere in the room; he did not go out by the window; he did not go out the *salon* door under my watching, nor the hall door under François'—but he was not there when we entered. Yet a murderer *had* beheaded his victim there; we know in this case above all others that the dead man did not kill himself."

And, as later events proved, Bencolin spoke the absolute truth. For the present, we were aware only of a confused and numbing sense of terrible things moving behind a veil. That room, with its amber lights and its black-and-white flagged floor, the two men who were my companions, suddenly took on an aspect of unreality which made me feel as though I were alone. It stripped away everything except the knowledge that somewhere in the house, unsuspected behind a familiar mask, was walking a man who had no heart or brain, but only a mechanism tuned to kill. I could fancy the smile on the featureless face as the thing stretched out its hand. I could fancy this horrible robot walking the halls with a copy of *Alice in Wonderland* under its arm. Its actions so violated the bounds of reason that one was almost willing to believe that it could vanish at will. I could understand now madame's feelings when she opened the bathroom door and saw the thing standing in the lightning-glare, looking at her.

Grafenstein's voice roused me. The doctor did not protest any more; he just sat down, shapeless and grim, and said, "I refuse to believe it."

He was rather pitiable, this spectacle of an intelligent man, a dogged and earnest and plodding man, seeing things undreamed of in his psychiatry. I had a crazy impulse to laugh; he bore such a weird resemblance to William Jennings Bryan reading Darwin. He looked up only when François entered again, bearing several sheets of paper and a book.

"Here are notes on all the other testimony I could get, monsieur," François explained; "you can correlate them with what you have learned. I did not think it necessary to hold anybody, but we are getting the names and addresses of everyone present, including servants. Here is the book you wanted; the bar steward does not remember who left it there, because the backs of the booths are high and he cannot at all times see who is in them from his place at the bar window. But he is positive that the book was not there when he opened up this evening. . . . Shall I tell the medical examiner that you will be out soon?"

"In a moment, François. Stay here; I may need you."

François put down the papers and the green-bound volume on the table.

"Hm!" said Bencolin. "No cloth like that will hold fingerprints. Besides, we have absolutely nothing to connect this book with the crime—at its face value, it is worth nothing. And yet what an extraordinary book to find in this place!—Just as a matter of form, François, you might enquire about this of the departing guests."

"I have already done so, monsieur. Nobody here professes to have left it."

"*Tiens!* that is interesting. Let's see. . . . Printed in America. Somebody's name has been taken off this title-page with an eraser that tore the paper. Well, we will put it aside for the moment. . . . Here, Doctor." He turned quizzically and tossed the book to Grafenstein. "If you can read English, this will interest you. You might psychoanalyse the mock turtle or the dormouse. . . .

"Now," he continued, settling himself to the papers, "wait while I straighten your notes, François. Excuse me, messieurs, for a few moments."

He was at once lost in the notes as completely as though shut in with sound-proof walls. The lean face grew rigid; the eyes narrowed; and now and then he would write down a sentence in his notebook. Under that twirled black hair the brain was sorting thoughts with the light-swift play of a conjuror handling cards. . . . For a time there was no sound except the deep murmuring that came from the people shifting in the halls. I looked at Grafenstein. The doctor had adjusted his square spectacles and opened *Alice in Wonderland*; he was reading haltingly, moustache moving and thick finger following the words. Gradually an expression of the most extraordinary bewilderment came over his face; he turned back a page, as though to make sure his eyes were not deceiving him. Then he shook his head to clear it, and plunged again into the text with the grim resolve of a prize-fighter coming up after the count of nine.

Bencolin pushed the notes aside. "François," he directed, "put a corps of men looking up the history of everybody here tonight: 'phone the Sûreté immediately. . . . Here is the most important order: have Saligny's house watched. If anybody attempts to go in—anybody, understand—hold him.

"Now, messieurs, here is a *résumé* of our knowledge. To fix the time element, I will go over it." He read from his notebook:

"10:15 P.M. Saligny, his wife, Vautrelle, M. and Mme. Kilard arrive at house. (Witnesses: Fenelli and G.H. Buisson, leader of orchestra.)

"10:20. M. and Mme. Kilard leave house. (Witnesses: Fenelli, Buisson, Vautrelle.)

"10:25 to 10:55. Vautrelle and Saligny in smoking-room. (Witnesses: bar steward, waiter.)

"10:30. Madame de Saligny has interview with

Fenelli upstairs. (Witness: Fenelli.)

"10:50 to 11:25. Fenelli remains alone upstairs. (Witness: the same.)

"10:55. Saligny leaves smoking-room. (Witnesses: bar steward, Vautrelle.)

"10:55 to 11:30. Vautrelle remains in smoking-room. (Witness: Vautrelle. Note: waiter remembers bringing him a drink—about—11:15.)

"11:18. Madame joins our party in main *salon*. (Witnesses: ourselves.)

"11:30. Saligny enters card-room. (Witnesses: ourselves, madame.)

"11:30. Vautrelle is talking to detective, enquires time. (Witness: François Dillsart.) Detective has just gone on duty.

"11:30 to 11:36. Vautrelle talks to detective before door of card-room. (Witness: the same.)

"11:37. Vautrelle joins us in alcove. (Witnesses: ourselves.)

"11:40. Murder is discovered by steward and François.

"Remarks: Nobody can be found who remembers seeing any of these people in the hallway from 10:20 to 11:30, the lapse of over an hour.

"Nobody remembers seeing Saligny from 10:55, when he left Vautrelle in smoking-room, until 11:30, when he entered card-room.

"It is quite possible for anyone outside the house to enter by a rear door giving on an alley communicating with the rue des Eaux. This door was not watched before time of murder.

"A document," commented Bencolin, "which tells us

much by its gaps. I hope you see its import without any comment from me. So, Doctor, I leave it for your consideration." He turned to me. "Come along; we will see what the medical examiner has to say."

VI. In the Black Parlours

We walked slowly down the hall again, Bencolin and I. Now that the scene was beginning to resolve itself into definite personalities, now that voices and emotions had lifted it in my mind to absorbing reality, I felt my brain crystal-clear and keyed to the highest.

Many people were thronging the hall, talking excitedly. Before the door of the card-room was a little group of significant black-hatted men who waited in a kind of gloom, hands thrust in their pockets. One of them carried a collapsible camera; he was leaning against the newel-post of the stairs, negligently smoking a cigarette. The peculiar bloodhound snoop of the press was also much in evidence.

When we entered the card-room again, there were more men studying the position of the body. They gathered at some little distance to avoid the nauseating welter of blood. With a detached and impersonal air, a fat man with whiskers—this must be the medical examiner—was taking notes and cocking his head at the body like an artist squinting for perspective. He made his last note with a flourish of the pen. Then he beckoned to two of the men.

One of them set up a camera, fiddled with it awhile, and the other prepared some powder in a flat pan. Presently there was a blinding flare of light; then the smoke and reek of flashlight powder drifting across the dull lamp-glow. While they were preparing for more pictures, I tried to get the scene firmly photographed in my mind.

There was the headless trunk, limbs frozen in that weird kneeling position. It was toppled forward so that the neck stump touched the floor, the back partly humped. One leg was doubled under, the other sprawled at a side angle. Both arms were doubled flat from the elbows, arms forward like the arms of the Sphinx, fingers dug with claw-like tension into the carpet. Altogether, it gave the impression that this headless beast was about to spring forward. The back of the dress-coat was soaked, the entire shirt front crimson, and both arms were splattered so that thin red splashes daubed the backs of the hands. Bencolin had replaced the head where it had been, some three feet away. . . . Again the flashlight powder glared over motionless men; blinding, like an instant of terrifying death.

One of the men stepped forward, and with an enormous lump of chalk, such as tailors use for suit markings, he drew a line around the edges of the body. Afterwards the medical examiner jerked a thumb over his shoulder, and in a tired voice said, "All right, boys."

Two of them lifted it up—it was becoming stiff, like a big plaster image in clothes—and started to bear it from the room. It passed by us, and Bencolin, coming out of his reverie, stopped for a moment the two who were carrying the burden. Pulling at his moustache, he looked down at it for a time. He unclasped one of the hands and bent close. What he extracted from under one finger nail I could not at first see; it was a tiny bit of thread, colourless and nearly invisible. Bencolin put it into an envelope, and motioned the bearers to go.

A matter-of-fact voice saying, "All right, boys," a jerk of the thumb towards the door—so that was how they carried a gentleman to his grave. . . . It was impersonal, and curiously pathetic, with a jazz band to play the requiem.

The medical examiner, notebook in hand, was addressing Bencolin:

"No more use for me here, monsieur the judge. What do you want done with the body? His relatives—"

"He had none," said the detective, "no close ones that I am aware of. Send it down for an autopsy—I want that report—and communicate with his attorneys. They will see to the undertaker, unless his friends"—Bencolin's smile was ugly—"care to take charge. That's all—"

Well, there seemed to be few friends here. I wandered out of earshot. It was a curious way to die, not so much in its tragedy as in its lack of simple dignity. Certainly the living Saligny must have cut a prouder figure than that, when you fancied the lift of that powerful body smashing a tennis-ball white against a glare of dust and sun. Was he, as I imagined, a sort of swashbuckling, back-slapping chap, ingenuous and hearty with everybody?—a conscious D'Artagnan with a ready jealousy and an equally ready sympathy? There was the head, with thick blond hair, and the startled wide-set eyes of an oxlike and docile brown, lips open on magnificent teeth. Now it was all smeared with a glaze. Yes, Raoul, you must have carried that head to better purpose than being surrounded by jabbering and paunchy men, to be accidentally kicked and set rolling by somebody's casual boot. . . .

I went to the window. It was still open, red curtains flapping, and I leaned out to peer around. A high-sailing moon lit the grey walls all about, and shimmered on darkened windows across the street. Lying just below was a little yard, cut off by a wall from the pavement of the rue des Eaux. Far across the street, beyond the walls of the apartment houses, the Eiffel Tower blazed its running electrics against the sky; a living thing in loneliness. All very still and cold. . . . I craned my neck. Bencolin was right.

It was—and I also say this in the light of what happened afterwards, and confirmed the statement that nobody had left that way—impossible to leave the room by that window. On the floor above there were no windows at all to that side; merely a smooth upward run of stone for some twenty-odd feet to an overhanging roof whose slope afforded neither a hold for fingers nor the attaching of a rope. The windows on either side were twenty feet away, and, of course, gave on the occupied *salon* and smoking-room where two dozen people were present. Below, the line of windows all had iron grills closely wrought: a fancy protection against housebreakers. . . . But most of all I saw the dust. It was thick over the outer and inner sill—an unbroken coating everywhere. The smallest body or part of a body could hardly have gone through without smearing the dust somewhere. The window was ordinarily kept closed. *Why, then, had it been opened tonight?*

I turned back to see Bencolin directing the group of men. They were looking for fingerprints now, with their lenses and their brushes and the little tins of powder like flour sifters. But there were few surfaces capable of holding prints, though they even went over the card tables folded against the wall. The photographing continued, and the room reeked terribly now. Two of them, at Bencolin's order, took off the cover of the divan, folded it together like a bag, and carried it out along with the pillows. A man was scraping into the rug; he appeared to be grubbing after ashes or something of the sort. . . . Then they got round to the window, these pecking chickens making a barnyard of justice, and yelped childishly at the discovery of some prints on the glass.

At length we were alone with the medical examiner. The sound of tramping in the hall had nearly ceased; out there the agents were at work taking the names of all who left, so that you sensed the grind of great wheels in motion. Alone in the room of the murder. Bencolin was leaning against the door to the *salon*, whistling between his teeth, his eyes a blank. The medical examiner, silk hat stuck on the side of his head, was standing in the middle of the room, frowning and jabbing at his notebook with a recalcitrant pen. Before him was the white chalk outline stark against the red of rug and blood.

In the silence Bencolin began to talk softly. "Four walls, of a room twenty feet by twenty—walls of red leather. A red glass lamp on a table by a divan. Half a dozen chairs in red plush, three card tables against the wall. That is all, except a body and a disappearing murderer—"

"*Hein?*" exclaimed the medical examiner, sticking the pen behind his ear.

Slowly, as though to get the situation clear in his own mind, Bencolin explained it.

The medical examiner struck his notebook.

"Oh, that's nonsense!" he said. His eyes wandered slowly round the square room.

"But it happened," stated the detective, going over and opening the door to the hall. "François!" he called, "stand where you were before!"

From my position by the window I could see out into the hall, see the staircase and the edge of the clock on the landing below. François appeared, poking his head around the corner. He was directly opposite me now, some five feet from the door. Bencolin then opened the door into the deserted *salon*.

"There we were," he explained, "at that lounge over there. We were watching the door all the time; after Saligny entered, nobody else either entered or left. Nobody escaped by that door François was guarding. . . . But there was nobody here when we came in."

After an interval the doctor pulled his hat down forcibly on his head. "But it's ridiculous! Ridiculous!" He made gestures. "Hiding, then!"

"So? Where? Can you show me a place I might have overlooked?"

The doctor preened his whiskers and probed about. He started to say, triumphantly, "The window—" but when he had poked his head outside he came back crestfallen.

"Well, name of a devil, it's your job, not mine! If you're sure nobody was hiding—"

"I am. Saligny comes into the room, we learn, at eleven-thirty. Almost immediately afterward he rings the bell. . . ." Bencolin scowled at the red cord hanging by the door into the hall. "Or does he? Somebody rang it, anyhow. At possibly fifteen minutes of twelve the servant enters from the hall door, carrying his tray. Saligny lies there, in the chalk circle, with his head cut off."

He stood motionless, with levelled finger. The murmur of departing people, the thrum of motors starting in the street, drifted up.

"All this time both doors have been carefully watched. But the murderer has disappeared." Bencolin beat his knuckles against the sides of his head, made a wry face, and continued with a gesture: "At any rate, why was the bell rung? That's the perplexing question. Why was the bell rung?"

"Well, why does anybody ring a bell?" asked the doctor, with some exasperation. "To summon the servant, apparently."

"And assuming, then, that he was ready for the servant to come in at any time?"

"Naturally."

"Whereupon the murderer, knowing that the servant may be in at any moment, proceeds to decapitate Saligny. What does he want?—a witness to his crime? If Saligny rang the bell, did the murderer go right ahead with his work, anyhow? By the same token, did the murderer himself ring it and proceed with the crime?"

"It needn't have bothered the murderer," said the medical examiner, "if he is as invisible as you claim. Either he made himself invisible and walked out one of two doors, or he made himself lighter than air and floated out the window. No bell-ringing is insaner than that. Either he was shut up in a cell with every door guarded, or else all of you others ought to be."

Bencolin, his face a mass of wrinkles, was thoughtfully rubbing his cheek. He said, suddenly, "There is an alternative."

"Well?" asked the doctor.

"Namely, that neither Saligny nor the murderer rang the bell."

"You mean that the servant never heard the bell at all?"

"No; I am sure that the servant is entirely innocent, and I am equally certain he did hear the bell. I mean just what I say."

The doctor bellowed: "A *third* person? Another one who disappeared, then?"

"No. I mean that the bell might have been rung by somebody who wasn't in the room at all."

The doctor was bubbling with anger, but he tried to show some calmness in yanking on his gloves. He stared at Bencolin and replied in an even voice: "Your alternative, monsieur, is beyond the furthest limits of unreason. Personally, I prefer the mere impossible. . . . You are absolutely sure that this detective, François Dillsart, is trustworthy, and that his testimony is true?"

"I would stake my life on it."

"And you swear equally to your own testimony?"

"Yes."

Without another word, the doctor made a gesture of high tragedy and stalked out of the room. In a moment we could see him standing with François at the head of the stairs. They were both waving their arms and jabbering excitedly at each other, engrossed with Gallic earnestness in the debate. Bencolin closed the door.

"The possibility of a secret entrance," he remarked, thumping his foot on the floor, "is out of the question; as I told you, I have looked along the line of all these walls. However, to satisfy the particular before I send an architect to look into it, we will see to the floor and ceiling. I will have the rug up in here. In the meantime, you might go upstairs and locate the room immediately above this; we can go over that floor and do some sounding between us. But I am convinced of the result."

Slowly he shook his head.

"Every character, every event at cross-purposes. Each event is brought about by precisely the *wrong* means; but too many of these wrong movements, combined, form a pattern that baffles us. I am inclined to believe that the thing is almost too consistently unnatural to be the work of a madman."

I went out into the hall, leaving him motionless in the middle of the room. The diminishing voices of François and the doctor echoed up the well of the staircase; an emptiness had settled on these chambers. The low light showed disarranged chairs at the end of the hall. One of the potted palms had been knocked over; a few cigarette butts lay on the marble floor with its strip of red carpet. The proprietor was nowhere in evidence, but a surly scrubwoman had appeared with mop and bucket, there was a clink of somebody gathering up glasses in the main *salon*, and cautious footfalls tiptoed round the smoking-room to the tune of a man whistling "Hallelujah" under his breath.

This stairway of marble and bronze rail was dark as it curved to the next floor. And—I might have known it, for it led to regions where ordinary patrons were not allowed—it had a closed door at the top. Tentatively I twisted the knob. The door was unlocked.

Double bolts on the inside; Fenelli had been taking no chances. I stood and studied the hallway. It was similar to the one below, except decorated with a defter hand. There were sombre tapestries, subdued in grey and green, with a grey carpet; it swam in a moonlight glow from a bronze Venetian lantern of pale glass. When you closed the door, it was so still that I suspected the walls were sound-proof. Four doors, numbered like private dining-rooms, were in the side facing the staircase, and on the staircase side three more. The numbers on the doors emerged with a greenish shine from their dull background. No guard, no noise.

Number three, it seemed, must be directly over the card-room. One moved like a phantom in this atmosphere. When I turned the knob of that door it moved in an oiled lock, and the hinges were oiled and soundless, so that the movement of the door had the odd and dreamlike quality of an opening gulf. . . . Inside there was a skylight in the roof, and in the blue over the well of shadows you could see bright, motionless stars. I saw, too, faint gleams from a perforated lamp, threading slow smoke against the weird moving rustle of the dark.

You may know the suggestion of incense to the brain. It transfigures any environment, it is a creeping drug to invest locked doors with mysterious promise, it mists the flowering entrance to dreams; light and heady in the nostrils, the mind, and then pungent in the heart . . . as it was now, stealing through the silent room with a scent of buried cities, of flowers and fleshly shrines.

I stood with a shudder at my heart, terrible and sweet. My grip on the chill door-knob was the only sense of reality, for the floor seemed to drop away in bottomless carpet. A voice in my brain whispered, "Ambergris," and another chanted in low refrain like a slow-swinging bell, "Ambergris for passion. . . ."

My first conscious movement was to fumble for a light-switch, involuntarily, in the wall towards the left. I groped, and found nothing, with a sensation as of one groping near a well. Then I hesitated, standing still, when I heard from over in the dark the sound of a low moan. . . . It was not repeated, that moan in the dark. I merely stood still, hand uplifted as against a blow.

VII. AN APPOINTMENT WITH THE WORMS

There were matches in my pocket, I realized. There . . . No, here they are, a little box that is clumsy in one's fingers. The flame sputtered up. Surprising how a match-flame can blind one against a darkness moving and breaking like whirls of foam on water! I do not believe that I was especially surprised at what I saw, for it fitted in such a breath-taking fashion with the pattern of the dead cities and the ambergris.

To see the face of a beautiful woman looking up into a match-flame is another part of the dream. The eyes were amber, turning to brown, and terror-stricken against a white face. The hair, waved and parted in dull gold, lay upon her shoulders. Except for a kimono over one shoulder, she was unclothed, a breathless mystery of flesh and shadow against pillows in the faint light; one hand was pressed hard against her teeth, and over it the wide black-fringed eyes dilated with that terror. . . . The hand moved, and she gasped. My match went out.

Ah, well, I thought, and shrugged and nearly laughed—ah, well, it is merely somebody's assignation, another branch of Fenelli's prosperous business. Nothing wrong or mysterious here. Then I was startled to hear her speaking in English, low and terrible.

"O God!" she whispered. "What do you want?"

Somehow this didn't fit the pattern; it shook one up, though I did not understand why it should. It was a sharp stab of that indefinable fear. It was as though something had whispered, "This is vital. . . ."

I said, slowly, trying to keep my voice even: "I did not intend to disturb you. I was told to come up here to—to look at the floor." (Well, what the devil was a person going to say, anyhow?)

"Who are you?"

"At present I am a representative of the prefect of police. Hence—"

I heard a rasp in the throat, a movement as of some one bitterly fighting to ward off knowledge, realization, like a physical thing. She said, "What has happened?" And then, with swift intentness, "Is he dead?"

Score one for intuition! But steady, now; hold yourself steady; no surprise. . . . You're getting somewhere.

"Is who dead?"

"Raoul. Raoul de Saligny."

There was no hesitation; the voice was trance-like, devoid now of terror or tears. She spoke with an English accent, light and slurred.

"That is correct. And," I said, "I am afraid I shall have to ask you some questions. Will you please turn on the light?"

I could hear her angry movement, and the creak of the springs on what I assumed to be a couch of some sort—I could sense her staring through the dark. A queer interview, this, without grace in the rather stupid futility and emptiness of a woman no longer desired. To be no longer desired, I think, is the one great shame. After a silence she said, bitterly:

"I know what you think. You think I'm a—a damned harlot." She snarled the word with the iron anger of what is known as the English good woman. "Well, I'm not; you can understand that now. You needn't treat me—"

"My dear girl, it makes no difference what you are. Why should it? If it spares your modesty, you will probably be able to dress in the dark. If not, I will gallantly close my eyes until you do, but I don't care to have you walk out on me by leaving the room. But, please, let's end this silly talking in the dark."

"I'll dress," she said. She was crying now.

There were more rustlings in the dark, and more creakings of the couch as she groped and tied, a lesser shadow under the starlight blue. I felt a cold and nameless gnawing, laughed at it, and fell to humming the fragment of a tune. But that cold surge came back, deadened by the perfume of ambergris. Ambergris for passion; bright star-points for romance, and downstairs a severed head grinning at the dark. . . . There was a smashing cold deluge at the remembrance, too, this time an impact. Simultaneously light came into the room, stealthily, by a low orchid lamp which threw only a little illumination over the long divan and warmed the reddish-purple tints of pillows. She sat there rather forlornly, clad in a chemise, pulling on one stocking. The shadows lay on her curved shoulders, white ivory against the orchid; the shadows gathered round her breast, Haunted the dark-gold hair as her head hung down, followed the supple outline of her hips. When she looked up, it was with a defiance of black lashes and amber eyes.

"I don't care," she said in that slurred accent. "I don't care." And she continued slowly pulling on the stocking. "You don't look like a policeman," she said, and after a moment's pondering added, reminiscently: "It was nice, lying there, dreaming. . . . I'm partly drunk, I think." Putting her hands against her temples in wonder, she nodded. "You'd be, too, if you had to put up with what I have." She shivered miserably.

Yes, it was going to be the same old story of being misunderstood; you could sense it all along. I hoped she wouldn't start it.

"Tell me about tonight," I suggested.

"Yes, I'll tell you," she said with an attempt at recklessness. "I don't know why I should, but I'll jolly well tell you. So Raoul is dead."

She talked in a small broken voice, steady, but full of self-pity. Her eyes met mine with a surly steadiness. In her face the sybarite struggled with the clinging vine; she seemed torn between an attempt at valiance and a temptation to throw herself on one's mercy. She asked, quietly, "He was murdered, wasn't he?"

"He was murdered. How did you know it?"

"I felt it. . . . I'll tell you the whole thing. If I don't," she muttered, biting her lips, her face growing half ugly with tears—"if I don't, I'll go crazy. You see, I loved Raoul, or I thought I did. I don't know. . . . When I know he's dead, it doesn't seem to mean so much."

Her eyes stared deep, through a veil.

"Only recently he changed. Before that, he wouldn't have anything to do with me. I wanted to be loved; I had to have him. But that injury did something to him; he was moodier, and when he came back from Austria I think he was maimed for life, and knew it. He'd been acting like—like one of those silly people in books," bitterly, "and talking about honour and the girl he was going to marry. But when he came back, he—took me. . . . It's a funny city, Paris," she said, reflectively. "You oughtn't to be lonely, but you are. You want to be loved, terribly, more so than anywhere else; but there ought to be people to love you, and there aren't. . . ."

The spent voice, maimed, fell to earth.

"He took me. We came here because he was afraid his *fiancée* might find out. But he was an odd one, Raoul; there were things in his nature that seemed to develop after he got hurt. He was more—I don't know—mystic. He always spoke French to me—I understand it, you know—and I used to hate to hear French; it got on my nerves, horribly, but he made it sound like music. He would sit here so you could see his face in the starlight, and tell me great lines from the 'Flowers of Evil.' Great music of poetry. And once, when his voice was hardly over a whisper, he suddenly quoted in English from another poet. It—it stopped my heart; it was a shock; it was like an anthem rising. . . ." Her voice floated thrillingly against the low light, " 'When the hounds of spring are on winter's traces, and the mother of months in meadow or plain.' . . ."

You could see the ghosts, shadows wreathed in stars, sitting there against the orchid light; you could see her own white face now, framed in dark-gold hair, with eyes closed and lips moving faintly.

"Today he said he wanted to see me, for the last time.

But there was something queer in his face; he looked—half mad. 'I want to see you tonight, in the same place about eleven. I want to tell you something; you'l appreciate the joke.' That was what he said.

"I came here before eleven; I lay and dreamed But—did you ever have a premonition—like—the fea of death—hollowing out the inside of your heart—wit a cold hook? I did tonight. I had the devils. I *knew* something was wrong. I got to thinking that with al the noise and music down there, I was alone, ou wandering somewhere, with nobody near. I knew ther was death downstairs; you didn't need to tell me.

"Then—I don't know what time it was—sometim before you came—then I saw that door over ther opening."

The terror had come back; she stared, fascinated

"I don't know why it should have struck me a horrible, because I expected Raoul, even though i must have been much later than eleven. But I saw th door opening, very slowly, and I saw a man's shadow i the doorway, against that light. I *knew* it wasn't Raoul It stayed there, not moving, for a long time. I felt—dizzy and scared. It walked over slowly, not making a sound, and I could feel it standing over me. Then, al of a sudden, it seized me by the wrist.

"Maybe I screamed; if I did, you wouldn't hav heard it downstairs. The man said in a low voice: 'I d not think Raoul will keep his appointment with you mademoiselle. He has another appointment, with th worms."

"That was all he said. I didn't faint, though, for I could still feel him holding my wrist and looking dow at me. Then he turned around, walked out, and th door closed without making a sound . . . but my wrist, where he had held it, felt *wet*. . . . I grew crazy. I struck a match, and . . . O God! . . . where he had held it my wrist was smeared with blood from his hand!"

Slowly the tension left her, and she sank back into the nightmare background. Abruptly there came into my brain a knocking, as of soldiers at castle gates in the night—a slow knocking of heavy blows: "Out, damned spot! out, I say!—One: two: why, then 'tis time to do't. Hell is murky!—Fie, my lord, fie! a soldier, and afeared? . . . Yet who would have thought the old man to have had so much blood in him. . . . Here's the smell of blood still: all the perfumes of Arabia will not sweeten this little hand."

The knocking ceased. The momentary terror was past, and here was only a rather frightened girl with hands before her face, trying to keep her wits and her poise. I said, gently:

"Did you recognize the man?"

"No. I—don't know who it was; I only saw him a second, and he spoke in a whisper."

"But you suspect—?"

"I don't know, I tell you! I don't know who it was!"

"Listen! We don't know who killed Raoul; we don't even know how. It is vital. Try to recall."

"I can't! . . ."

"Can you think of anybody who might have killed him?"

"No!" It was almost a cry of hysteria. She took her hands away from her face and looked up dazedly. "I—wouldn't dare tell you if I could."

I was surprised at the vigour of my own words:

"Look here, you needn't be afraid. Nobody's going to hurt you. . . ."

She studied me bending over her.

"Please," she said, "won't you let me go? You can ask me all this again. I don't feel like talking. I . . . I'll come back here. My name is Sharon Grey; I live at Versailles; you can find me. . . . If you let me go, I can get out the back way, without anybody seeing, and nobody will know I was . . . like this."

It had seemed natural that we should be talking thus, not odd at all; there was in it a sense of frankness and security, and the solid order of things. It was a bit astonishing to discover conventionality coming in like daylight. Somehow I feared its coming. It would be like a dashing-down of china to join the other broken jars of romance. Without conscious intent I said: "Yes, you may go. If there is a back way, don't let anybody see you go out." An odd stab shot through me, almost of anger. "But this isn't the last, remember! The police will want to question you."

"Of course," she answered, thoughtfully, "the police." Then, irrelevantly, with a lift of her eyebrows, "I don't know your name."

So—were the social amenities going to intrude at the very last moment? This was irritating, too; ordinarily it would have been laughable. When I had told her, she remarked, "Oh, then you're not a Frenchman. . . ."

"No!" I said, and went to the door. It would never do to let that brief dream-scene dissolve in commonplaces. Stars and orchid light, dark-gold hair and amber eyes poised in motionless fragile beauty, were shut back into night by the closing door. I realized, wryly, that I should never make a detective.

When I walked down the grey-tapestried hall, my rueful chuckle was echoed aloud. I stopped, staring, and saw Bencolin leaning against the wall, smiling mockingly. This goblin quality of sudden appearances never left him. He looked like the quizzical black-bearded goblin squatting on the tombstone in the story.

"My dear Jeff," he said with faint expostulation, "in the excitement of your tête-à-tête you seem to have forgotten the reason why I sent you up to this very artistic place."

Then he scratched his head.

"However," continued this unsurprised person, with a sigh, "it doesn't matter. During your somewhat idyllic peregrination we have been at work downstairs. The room, I fear, is torn to pieces, but at least we have established that there is absolutely no trap-door or any hidden means of leaving the room, in either the floor or the ceiling. *Voilà*."

As we started to go down the stairs, he hooked his arm in mine.

"The card-room has just been sealed and the work is done. Now we can go out and meditate, if you don't mind. . . . By the way, I took the liberty of listening to your very illuminating conversation with the English lady. Your deportment, I may say, was discreet and quite commendable. Now—"

I swore at him. "Well, you know I let her go, then. It was a stupid trick, I admit. I—"

Bencolin looked at me with eyebrows raised in astonishment.

"Stupid, you say? It was the only thing to do. I am inclined to think you extracted from her more information than I ever could. A lady *sans* garments is a lady *sans* reticence. She will be shadowed from here, of course, like all the rest of them; but in giving her name and address I can testify that she told you the absolute truth. I am not well acquainted with the lady, but I know who she is."

"Oh! Have I by any chance stumbled on some famous person I should have known?"

"Not exactly. She has money and, I think, a title somewhere back, but she is not especially famous. She is the mistress of our friend Vautrelle."

VIII. "We Talked of Poe"

It was a relief to get out of that house and smell the warm, rain-tinged air, and over everything a scent of opening green made more haunting by the dark. The three of us drove along the river in a wide swing to the Place de l'Alma, where the white-flowing lights all converged. The yellow glitter shining from Chez Francis on the sidewalk tables drew us in for a drink; inside it was buzzing with the after-theatre crowd of dignitaries from the stages where they do not dance the Shar-le-stone, and with the longer-quilled members of the press. There was an abrupt silence when Bencolin entered—the news must have got round, of course—but though we nodded to several of the newspaper men I was glad to see that they did not swoop down and besiege us with questions. They merely smiled politely and returned to their vermouth and their poker-dice. *That* was for business hours. We went into one of the leather-seated booths and discussed the case until three o'clock. Rather, Grafenstein and I discussed it, for Bencolin remained silent and shadowy, with a dead cigar in his fingers and moving his hand only to order more brandy.

At last we left our curtain of tobacco smoke for the spring night. And as we stood among the forlorn tables, Grafenstein was talking about beer and I was talking about Swinburne; but why we dwelt on these things with such heat I am not sure.

When they had been driven home—Bencolin to his apartments on the Avenue George V, just around the corner, and Grafenstein to his hotel on the Champs Élysées—I came back in a kind of detached fuddle, circling the Rondpoint to my own apartments in the Avenue Montaigne. It was impossible to think. I stood a long time by a tall window in my drawing-room, smoking many pipes in the dark; but the weird piecing of images that rose from the night only served to make me queerly and inexplicably unhappy.

I woke in the warmth of clear blue sunlight, one of those mornings that flood you with a swashbuckling joyousness, so that you want to sing and hit somebody for sheer exuberance. The high windows were all swimming in a dazzle of sun, and up in their corners lay a trace of white clouds, like angels' washing hung out on a line over the grey roofs of Paris. The trees had crept into green overnight; they filled the whole apartment with slow rustling; they caught and sifted the light; in short, it was a springtime to make you laugh at the cynical paragraph you had written the night before. I roused and stretched in energetic laziness. I could hear the sound of water running for my bath, and smell the coffee bubbling in the percolator. Thomas—have I mentioned that invaluable servitor?—was fussing about the room in his daily agony of spirit over what clothing to select, and smiling in the depths of his staid old British soul as he inspected the weather.

I was having breakfast by the window when Thomas announced a visitor. It was Bencolin. He entered in the effulgence of topper and morning coat, looking almost too much like a Frenchman to be one. His beard was freshly barbered, his expression gay and quizzical; but I knew by the deep hollows under his eyes that there had been no sleep for him the night before. Sitting down on the other side of the breakfast table, he folded his hands over his stick and looked thoughtful.

"Coffee?" says I.

"Brandy," says he, absently. It was some very choice apricot, and a most disapproving Thomas brought in the decanter. Its colour glowed against the sun as he held up the little *aventurine* glass and studied it; but his eyes seemed to be looking deep into a fathomless crystal. I wondered if the man had been drinking all night. He drained the glass and pushed it thoughtfully away. "I do not like the tone of the morning papers," he said, "I think I shall finish up this case tomorrow. . . .

"I once promised your father," he continued, after a pause, "that I would see to your welfare when you came, inevitably, to Paris. I suppose that now includes your participation in the present events. And yet—I think you are rather too much like him to be of use—there is too much of the Irish in you both. Still, for that very reason you may be of service."

He studied me as though I were being cast for a rôle. Or say, rather, that he resembled a general, thinking in numbers and geography without regard to the little men who are only battalion-units to G. H. Q. In his beard was a thin Borgian smile.

"The reports from the laboratory, and my check-up

on certain people will be in this afternoon. Until then we have work. Finish your breakfast. We are going to interview M. Kilard."

"Good! Where is the doctor?"

"We are to pick him up at his hotel. I've brought my own car, but I want you to drive yours. . . . The doctor will be very valuable. I shall be interested in hearing the doctor explain the thought-processes of the murderer after I have caught him."

"Bencolin," I said, slowly, "I am wondering whether you believe that nobody notices things except yourself."

"Ah, now we're getting down to it! Let us have your opinions on the matter."

"I don't claim to be able to understand much of it. But don't underestimate Grafenstein. That man is no ass. He noticed something last night that so shook him up that he was hardly able to think at all; he was almost too stupid to be true."

"What, do you think, did he notice?"

"I don't know. But I have a suspicion it's something that wasn't brought out at all; he thought it was too incredible to mention. And there were lots of other things that weren't brought out, either. . . ."

"Such as what?"

"Two people, namely our obstreperous friend Golton and the English lady upstairs, told about holding conversations in English with Saligny. Then—whatever was in the back of your mind—you questioned Vautrelle about that very thing. Saligny, according to him, spoke no English. Somebody is a most engaging liar."

Bencolin chuckled. "Distinctly you are improving, my friend. You are now quite able to see the obvious.

Now, can you suggest a reason why somebody lied?"

"No. It doesn't seem to be of any importance at all—in fact, it's a ridiculous point to lie about, anyhow; I was only trying to apply the doctrine of *falsus in uno*."

"Applying it to whom?"

"To Vautrelle, it would seem. Then, about that copy of *Alice*—"

Bencolin dropped his bantering manner. He struck the head of his stick with gay approval. "Good! You commence to be interesting. Go on."

"I have a theory. That smoking-room last night was practically deserted; so much so that the bar steward noticed when Saligny went out. There couldn't have been many people who could have left a copy of *Alice in Wonderland* there, and, furthermore, nobody admitted having left it. On the other hand, Vautrelle and Saligny were very much there. They occupied their booth for something over half an hour, and then Vautrelle stayed on himself for another half-hour. . . . I suggest that the book was left there by Saligny, accidentally. I suggest he was taking that book up to the lady on the third floor, with whom he seems to have shared his—literary tastes." I had unconsciously put a good deal of acid into that last remark; but I continued: "In any case, why didn't Vautrelle tell us that Saligny left the book there?"

"You are stating an excellent objection to your theory, my friend. You imply, then, that Vautrelle has an excellent reason for making us believe Saligny spoke no English?"

"If Saligny left the book there, Vautrelle must have known of it. But he didn't tell us. The alternative is that he left it there himself—"

"Yes . . . if one grants your original premise that

nobody else did. Well, Vautrelle may have said what he did because he didn't notice Saligny had left the book in the booth; that is entirely possible, you know."

"It seems to me," I remarked with some asperity, "that Saligny is having entirely too damned many appointments for one evening. One with the woman upstairs and one with his murderer. He seems to have planned for an exceptionally busy wedding-night which in no way concerned his bride. Then—what possible connection is there between Laurent and Saligny's paramour, Miss Grey? This mysterious man, Laurent, pays a visit to Miss Grey, smears her hand with blood, and informs her that Saligny will not keep his appointment with her. . . . Is Laurent taking a paternal interest in *all* the women in this case?"

"Softly!" said Bencolin, laughing. "In your efforts to elucidate the matter you are almost contriving to give *me* a headache. You might also enquire whether Saligny was taking a personal interest in all the women in this case. *Tiens!* he was a cool one, Saligny! Our big athlete's character becomes more muddled as we continue. In his simple, frank, straightforward manner he arranges for a meeting, on the night of his wedding, with the mistress of his best friend. According to you, he is even so thoughtful as to bring along a copy of *Alice in Wonderland* in order that no moment shall be wasted. *Diable!* He has efficiency, that one! He is what you call in America a Rotarian."

. . . While Thomas was 'phoning for the car, Bencolin strolled into the drawing-room. I heard him strumming at the piano, picking out a careless bar or two with the dalliance of one who knows himself to be a master; and I was not at all pleased with his debonair patronizing of one's ideas. But when I came into the room he looked up from the piano with a wry grin, and observed:

"Listen, old man. It may interest you to know that I am afraid you're right." He shrugged, and plinked out a "ta, ta-ta-ta-ta-ta—*ta-ta*" at the end of the keyboard. Then he rose to go.

Out in the street, the garage-man had brought round my car. Bencolin's Voisin led the way down the avenue. We circled, and he picked up Grafenstein at the hotel, after which I trailed him down the Champs Élysées, across the Place de la Concorde, and over the river, then round the curve into the Boulevard St.-Germain. We stopped before a grey and battered building not far from that famous restaurant which has annexed the boulevard as a secondary attraction. An archway with massive doors like a prison led into a tunnel, where a troll-faced *concierge* poked his neck out suspiciously as we passed through the tunnel into a weedy quadrangle shadowed by grey gloomy walls. When we found M. Kilard's offices, a morose clerk lined us up in a long waiting-room with barred windows and decorated tastefully by a picture of the eminent Dr. Guillotine. Presently we were led into the lawyer's presence.

He had been either rehearsing a speech or bawling out a clerk, for he exhibited signs of a passionate and Jovian calm. He was a gaunt man, whose body looked collapsible; he possessed a high bald skull, with a beaked nose and cold eyes under carven lids. The whites of those eyes gleamed with startling purity out of his dusty face. Standing behind a broad desk in a room lined with books, he wore an advocate's black robe, and bowed loftily as we entered.

"Ah," he said, "you've come about the Saligny affair. It was very sad, that. Have chairs, please."

His manner was that of a dentist reaching for his forceps. We sat down in chairs which squeaked in chorus, the loudest creak emanating from that of M. Kilard. The lawyer glanced at us in turn questioningly.

"I am sure, M. Kilard," said Bencolin, "that you will be violating no professional confidences if you answer us a few questions. . . . You knew M. de Saligny well, of course?"

The lawyer considered, cocking his head on one side.

"No, monsieur, I can't say that I did. I handled his affairs, but it was his father I knew well. I met his father in the spring of '92; no it was '93—April 7, 1893, to be exact, that being the day, a cloudy day, with occasional showers, on which I defended Jules Lefer for burglary." He cleared his throat and looked hard at us, as though to say, "Will you please tell the jury where *you* were on April 7, 1893?" "Technically, I have been Raoul's adviser since his birth, but I seldom saw him. He was not a young man who interested himself in financial affairs. So long as he could draw a cheque he was incurious."

"But you entertained for him yesterday, I understand?"

"Yes. Yes. As you understand, it was only fitting that I should add my blessing and coöperation to this union. Besides, it was Madame Kilard's idea. . . . And I must say"—he had lost interest, and the carven lids were blinking at a corner of the ceiling—"that, having had several talks with him as his marriage-day approached, I formed a much higher opinion of the young man than I had originally possessed. Yes, that's it."

"He consulted you, then?"

"Naturally, monsieur! He was worried, and I do not blame him. He wished to provide for the future." Suddenly the whitish eyes were fixed on us; Kilard's shoulders hunched under the black robe.

"He made a will, then?"

"Yes. He also arranged for me to get him the sum of one million francs."

There was a silence. Bencolin murmured, *"Tiens!* So? Wasn't that a bit unusual?"

"If I never dealt with the unusual, monsieur, I should not be practising this profession. When M. de Saligny wanted a million francs in cash, his securities and my connections were such that the bank at least did not think it unusual." Abruptly Kilard added: "Perhaps I had better tell you. M. de Saligny explained to me. His quiet honeymoon at home was a blind. He wished that published in the papers to deceive . . . any, let us say malevolent, force watching him. He planned to start today with madame, whereabouts unknown, and with cash enough to keep them supplied without communicating with anybody until the police should be apprehend . . . this malefactor. (Of course, I do not use the word in its accepted legal sense.) And I am wondering whether a million francs was enough to cover such a time. . . ."

All antagonistic! Everybody we met seemed guardedly to bare claws, to skirt and avoid the open; but there was another element in a vague doubt that even harassed this dry old vulture in the black robe. He told us what he did, you sensed, not out of any desire to be frank; rather to test its effect on us. The bare skull was leaning forward against the light from a window, his elbow crooked on the desk, and long fingers playing with a steel paper-knife.

During the long stillness I could hear a wind through the open window rustling papers, and a hopping twitter of birds in the courtyard. A cloud stirred across the face of the sun, and slow shadow was drawn over Kilard's tense figure. Bencolin asked:

"Tell me, M. Kilard, do you know if by any chance your wife found a trowel in the medicine-chest of her bathroom?"

The effect of the question in this place was rather ludicrous. Kilard stiffened, and put down the paper-knife.

"I fail to follow monsieur's humour. A trowel. A *trowel*! . . ." As he repeated the word, his eyes flashed open and his body snapped with the sudden rustling dart of a rattlesnake. "What should a trowel be doing there?"

"You place the reference, then?"

"Yes. It is not the first time I have heard mention of a trowel."

I should not have thought it possible for last night's terror to come back; but insensibly, as the long shadow crept across the dusty room of books, it was as though Laurent's shadow were on us again. Kilard continued, slowly:

"I am going to tell you about it. It has preyed on my mind. . . .

"Well"—he made a gesture in his flowing sleeve—"on the night before last, Thursday, April 22, M. de

Saligny gave a bachelor dinner at his home. It was not a sporting affair such as he used to give. Madame Kilard tells me that at one time his dinners were highly undignified, even roystering, I may say, and included as guests professional men from the race-track, swordsmen, boxers, and others whom we come to look on in this day and age," he said, bitterly, "as the equal of a nobleman of France. . . ."

The skinny figure straightened up. I caught my breath. In his eyes was now a look curiously proud and poignant, as at the sight of torn battle-flags going by; as, once upon a time, a guardsman would have said, "The Emperor!" with his hands at salute, even when the crushed and beaten eagles fluttered down.

"We are of the old school that dies. . . . I remember that grey house in the Bois, within sight of the Arch, when his father owned it, and stately people walked in its halls. He was a great man, that one. . . ." Kilard brooded. Suddenly he went on: "You will not know, you will not understand, what it means to some of us when the last of the aristocrats pass one by one from the world. It is like the blowing out of candles, in a *château*, one by one, until all the house is dark. God in heaven! It strikes home! It leaves us lost! . . . I saw Raoul's father die in that house; and ever afterward all those big rooms seemed to smell of medicine and death. . . ."

He was spasmodically opening and shutting the fingers of his hand, and his words were like falling timbers of a house knocked down in dust and clatter, to show long-imprisoned things to the light. The dry precision had left him. The man was trying to tell us something!—hesitant, peering at us, urged to convey some nameless doubt.

"But that night it was like the old days. No sporting dinner, but guests from the *Almanach*, people whose fathers Raoul knew, but who scarcely knew him. It was astonishing, in this day, to find a dinner so perfectly prepared, and to eat it with people with intelligence enough to realize that Brillat-Savarin was one of France's greatest men. Nowadays they cannot tell Chambertin from Sauterne; they will drink champagne from a bottle with a soft cork, and decant port as you would pour out water, without attention to the sediment. Zut! it is blasphemy! They will serve Chablis with anything but the oysters, and I say to you, messieurs, that a host who would offer Médoc instead of a Burgundy with the game should be shot without mer—I ask your pardon, messieurs! I digress.

"Yes, it was an excellent dinner, at a long table with flowers. But it was a very cold and gloomy one. I like—I must confess—to see a certain mellow expansion with the wine; nothing undignified, you understand; but here were just a number of people with faces as expressionless as their shirt fronts, sitting at a long table with candles burning like the candles round a coffin. It should have been merry. But no merriment was there.

"Finally the guests left, all with their precise bows and congratulations, but not with the fine real courtesy we used to know. . . . At any rate, there remained only two of us, a certain M. Vautrelle—possibly you know him?—and myself. We sat at that long table, in the gloom of the tall house which smelled of medicine and death, with our elbows among the roses. . . .

"There were many windows, with little diamond

panes, slanted open to catch the low sheen of the candles, and outside the windows was a plum-blue sky lighted by a single star. There came a sweep of wind rustling through the long grasses, stirring a froth of blossom to the tops of dark trees in a tremulous whispering. The flames of the tall candles undulated slightly above the white table, over the faded upholstery of the chairs, until everything seemed to move except the faces of my companions and their clenched fingers hooked round the stem of a wineglass. But a cold presence had come like another shadow across the light, and as we waited for its approach we talked—we talked of famous murders."

Here was Kilard emerging from his dry shell, the man who brooded so long on the past that he had become fey with a kind of dim poetry. . . .

"Famous murders! The table piled with roses put the idea into Vautrelle's mind of Landru decorating the room for his sweetheart; we talked of Troppmann; of Basson, Vacher, Crippen, and Spring-heel Jack; of Major Armstrong with his hypodermic needle and Smith with his tin baths; of Durrant, Haarmann, and la Pommerais; of Cream, Thurtell, and Hunt; of Hoche and Wainright the poisoners, and the demure Constance Kent. . . . There we sat, with that insane repulsion which makes men go into the thing, and Vautrelle talked of the 'artistry of crimes planned like a play,' and laughed . . . so Raoul's hand shook when he drank his red wine, among the candle-flames and the shadows. . . ."

Now into Kilard's dusty countenance had come a pale shine like marble, and the blue veins stood out at his temples; his black robe rustled, and the eyes under the carven lids fixed us with a hypnotic stare.

"We went into history and fiction; it was a nightmare. . . . Vautrelle was more than half drunk; but we all preserved that low tone of voice, and Raoul was sitting back with the glass dangling from his hand hunched up against his breast, and a kind of fierce glare in his eyes. So Vautrelle, in his silky tone, said, 'To my mind, the most artistic scene in all literature comes from Poe. . . You know Poe, don't you, Raoul?'—and he smiled. . . . 'It is in the story about the Amontillado, where Montressor takes Fortunato down into the catacombs to bury him in the wall forever, walled up with blocks of stone and bones. . . . You're *very* familiar with that story, aren't you, Raoul? . . . Fortunato, not knowing of his impending doom, asks his companion if he is a member of the brotherhood of Masons. Montressor says yes. "A sign!" cries Fortunato; whereat Montressor, with his own grisly humour, takes from under his robe—a trowel. I said, 'You're *very* familiar with that story, eh, Raoul?' And he laughed in an arrogant drunkenness. . . .

"Name of God! the expression on Raoul's face!—partly of fear, partly of amazement—as he looked at Vautrelle, as though he suspected something he could not believe. He staggered up against the table, and his glass rolled over among the roses. His elbow knocked down a candle, and I cried, 'Watch out, man; you'll set the place on fire!' I leaned over to thump it out with my hand, and called for the butler, and felt the hot wax under my hand. . . . But there were these two looking at each other, Raoul with his hair hanging down in his face, and Vautrelle with a quirk of his eyelid like a diabolical wink."

Kilard caught himself up; the picture vanished. He was once again dry and business-like, in a business-like room that smelt of books and mice.

"That is all, messieurs," he said. "There was no fire, of course. The candle merely damaged a very valuable tablecloth."

IX. The Shadow of the Murderer

It was mid-afternoon before we stood in the park of the house of which Kilard had spoken.

We had got nothing more out of the lawyer. He was very helpful, very earnest, but he could shed no light on the matter. When he had bowed us out of his office, I sensed that the relief which settled on him was a relief at having done what he fancied to be his duty. Nor had Bencolin been more communicative. Grafenstein, launching into excited speculation, he had cut short with: "Please, Doctor, let me warn you against jumping at conclusions. I do not ask you to distrust the obvious; I merely urge you to be sure you know just what the obvious is. And I think it would be better, my friends, if we all kept our suspicions to ourselves, whatever they may be. We shall only be confusing the issue if we attempt to argue without knowing all the factors of the case." There it rested. We had lunch at Foyot's, for the most part in silence, before we set out for the Bois. . . .

Here in these woods you sensed the clamour of Paris only in dim echoes—the rattle of a tram crawling thinly, the faint mutter of auto horns calling and answering. The trees were murmurous with the sound of running water and an idle stir and twitter of birds. . . .

We had left our cars, and we walked a path that was

soggy underfoot. To our right I could see the iron fence that marked the property. Then we emerged into a clearing; and risen up before us, gaunt and grey-ribbed, the house looked out from under its dark roof, inscrutably, as from under a mask. It was a tall grey house, whose windows swam in low still slants of sunlight. Behind it a line of thin poplars moved slightly, and contrasted with grim, motionless chimney-stacks piled against the sky. . . . The noises of Paris came with a muted and mournful quality into this stillness. We walked up to the place through rosebeds of Gloire de Dijon and La France, bright swaying things which heightened the effect of the grey house's blank and empty stare.

The bell-peal jangled aloud. Presently the door was opened by a secretive manservant, dressed all in black, with a high white collar and a *toupet* parted down over the sides of his narrow face. He hesitated to admit us until Bencolin showed his card; then we were ushered through a vast hall of drawn blinds and into a tall room in the gingerbread gilt and blue plush of Louis Quinze. There were many windows, muffled in white shades. Automatically, our voices were lowered.

"We shall put the casket *there*," said the servant, pointing. "I am making all the arrangements, messieurs. . . ."

"You are in charge here?" asked Bencolin. "Odd. I have been here before—I don't seem to recall—"

"Alas, no, monsieur! I am Gersault, M. de Saligny's valet. I have been employed only a few weeks."

"Where are the others?"

"The house servants, monsieur? They are gone. M. de Saligny let them go day before yesterday. . . . He and madame did not intend to remain here."

"Ah! You are familiar with his affairs, then?"

"He trusted me very much. Yes. I did my best to see to it that he was well served. He sent away all the others, temporarily, except the grooms at the racing-stable and the *concierge*. I myself intended to leave last night, after I had prepared a cold supper for monsieur and his bride and tidied up a little." He smiled in a wan, spectral way. "I intended to welcome them, as a good servant should." After a pause he added, softly, "It is hard to believe that he is dead. . . ."

"You remained here last night, then?"

"Yes. And it is not a pleasant place to be, alone, wandering from room to room. . . . I ask your pardon, monsieur; I should confine myself to answering your questions. They telephoned me at two o'clock to tell the news. It is strange," he murmured with that smile and shrug, "because a bit earlier than that I could have sworn I heard M. de Saligny's key in the front door. However, I was mistaken. I came downstairs with a bridal wreath I had bought with my own money, but there was nobody there."

Through the dusk I looked over at Grafenstein, who nodded his big head. The valet, Gersault, was standing with folded hands, rather like the image of a saint, and you noticed how the corners of his wig curled down almost to his eyebrows. He waited patiently, soft and apologetic, for Bencolin to continue.

"His key in the door?" repeated the detective. "He carried a bunch of keys, then, I suppose?"

"Why, naturally, monsieur!"

"And, of course, he had them with him when he left for the wedding ceremony yesterday?"

"Yes. I helped him dress, you understand, and I remember laying them out and seeing him put them in his pocket."

"The keys to what?"

"Why—the regular thing," said the valet, wrinkling his forehead. "A key to the front door, one for the back, one for each of his cars, several to the stable paddocks, his desk, the wine-cellar, the strong-box—"

"He had a strong-box, you say?"

"Yes, monsieur. I know, because I handled his correspondence since he hurt his hand, and I know that he used it; but for nothing of much importance. He never kept large sums of money at hand."

"Not last night, for instance?"

"Why—no, monsieur! Why should he? Pardon me. I mean, not to my knowledge."

"Hm! . . . M. de Saligny had many visitors?"

"Very few, monsieur. He seemed to be afraid of something."

"At what time was this when you thought you heard him coming in last night?"

"I am not sure. It must have been after one o'clock."

Bencolin suddenly wheeled round. "Show us his strong-box, Gersault. . . ."

When Gersault was moving soundlessly over the floor, his outline wavering, as though he were hung there and floating in space, I heard Bencolin mutter: "Are there *nothing* but fools in my department? Am I *always* going to be too late?" And I thought for a second that Gersault looked over his shoulder and lifted a long upper lip to smile, as though he were saying, "Yes. . . ."

We went upstairs, along another hallway of the

drawn blinds; and the only sound was Grafenstein's asthmatic wheezing. The three dusky figures of my companions stopped before a closed door. . . . Then there was a strained movement through them. I saw Gersault's narrow face turn on its high collar as on a pivot, his jaw fall open a little, and one hand with drooping fingers extended motionless towards the door.

"This is his study, messieurs," said the valet. "And there are his keys in the door."

One of them was in the lock, the others hanging from the ring. You cannot be so weirdly reminded of somebody's presence as at seeing a key in a door when nobody is there. The lock was not even caught.

"The person you heard coming in, of course," Bencolin said, quietly, "was the murderer. . . ." Then with a spasmodic motion he pushed the door open.

In contrast to the other rooms, the blinds here were up, but the place smelt stale and stuffy. A fly buzzed against one bright pane. It was a fairly large room, panelled in oak and with yellow straw matting on the floor. There was a profusion of tarnished silver cups on the panel-rail, more of them on top of a big stone fireplace, and most of the wall space was taken up with framed photographs. The chairs were wicker, and on a wicker table charred with cigarette-burns stood three glasses, partly filled with whisky. A riding-boot lay in one corner, a dirty shirt was thrown over a chair; you would have said that the occupant had dressed hurriedly and gone out whistling. . . .

"I am very sorry, messieurs," said Gersault, "but I have not had time to clean up—"

"Who was drinking here?" asked Bencolin, pointing to the glasses.

"M. Kilard and M. Vautrelle, monsieur. They came here to wake up M. de Saligny on the morning after his bachelor dinner."

"And that door?" Bencolin indicated one at our right.

"To his bedroom, by way of a bath."

Except for the droning of the fly, there was silence while Bencolin walked about the room. He inspected a row of lockers under the windows, raising their lids with his stick, and he was muttering aloud:

"Davis Cup racquets . . . warped; not even in a press. *Tiens!*" We hearda singing *plung* as he struck the gut. "Haven't been used in a long time. . . . What's this? Rifles. Out of their cases; breeches jammed—no oil—*diable*! He treats them cavalierly." Another locker lid banged. He looked at a stuffed leopard's head hung over a small bookcase. "Sumatran. He was a dead shot to get *that*, too." Suddenly Bencolin turned, with the fangs of the leopard over his shoulder. "Messieurs, you remember that story which Charcot published in his book, *The Beast Hunters*? He said that there were only two men he had ever known to attack a mountain lion with a hunting-knife. One was the late M. Roosevelt of America, and the other this young Duc de Saligny. . . ." He turned to the pictures. "His prize filly; he was getting her in shape for Auteuil this year. . . . Here he is; he was in the finals at Wimbledon last year. . . ."

Grafenstein protested, "Very interesting, but we came up here to see the strong-box."

The detective sat down on the window-locker, put his forehead against the glass, and for a long time he stared out at the trees. The low afternoon sun crept along the carpet in a thin hover of dust, shining on Bencolin's top-hat and the silver head of his stick as he gripped them. Then the grip relaxed in a small gesture of weariness. . . . And as the shadows gathered against hot dying light, so there rose now all the grim reminders of the man who would not come back—the shirt flung carelessly over the chair, the three glasses standing forlorn on the table.

Gersault, padding into the room, said, softly, "I will get the strong-box for monsieur," and jingled the keys he had taken from the door.

"Oh—yes," observed Bencolin, looking up with a vague stare. "Where is it? In that desk over there on the wall towards the bedroom?"

"Yes, monsieur; the key to the desk is here. He kept his papers there, In think; he never allowed me to see them." The man's lean face was palely eager, his eyes glistened, and his wig had slipped a bit to one side. I fancied that his handshake must be cold, like a toad. He seemed to rustle when he walked.

"All right—but don't touch anything. Just put the key in and let down the lid of the desk; don't put your fingers on it."

We all gathered round the high desk with its lid that swung like a trap, outwards. Gently Gersault eased down the lid. The desk was empty.

"Yes, monsieur, somebody has been here," the valet told us. "The desk had papers in it; in those drawers, and stuffed in the pigeonholes."

"Naturally," snapped Bencolin. "Now"—he pointed at a heavy tin box pushed back in a corner—"open that."

. . . Gersault sucked in his breath in a tiny gasp. The cash-box was stuffed to the brim with bank notes, the topmost one for two thousand francs. Bencolin's wry laughter jarred on the silence.

"Our thief," he remarked, "has taken all Saligny's papers, and passed up a million francs in cash. . . . You don't know what these papers were, do you, Gersault?"

"No, monsieur. I—I never worked here. He dictated his correspondence to me on a typewriter downstairs. A million francs—!"

"Shut up the desk. We have finished. I shall want a telephone, Gersault. Is there one up here?"

"In the bedroom, monsieur."

"Very well." He turned to us. "You might wait for me outside while I have a further look around. By the way, Gersault, can you tell me if there are any keys missing?"

The valet ran over them and pondered. "Yes! Yes, I am sure! The key to the wine-cellar is not here!"

"To the wine-cellar? Surely the butler carried that?"

"Not to my knowledge. For his dinner, M. de Saligny supervised the wines himself. When he dined here alone, he rarely drank; and he kept the key himself. I remember his saying he was forced to discharge one butler for being too interested in the wine-supply. Zut! The man we have now—" Gersault spread out his hands. His long lip wrinkled in distaste.

So Grafenstein and I left the two in the room; as we went out Bencolin had walked over to inspect the lion skin spread before the fireplace. . . .

We tramped down the great staircase, as though we descended into a dim gulf from which rose voices of the past, all those portraits on the walls stretching out their mimic arms, stirring and rustling in brocade through the whitish dusk; as though the candles in those silver sconces drew back their ghostly light, and into the carpets crept the bloom they had lost for a hundred years. . . . I could not put down the impulse to wander through this place, to feel the pull of the memories that must have haunted it for so many. So, while Grafenstein lumbered out the front door, I turned back.

I those stately shadowed rooms of cream panels, far up in the ceiling glass prisms tingled faintly to your step echoing on the parquetry. You could hear, too, the voices of many clocks all ticking through deserted rooms. Thin level slits of light were built up high in closed shutters, to show dimly the outlines of marble mantels, mirrors reflecting the past, and murals, delicately tinted, of simpering shepherdesses curtsying forever with a crook tied in a blue ribbon. What was that song?—"*Il pleut, il pleut, bergère; ramenez vos moutons*. . . ." You could almost hear tinkling the Swiss music-box of the eighteenth century, and see the porcelain figurines dipping white wigs for a minuet. Yes, here was a spinet in a little music-room off the banquet-hall Kilard had described; through the door you could see the white of the table laid for that supper which Saligny and his bride would never eat. Above that spinet I could see another tall portrait looking down. . . . What was the plate? "Jourdain de Saligny, May 30, 1858—August 21, 1914."—A white-haired aristocrat with his hand in the breast of his coat. Raoul's father. Queer how Kilard's voice kept coming back, speaking dry through the house, through the dimness and the stale scent of rose-leaves:—"I saw him die." Then I touched the keys of the spinet, which gave forth a throaty rasp, and when I looked up again at the pictured face in the dusk it suddenly smote me, chilling and weird in grandeur, how the history of this house had been written in songs. Changing fingers on these keys, changing dresses under the wax-lights; satin and small-clothes, sweeping beaver hats and silly little love-tunes through a hundred years in a chime of gurgling voices. But when that grim old aristocrat died, the medley of eternal clocks, the medley of eternal swishing trees, the eternal chiming voices had all passed from the music-box jingle of *"Il pleut, il pleut, bergère"* . . . it had the terrible beat of marching rhythm, the heartbreak of glasses wild-clinked in a final toast: *"Quand Madelon vient nous servir à boire!"* . . .

And so I sat a long time before the spinet, hearing nothing except those echoes, or possibly last night a jazz band banging another final tune. I felt a rage at this ugly and senseless business, at the madman and his cheap terrorism, but I did not know then how ironic was even my rage.

Presently I wandered out through the banquet-hall, through creaking doors into pantry and kitchen. In the kitchen I noticed an inner door partly open; it apparently led to the cellar, for I could see a whitewashed wall on the inside. And then, as I walked across the linoleum towards the back porch, I came face to face with Bencolin. He had emerged suddenly from the cellar door. In the low light through curtained windows I scarcely think he saw me; his eyes were blank, and on his face was a devilish smile of triumph. He passed me without a word, like a ghost, disappearing through the door towards the front of the house.

Well, it was none of my business! It was none of my business, either, I suppose, to open the back door and go out into the garden behind the house; but even there I found no lifting of the unreality. The garden was shut in by poplars, held through the branches in a hush of dying sun on gravel walks . . . it was there, sitting on a bench, that I saw Miss Sharon Grey.

She wore something that looked like grey tweeds, queerly mannish for a figure that was not mannish at all, and had a small grey hat pulled over the shining hair. She was sitting there, chin in her hand, scraping at the gravel with her slipper—or maybe it was a brogue—and it was surprising at what a distance a fool like myself, say, could see the line of her eyelash. I was going to turn back (why embarrass anybody unnecessarily?), but she heard my step coming down from the porch, and raised her head.

I give you my word that it was impossible to judge that girl calmly. The amber eyes woke from their abstraction; recognition passed over them; a strange expression came to her lips. Not knowing what else to do, I walked closer. There was an utter emptiness of sound and thought, while I seemed to be standing over her again. Then, with an unexpected inner flip of astonishment, I noticed the cold, stabbing look in her eyes.

"I thought you'd keep your word," she was saying, suddenly and bitterly, "and you didn't. You didn't keep it. You said nobody would see me go out, and they followed me; I saw them follow me."

"Look here," I said, with some heat, "that wasn't me; it was Bencolin. *I* didn't know anything about it! I didn't know they were going to—"

"You have no more regard for truth," she added, "than you have for grammar. You are quite as nasty as you were when you—when you first came in there, and—and—" Wings of the dark-gold hair were drawn low on her cheeks; I could see them glint as she gave an angry flirt of her head and turned away and twisted a handkerchief.

I thought, furiously, "All right. You can go to hell, then!" and so I said, "What's more, if you hadn't been there in the first place—"

"Aoh, I like *that*!" she cried, opening her eyes wide. "Fancy your telling me—as if you had bothered anything about me—"

The darkening eyes held no surprise, but a kind of defiant hostility. Everything faded before that argument,—trees, flowers, sunlight; we were both engrossed in hurling out words—until suddenly we stopped, rather appalled. There was a long silence, while reality flowed over me, and I realized I was looking into the blank gaze of a stranger.

Then we both laughed. When the tension left, it was like a lifting from the heart; a warm rush of scent and sound came back, the wet perfume of lilac, the yellow flash of a bee, and the hot still sun low-lying on the ground. We laughed, as though we found relief in that garden; and she put out her hand and said, "How *are* you?" and I said, idiotically, "Great!" and sat down beside her on the bench.

In talking, you forgot everything except the immediate presence of this girl: her very face and gestures; the way the dark fringed eyelashes rose and fell on luminous eyes that ran over you, penetrated—a sweetish-sickening stab—and turned away, the flush on her cheeks, the quick low slur of her voice, all bound the brain with a power of what can only be called dreaming vitality. We spoke in commonplaces; in fact, I do not remember what we spoke about at all. Conversation was halting, in that groping, that sense of a barrier never referred to, which could be broken in an instant, but was not broken by either. Suddenly she said:

"I came up here this afternoon—you like to be alone with yourself—and there had been an unpleasant experience"—she moved her head vaguely—"down there. I wanted to see if I could feel anything about this house. I can't explain it, just to sit here, and maybe gather a flower—or see if there were anything to draw me to *him*, now that he's dead. . . . You won't understand, but it's all so *empty*."

She paused, trying to choose words.

"I mean, when a person dies, you don't have any sense of him any more; you don't think of him as really living"—she gestured—"up there. It's as though he had never lived, do you see? He isn't real any more. You wonder what he was like, and you can't even visualize him, when you try, except as—as a kind of magic-lantern picture on the wall. I wonder what's wrong with me? It doesn't mean anything to me. . . ."

Again that trancelike voice of a woman trying to punish herself, and not succeeding; the quick emphasis on some words, the deep brooding in the amber eyes—a sense of wonder, and almost of communion with unseen things behind a veil. Then she looked at me, as though she was searching, and something quickened behind the gaze.

It was then that there rose sharply from the front of the house a series of reports, an automobile back-firing, the scrunch of wheels on gravel, and the babble of excited voices. The sounds beat against the grey house, stirring a cloud of startled birds towards the sun. We rose and went to look. There was dead finality in the sound.

Circling the path in the shadow of the damp walls, we emerged round the angle of the house into the full westering light. A black van was backing up to the great front door, the driver twisting his neck around and gesticulating with his free hand, and two other men were unlocking the rear of the van. Exhaust smoke drifted across the dead colour of the roses, gravel scruffed and pattered from the men's feet. Somebody triumphantly said, *"Voilà!"* We heard the rasp of a bolt, a grunt, a long stretcher, dark-covered, was eased out from the van into the men's hands. "Softly, there. Don't bump—easy, *mes enfants*!" cried a gendarme in uniform. "Diable! my receipt! Softly, now! Ah!"

The sun dipped beyond the trees, falling in shattered light. A tide of shadows crept up round the house; it seeped like water—rising slow over this proud place whose windows were drowning eyes, sinking as the water swept it; but every chimney, every window, every dark stone stiff and arrogant in the stoicism of its death. "Up the stairs, now. . . . Monsieur, will you sign for this?" From the corner of my eye I could see Gersault standing on the steps, and the gendarme, flourishing a little notebook as the black burden was trundled up over the treshold. And Gersault turned, and made a queer stiff bow as for a last welcoming.

The songs were over. The master was coming home.

X. Bencolin Weaves

She put her hands in the pockets of her tweed skirt and looked up jauntily. She drew a long breath and said:

"No good moaning; that's over with. Have you a cigarette?"

"Look here—aren't you dramatizing this a bit?"

"Most of us do. A light? Thanks." She blew up a plume of smoke thoughtfully. "Most of us do; we can't help it. Pernicious influence of the cinema. We have to find a substitute for the standards of acting laid down in Victorian novels. . . ."

Now the moment anybody mentions the word "Victorian," you can take it for granted that the conversation is going to become artificial, and that the person who says it is avoiding all pretensions to frank discourse. But she laid her hand on my arm as we went back to the garden.

"No, but really—that's what's behind all this. I've read the morning papers, and I know all about it. Don't you see? The whole thing is dramatized, expertly staged; this murderer they're talking about is all kinds of a stagy curtain-line artist. That's his trouble."

She sat down on the bench and stared unseeingly at the tip of her cigarette. "The French can't realize it, because they love gestures so that they come to associate them with life. The point is that they rarely indulge in them. . . . I'm sick of aliens; and I'm afraid." She shivered. Her eyes regarded corners of the garden. "O God! Last night I—"

"Steady, now!"

"And today I got shaken up again. It was horrible."

"Do you mean to say that this person came again—"

"Oh no! nothing like that. I can't tell you. . . . Yes, I will, though. Well"—she looked at me defiantly—"I thought I'd go round and see how Louise was taking this. It was horrid of me, all right, but I felt—well, savage, as though it didn't hurt *me* any more, and I wanted to see whether it hurt her. . . . Oh, this is putting me in a rotten light, but I can't help it! I knew her, you see; that was the way I met—Raoul."

She chewed a moment at the cigarette, looked at it as though she had never seen it before, and threw it away. "I went over this afternoon; she lives not far from here. Avenue Bois. They say the French are emotional. They are, if it's a question of a new way of preparing caviare or something; but there's a terrible silent grief in them when they . . . lose somebody. I saw it when I was a little girl; I was here when the war broke out. The postman with his funny bicycle would come around, and say, 'Pardon, madame,' and give a letter to some woman—'pardon, madame. Your son has been killed in action'—big brawny women, like those statues of La République. 'Pardon, madame,' with a bow—and the light would go out of them and they'd walk queerly, but if they could talk at all they would just murmur, '*Tiens!*

it's war—!'

"Louise was like that. She sat in her room, and smiled occasionally. She's lovely, you know. I tried to buck her up, and felt—no end of a hypocrite, though I did mean it! She just sat there, stroking a cat, with no expression on her face at all. Then in burst a horrible person, all buttery and sympathetic, who banged the door when he came in—an American named Golton.

"I don't know how he got in. But immediately he began to pour out condolences; said he was one of Raoul's best friends, and, while he hadn't the honour of Louise's acquaintance, he thought he should extend his heartiest sympathies . . . and if she wanted his heartiest sympathies . . . and if she wanted to be taken out to dinner any time, he was the man. Ugh!" She threw back her head and laughed wryly, almost hysterically. "That, you see, was bad enough. He kept scraping his boots together, and dropping his hat, and he talked ghastly loud and fast. She had to introduce me. The moment he heard my name he gave a ponderous wink and leer, and—where he's picked up this gossip I don't know; he seems to know every . . . anyhow, he practically accused me of being—well, the mistress of a man named Vautrelle."

She paused, and looked at me intently. All of a sudden I grew weary of this roundabout way of drawing a person out. I said, politely:

"Indeed? Yes, terrible, isn't it . . . ?"

"It doesn't seem to surprise you."

"Well, after all, why should it?"

She rose, breathless, her face flushed and her eyes dark with a questing, futile rage. The throb and fire of her loveliness, a languor that struggled to burn, swept a wave over the heart; that whole expression said, "Damn you!" but something quivered in her lip.

"So you don't understand," she said in a quick short voice. "There's nobody I can go to," she gestured. "They all want to preach—"

"My dear girl, who's preaching to you? I'm not. I think it's fine—"

She blazed, "Well, why aren't you, then?"

Round in a circle again, round in this endless bickering that was not only rather ludicrous, but entirely without sense or point! Yet for no reason at all both of us felt stubbornly impelled to flounder through it. I tried to point out to her where, in the statements she made, her logic was at fault, but she couldn't see it—she went right on in the same vein until her talk grew positively unreasonable. To tell the absolute truth, I was considering the expediency of taking her by the neck and choking her until she could see the rightness of my logic; but the storm passed, and a curious feeling of intimacy descended in those old trees.

"I don't like him," she said; "I haven't liked him, either; and I'll tell you this, he never supported me." She made this assertion with pride. "I have a villa of my own at Versailles. . . . I say," hesitating, "why don't you come out and dine with me tonight?"

We argued this for a while, for neither of us could quite conceive of the idea as a good one. But we finally agreed that it had enough points of merit to be worth trying; then she said it was late and that she had to go; and I suddenly remembered that I had come here as a grim detective. . . .

"I'll tell you the address," she said; "and don't write it

down, please; it would look like—Never mind. No, you needn't take me anywhere; I have my own car down by Louise's. I just walked up here. . . ." As she rose to go she turned and held out her hand with a queer little smile. "Cheers! We get along rather beautifully, don't we?"

I watched her go towards the house, past a clump of bushes and out of sight. With her passing a jumble of ideas rolled about in my mind—back there came, stinging, the questions I had forgotten to ask, the information I should have obtained, put off once again. It was like thinking afterwards of the speech we should have made in the conversation in which we were worsted at repartee, futile and not a little irritating. It reminded me of last night, still more so when I heard behind me a dry chuckle. . . .

Bencolin was lounging against a hedge, negligently smoking a cigar. He raised his eyebrows, lifted a finger profoundly, and all he said was, "Ah!"

"I suppose," I remarked, "you were listening to that conversation, too?"

He shrugged, regarding me with approval. "For a fledgling," he returned, thoughtfully, "a young man who is not yet what we call 'unsalted,' you play the game not at all badly. Well! For the greater glory of my profession, I sacrifice and crucify myself in the pleasure of listening to people's confidences. Come, we have work. . . ."

"Bencolin, listen! You didn't by any chance *arrange* for this—?"

"My dear young man," he expostulated, giving me a glance of injured surprise, "I am a detective, not the proprietor of a *maison de tolérance*. Besides, what could I hope to learn from such—you will pardon me?—nursery prattle as I heard this afternoon? Is it not unfortunate that true emotion is so imbecilic? . . . At any rate, we must go now. I have finished."

"Did you find anything?"

"I was searching for something in the nature of handwriting; unfortunately, it has been removed. *Tiens!* we've a clever antagonist!—but I did find a sheet of paper and a pencil—a Zodiac No. 4 pencil." He tapped his breast pocket with satisfaction. "Now we can go serenely. The good Dr. Grafenstein, I believe, is peacefully asleep in the front room. . . ."

As he rose, his fingers descended on my shoulder. They were fingers of crushing strength. The mockery was gone from his voice when he said:

"Miss Grey was good enough to favour you with a few comments on my race. Let me add at least one comment on your own. You profess to deny that flames flare and die easily; let me warn you to enjoy their warmth when they rise, and realize that they are only momentary, as we realize it. Why not philosophically admit that it will not last, and therefore savour it the more?—the great danger is that it *will* by your own stubbornness remain longer than you want it. *Pardieu!* Would you not grow unutterably weary of eating every evening of the same dish?"

With a shrug he released his grip. "Let each dawn find a new nymph beside you, and you will be happy; otherwise you will be either hurt or bored. I speak"—his head inclined politely—"as a father. Now let us go and find Grafenstein."

We found the doctor, as Bencolin had predicted, asleep in the drawing-room. He had one shoe off as he sprawled on a Louis Quinze sofa, and he was emitting an ascending series of gurgles from the corner of his moustache. Across the dim room, on a table, the body of Saligny lay under its black robe on the stretcher, waiting for the undertaker. Bencolin looked thoughtfully from one figure to the other, and then he woke Grafenstein. Gersault appeared again to escort us all to the front door and assured us: "Yes, monsieur, I will see to all the arrangements. I expect the undertaker before long, and I shall attend to the flowers and the condolence cards when they arrive. Trust me, monsieur. . . ."

"The autopsy is over," Bencolin observed, as we tramped down the path towards the cars, "and I shall have the reports I am waiting for. In the meantime I think we had better pay a visit to Madame de Saligny. That was a very illuminating conversation you had with Miss Grey, my friend."

"But I can't see that we're getting anywhere," grumbled the doctor, who looked morose and yawning. "Nothing tangible. We want evidence—clues," he explained, vaguely. He subsided again into a doze when he entered Bencolin's car.

It was not a long drive to the apartment-house in the Avenue Bois where madame lived. A pink afterglow was climbing the roof-tops when we sent up our cards, but no lamps had been lighted in the foyer or in the halls. The whir and creak of the automatic lift bore us into dim regions, hushed like a sick-room. A maid admitted us into the outer corridor; immediately, through open glass doors to the drawing-room, we could hear a voice upraised, ". . . and I says to him, I says, 'Say, brother, it'll take you and what army to put me outa this place? Lookit,' I says, 'I paid my money, didn't I—?"

Against a line of long windows through which the pinkish light made many shadows, Madame de Saligny sat in a winged chair before a tea-table. Opposite her, perched on the edge of a chaise-longue, Mr. Sid Golton was wiggling a glass of port in one hand and gesturing argumentatively with the other. Madame's head turned slowly, clear white profile and night-black hair swimming in the elfin light; there was an infinite weariness of pain in her eyes, and at intervals she smiled mechanically at her visitor. She greeted us with an eager relief, but Golton was palpably annoyed. He gulped off the rest of his port and sat glowering.

". . . and I regret very much having to disturb you for a moment," Bencolin was saying (he ignored Golton, and spoke in French), "but I was certain you would be interested in running down the culprit in this affair."

"Naturally. Please sit down. Will you have tea or port?"

"Neither, thank you. We cannot stay." Bencolin was standing there with his hands folded over his cane, a weird figure against the dying light, and there was a queer gentleness in his voice. "I merely wanted to ask you how much you know about a certain M. Vautrelle."

For an instant she quivered as though she had been stabbed. Golton demanded in a hoarse stage-whisper, "What are they parley-vooin' about?" Then madame's bracelets jingled faintly from the depths of the chair.

"He is a devil, that man," she said in a suppressed voice. "I, who know, tell you that."

"He was a close friend of M. de Saligny's?"

"For what he could get out of it—yes. He was interested in trying to get Raoul to back him financially with a play he had written."

"How long had he known him?"

A faint, wan smile went over her face, like the smile of one who sleeps.

"No—I know what you are thinking; I thought of that, too. He is not . . . Laurent. He is evil, that man, but he is not Laurent. He knew Raoul at a time when Laurent was confined." Her eyes flashed open; from the depths of that chair it was oddly as though she were struggling in water. Her voice sank to a crooning: "But Laurent is somewhere. I sense his presence . . . they cannot deceive me . . . I sense his presence. . . ."

The thought shot through my mind, "The woman's mad!" and was answered only by that eerie jingle of bracelets. "No," it struck me again, "she's not mad; she's terribly sane," and I looked round me, half expecting to see Laurent standing over among the shadows.

After a pause, Golton said, loudly and plaintively, "Well, if nobody's going to pay any attention to me, I guess I'd better leave—!" and heaved up from the couch with a tentative motion. Nobody did pay any attention to him. The three of us were all deliberately ignoring him, and as for madame, I doubt that she knew he was there at all.—We heard him in the hallway, calling for his hat, and he hesitated round the door as though waiting for recall; but presently the door banged, and little quivers shook the windows of the room where we stood motionless round madame's chair.

Still those dark eyes searched our faces.

"I do not hesitate to speak before you," she continued. "I even felt impelled to talk last night . . . *last night*. . . .

"M. Vautrelle gets money. And I think he has an agreement with some one, the proprietor of that place we visited. *Vous savez*, that droll little man," she made strutting gestures. "That is all I am sure about. That droll little man who keeps telling you he is an artist."

Her eyes wandered out the window over the trees.

"Is M. Vautrelle usually to be found at home in the afternoons?" Bencolin asked. "I have his address, and I thought perhaps—?"

"I am always sure where he is in the afternoons, because Raoul used to go with him before his injury. They would practise at Maître Terlin's fencing-rooms just off the Étoile. It hurt Raoul not to—" She stopped.

"Of course. . . . Madame, I suppose you are acquainted with a Miss Sharon Grey?"

"Sharon?" She nodded listlessly. "Sharon is related to some very good friends of mine in England. . . . She is very nice, but she is—the flesh, solely. Why do you ask?"

"She knew M. de Saligny, I suppose?"

For the first time madame smiled, but it was with a trace of bitterness.

"You understand, she cannot let the men alone. Yes, she knew him; she went quite mad over him, I happened to know, although she had seen him only twice. . . ."

"Ah!" said Bencolin. In shifting his position he accidentally knocked against my arm. "Yes, I can understand that."

". . . and she wrote him constantly, even when he was in Vienna. Personally, I did not care. Raoul was not that sort. He used to show me her letters."

She looked very proud when she said this, because she believed it. I found myself thinking—irrationally—that Saligny was rather a fool in his preference of Miss Grey. Bencolin changed the subject.

"Please forgive me, madame, if I bring up unpleasant subjects. But you understand we are engaged in a criminal investigation. We have reason to believe that—your first husband has taken the guise of somebody almost certainly known to M. de Saligny and very possibly known to you. . . ."

She put her hands over her face suddenly, and said, "No!"

". . . and, madame, you knew him better than anyone else. Is it your opinion that he would be capable of doing this?"

"Doing what?"

She had been staring at him, but when he replied she settled back again.

"I mean, could he—let us say—assume the guise of a character alien to his own—another nationality, perhaps?"

"No doubt he was a clever actor," she said in a hard voice. "He deceived me into thinking he was not . . . mad. No, don't bother to spare my feelings, M. Bencolin; please, now. I understand. Yes, he had a gift of mimicry; it usually is a part of a great aptitude for foreign languages, you know, and that was his hobby. He used to clown sometimes; a relief from restraint, he called it. Relief from restraint!" She laughed. "I have seen him imitate everybody, and people of many nationalities. Given a half-hour to watch a German—I have seen him do it with Hindenburg, whom he admired—and you would swear you were listening to a real German—gestures, mannerisms, everything. . . . But all the time you had the idea those horrible eyes were on you. . . ."

She paused, fascinated, impelled against her will to go on.

"How he would sit in his study and plan what he called his 'jokes'! I did not understand then. I thought his silky beard was rather comical; I used to feel him stroking my throat, and see him open his eyes . . . but I did not know. It was when he took off his spectacles that you noticed a change. . . . He put on weight easily, too; it made him look . . . I was drawn to him; I don't know why—it was almost a repulsion. . . . I'm tired," she said, suddenly. "I'm tired."

We left her, head on her hand, looking out into the red sunset. Once again we heard the whir of the elevator in darkened halls, and emerged on the Avenue Bois among the tall trees.

"And now," remarked Bencolin, "one last interview before the *apértif*. We go to the *salle d'armes* of Maître Terlin. Possibly we may get a bit of illumination from M. Vautrelle."

XI. Swordplay

Just off the Étoile, in its angle with the Avenue de la Grande Armée, is the fencing-school of Maître Jérôme Terlin. I have not been inside its cobblestoned court for a year, but I am as sure it is still there as I am that the unknown soldier still lies under the Arch. M. Terlin, in his browned age and his agility with the foil, resembles a mummy touched by a galvanic battery. He taught me to fence when I was eight years old, with a miniature foil which—he said—had been used by Louis Napoleon. People thirty years older than I have early memories of him dancing about while he bade them spend wearisome hours of practice lunges, the *tirer au mur*, or stroke at the wall, before ever you might learn the simplest parry at tierce. We can recall this animated mummy hopping under his dingy walls, crying: "Clumsy camel! Species of elephant! Do not *hit*; this is no boxing-match! The steel rod is not more rigid than your arm, can you see? and body and arm are one, moving together, when you lunge—!"

There it was, the same huddled gate with the lamp, when Bencolin, Grafenstein, and I arrived that late afternoon. Tall lights were winking out in the tall trees;

a pale glitter rose along the Champs Élysées, deepening to blue-grey and twinkling gleams as it swept down beyond the Arch. Out towards Neuilly the red sky hung between the dark throats of buildings, glittering with car lamps. From this we went through the door, down a little alley to the *salle d'armes*. This place of Maître Terlin's had now become a sort of occasional club, to which came only the great names of the fencing world for an exchange of reminiscences, a cigarette, and a glass of *fine*, or lightning bouts wherein a touch was somewhat of a rarity.

In the long *salle*, of which I knew every trophy and rapier on the racks, I felt a sense of coming home. That smell of dust and liniment and oiled steel; the old mats, the masks, the tiny windows of pale glass high up in a dusky roof . . . it was a background for the embalmed elegance of M. Terlin. He loomed up, courtly and black-clad, with his face wrinkled and bald like a brown apple; and when his sharp eyes picked me out he descended on me with a flourish. Ah, where had I been these five months, that I forgot my old master? Did I go well? And had I learned, as I never should, alas! not to slap in that outlandish Italian fashion in the parrying of *seconde*? And here, if his eyes did not deceive, was his friend M. Bencolin, the pupil of Merignac! When we had shaken hands all around, M. Terlin said:

"I sit in my back room, messieurs, this afternoon, and with a toast I mourn the dead." The climax of each speech had a dramatic swish, as of a rapier through the air. He pointed at a picture on the wall by the door; it was the famous one of Saligny in fencing costume, right hand with foil up at salute. It was a gay and joyous thing in that dim palace.

"A great swordsman, messieurs," declared Terlin. . . .

And now, coming up out of the dusk in the great room, I saw another figure that wore white. It was Vautrelle, broad of shoulder, conscious of his carriage. He smiled through cleft teeth, and in his hand he carried a rapier with great bellguard and quillons. M. Terlin chattered on, throwing out gossip of 1885 mingled with criticisms of all our fighting styles, quite unconscious of our errand or of the way Bencolin and Vautrelle regarded each other. We must come with him to the back room, where the great ones used to sit.

Presently we were seated at a round table in a small chamber off the pale-lit *salon*, and M. Terlin went to get the wine. You had a feeling of ghostliness among the high rafters in this semi-darkness. Vautrelle was leaning back, one arm akimbo, and the guard of his big rapier shining across the table. I could see that he was smouldering, aching to show off; when he spoke, his voice was soggy with sarcasm, and he looked down from his great height with the speculative expression of a man turning over in his mind the most effective insult. To my surprise, Bencolin said nothing whatever about Saligny. Vautrelle must have known that was why we had come, and this social-call attitude chafed him. But instead the detective discussed with Grafenstein the merits of the foil as contrasted with the *schlager*. . . . Terlin brought in a dusty bottle and four glasses, that we might drink to Saligny. Vautrelle rose, lifting his glass, and as Terlin proposed the toast Vautrelle laughed and in a stage voice quoted the cholera-hymn, "Here's a glass to the dead already. . . . Hurrah for the next that dies!" After he drank he somewhat unnecessarily smashed the glass against the edge of the table.

"Take my word for it, there will be another," he added, flipping up the blade from the table and catching it. "Does any of you gentlemen fence? I need a workout. I am like Paderewski with the piano. If I neglect practice a day—" Again he flipped the blade.

"Ah, that is the spirit I like," said Terlin, chuckling. "In the old days, mark it! they practiced every day, and they did not use leather buttons, either. I remember—"

"Never mind that," said Vautrelle. "How about you?" he asked Bencolin. "Does monsieur's dignity permit? Seven touches, no masks. What do you say? I need exercise. I'll give you a handicap if you like."

"Kindness itself," said Bencolin, twirling his glass. "No, thank you. I should need to change, and I am not so spry as young people like you and M. Terlin."

"Three touches handicap," offered the other. "Even a *juge d'instruction* can come off his dignity, you know." He was growing exultant, and his voice grew more heavily patronizing; he had not forgotten last night. "Let's run it off. *Hein?* I shall have to go soon; I've got a little mission in Versailles this evening, and I must dress."

Bencolin looked up with mild surprise. "How interesting! . . . We must go, too. My friend, M. Marle here, also must go to Versailles tonight." He paused and added, deliberately: "What is it, my friend?—I forget. Don't you have a dinner engagement with Miss Grey?" His question as he glanced at me was innocence itself.

I got a rush of blood to the head, and stared at

Bencolin for the tactlessness of that remark, but the detective was finishing off his wine. Vautrelle's eyes opened wide, and then narrowed. He held the blade out levelly, motionless. There rose the dry shrillness of Terlin's voice, crying in all unconsciousness:

"*There's* an idea. Not M. Bencolin—why don't *you two* fight?"

Bencolin said, *"Tiens! tiens!"* and clucked his tongue. Grinning, he glanced round the circle with raised eyebrows; then sighed and returned studiously to his wine. He had a knack of making these gestures seem almost rowdy. So that was the idea—baiting Vautrelle!

"Oh!" Vautrelle said at length. For the first time he studied me from head to foot, and asked sweetly, "Do you care to engage, monsieur?"

"In what?" I asked. My blood was pounding quite fast, and I wanted to cry out, "You're damn right I will!"

"A fencing bout, of course."

"Of course," said Bencolin, shocked. Vautrelle turned to him savagely; then closed his mouth hard. Vautrelle and I had singled each other out. Why we should both be grimly polite, and why I should commence inwardly to call him a grandstand swordsman, I was not sure; but I think we both got the feeling that we were both as small and foolish as chessmen whom Bencolin was pushing about the board.

"Delighted," I said. "I used to have a locker here, if M. Terlin hasn't given it to somebody else. What's it to be—foils or duelling swords?"

"Neither," interposed Bencolin. "Zut! you two can fence to your hearts' desire when you have time, but not now! You don't seem to realize it's getting late. We have too much to do to waste time with dress-rehearsals. Encounters behind the Luxembourg can wait."

"Oh!" said Vautrelle, "I see! Well"—he swished his blade through the air—"another time, perhaps, when you have nothing better to do than—your present activities, M. Marle." He oozed thick sarcasm all over.

Bencolin agreed: "By all means. . . . 'You have not seen the last of me, monsieur; we shall meet again,' " he quoted, and struck an attitude. Then he laughed.

"Look here," said Vautrelle, leaning across the table. "You've done nothing but insult me ever since we had the misfortune to meet last night. Did you come here just to do it? I want to know what the point is."

"When I am endeavouring to learn something," the detective answered, "I try to do so, if possible, without asking questions. That, I believe, is your own amiable technique, M. Vautrelle. . . . Do we understand each other?"

He had risen, and was moving his sleeve around his top-hat absently. Vautrelle said nothing more. After a glance at me he turned and walked away towards the locker-rooms. I think he saw in my look the thing I was thinking, "You're getting old," and that thought had no connection with his agility in the fencing-room. I heard him murmur, "Damned boors!"

The swordplay that underlay this conversation had never been recognized by M. Terlin. He expressed sorrow that the rooms should be so deserted that afternoon, and he was engaged in telling us some anecdote of Conte, the Italian master, as he escorted us to the door. It was only when we were taking our leave that it seemed to dawn on him that our visit had some connection with the murder of Saligny. We left him among the ghosts of the swashbucklers, pointing his finger first at the portrait of Saligny and then towards the interior where Vautrelle was, thinking. Looking back over my shoulder, I saw him smite his forehead in the twilight.

"Now what was the purpose of that?" demanded Grafenstein, when we were in the Avenue.

"Wait!" cried Bencolin, struck with an idea. "I forgot something. I forgot the most important thing of all. . . ." He turned and went back into the alleyway, where I could see him conversing with M. Terlin.

"Yes, that was correct. I thought so, and M. Terlin confirms it."

"Confirms what?"

"That Saligny's prowess has been honoured by many nations. When they can't give a person any signal honour with a medal—note how our Legion of Honour has degenerated—they do the next best thing. France did it with her most distinguished athlete. He enjoyed the privilege of royalty; he could go through our customs-houses without having his luggage searched."

"Bah!" said Grafenstein, expressing much. Suddenly he smote his hands together. "You mean . . . it might have something to do with the opium?"

"It has very much to do with opium, but that wasn't my point. Patience, Doctor; I will satisfy your curiosity very soon. In the meantime let us go to the offices of the Sûreté."

On the drive to the Quai des Orfèvres my thoughts were taken up with Edouard Vautrelle and Miss Sharon Grey. Bencolin had caught him off guard, as surely as a fencer breaks up a complicated feint with a me-thrust, but it seemed to prove nothing except that autrelle was very much bound up with Miss Grey. et the connection was obvious; it would all have been straightforward matter except for that extraordinary uestion about Saligny's luggage. And even Saligny's ggage was not so bothersome as—what had Madame ouise said?—"the flesh, solely. . . ."

It was dark when Bencolin led us through the side oor of the Sûreté offices, down a corridor, and into a oom of bookcases and green-shaded lamps. I dropped to an easy-chair, meditating on the prospect of the ening. Grafenstein went to look over Bencolin's oulder when the latter sat down at a littered desk. A ell tinkled somewhere in the next room, and François tered.

"Anybody in the laboratory?" Bencolin asked.

"Doctor Bayle has gone, monsieur; but Sannoy can o any work you like."

"Let him make the tests on this pencil, then. Find its roup. Have they developed the last plates on that ook?"

"The negatives are drying, monsieur. I saw them hen I came through. Doctor Bayle says that the ink is o common to be traced, but the name is distinct."

"Good! I'll look at it presently.—He phoned me this orning that there was no doubt about the drug."

"None whatever, monsieur. They have been comparg specimens all day."

This talk made no sense whatever. Grafenstein and I rotested simultaneously, but Bencolin waved us into lence.

"Later, later! . . . Give me the autopsy reports, rançois, I regret that there was something I neglected to require in that work, which the medical examine wouldn't have done as a matter of routine, but I ca attend to it myself." He glanced at the typewritte sheets which François handed him. "Doctor, the med cal examiner reports that Saligny's blood and hea condition indicates he has been using opium for over year."

The big Austrian grunted, and Bencolin continue

"Here is a cable received from Doctor Ardesbur the specialist who attended to Saligny's injuries:

> "Hurts not permanent, but painful. Ligaments of spine strained; no difficulty, however, in walking, if he does not indulge in violent exercise. Anterior bone, left wrist, broken; used cast, but removed it before he left. He can go without any brace if he does not use the arm.

"So much for that. What about the fingerprints o the window of the card-room?"

"They are unquestionably those of Laurent, mon sieur."

"Ah! That established it pretty definitely, then. N fingerprints on the sword?"

"No distinct ones. There are several half-prints su perimposed on the brass nail-heads, but, though w used Doctor Locard's photographic process, we cann use half a point to identify anymore."

"And the thread?"

"We have identified it. It is precisely as monsieur ha predicted. It is a product distinct to the Merveil factory, moreover. Another similar particle was foun under the finger nail. . . . And, oh yes! We looke under the window, as you suggested, and found that other specimen. It corresponds with the ash traces when we submitted it to the test-glass."

"In short," said Bencolin, "you have confirmed my reconstruction of the crime?"

"To the very last detail, monsieur. You were even right about the sword having been concealed under the pillows."

"I fear, François, that we are talking the veriest abracadabra before these gentlemen. You may go. . . . For the present, I must ask you to excuse this talking in the dark," he added to us. He was silent awhile, his chin in his hand, tapping a pencil against the blotting-pad. Then he made a slight gesture.

"I suppose you have never been through our laboratories, or inspected our gallery of exhibits. It is late in the day, or I should take you through. I could promise you many interesting curiosities. However, I prefer to use a practical example rather than generalities. You shall see how we work when you see how this case has been worked out."

The vast building was silent except for a door slammed in some distant corridor.

"One of the popular fallacies of the day," Bencolin continued, thoughtfully, "is that the detection of crime is *not* a science, and that its investigators do *not* achieve almost magical results. I do not know why this error should be so prevalent, unless it is because extraordinary analyses occur so often in fiction; therefore, the careful public reasons, they cannot possibly occur in life. . . . Still, it is difficult to understand why the man on the street is prone to be so suspicious of what he is pleased to call 'book stuff' in this business. Tell him that a doctor—preferably a German with a sonorous name—has discovered a cure for cancer, and he will be very apt to believe you; but tell him the simple truth that by a single trace of mud-stain on a coat the identity of a murderer may be established, and he will probably sneer, 'Pah! you've been reading Gaston Leroux!' Yet we do not say, because the doctor's naked eye cannot see into a man's appendix, that the doctor cannot know this man has appendicitis. It is a field for specialized investigation, precisely like medicine.

"On the other hand, there is an astonishing idea that anybody at all is quite capable of being a criminal investigator: 'Knowledge and experience unnecessary; all that is required is a certain native shrewdness.' Messieurs, I should be most unwilling to put myself into the hands of a doctor who had no knowledge of medicine, but only a certain native shrewdness. I should not even go to a barber of that sort to get my hair cut."

He paused and looked at me.

"Particularly, I have found, is this the conception prevalent in America. Police officials with whom I have talked there have assured me that what we did here was all nonsense. In that country, I believe, the chief weapons of the detective are the 'stool pigeon' and the 'third degree,' just as the criminal's chief weapons are the alienist and the police department. Both forces are also materially aided by the ballot-box. . . . In regard to the weapons of the detective, there is consolation in the thought that the detective can always get his work done for him by the criminal. There is also consolation in the knowledge that a piece of lead pipe, judiciously applied for a long enough time, is sure to extract a confession of something from somebody; whether the right man or the right crime, it would be superfluous to enquire. Besides, no injustice is done—a quiet word in political circles will always exonerate him at the trial. *Voilà*! What could be simpler? The 'patient, plodding, tenacious investigator'—there is an ideal. You will pardon me if I believe it to be a most ignorant and useless one. You do not have uneducated men at the head of your school systems; I fail to comprehend, therefore, why there should be uneducated men to guard your most cherished possession, the law. Reflect, messieurs, and see in what appalling manner standards of mediocrity are applied, as a matter of course, to criminal investigation departments! To designate a person whom we *admire*, remembering, we say, 'Not a brilliant man, but a human, patient, thorough worker, who often makes mistakes and is frequently baffled'—and isn't it rather deplorable?"

Bencolin straightened his shoulders, and his eyes narrowed. He made a gesture as though he were spreading his fingers over the city of Paris. He added:

"I have never been baffled, and I have never been more than twenty-four hours in understanding the entire truth of any case on which I have been engaged. That should be the rule, not the exception, and I have no patience with the stupidity which takes any longer time." Presently he rose, slapping the chair arms. "However! It's getting late and we shall have to adjourn. Before we go, I want to call your attention to the dossier I have collected on our friend Vautrelle. Read it."

He spread out a typewritten sheet under the lamp. Grafenstein and I approached, and bent over it.

VAUTRELLE, EDOUARD. Investigation discloses that there is no substantiation of statement on this man's identity card and application for citizenship that he was a Russian officer. First came to Paris October, 1925, from Marseilles. Marseilles bureau wires that there is record of birth certificate of a man of that name in Hôtel de Ville, September 4, 1881; son of Michel Vautrelle, fish merchant, and Agnes Vautrelle, proprietress of wineshop on the waterfront. May be mistaken in the names, but Russian claim cannot be verified; no imperial records kept at Moscow. Since coming to Paris, there is no record of employment anywhere. Bank account at Crédit Lyonnais shows monthly cheque of four thousand francs, signed by Luigi Fenelli.

Bencolin looked at us with the suggestion of a smile, and then he put away the paper in a drawer of the desk.

XII. A Hand is Motionless Beneath the Cypress

So here was I at eight o'clock of the evening, fighting a dress tie before a mirror which on that magic night reflected my image as I should have liked it to be, for all the world like an author reflected in his book. I believe that I have said very little about myself in the way of data. This is as it should be, for it is too late to begin now, even if I were so minded; and I should not have included what I have if it did not have a bearing on the investigation in hand. Had it not been for the spring, and the night, and the way of young men in Paris at blossom-time, there might not have been hideous events in store. But I can see that only in retrospect. It comes back like a tune from over the hills and far away, and you can no more recapture its weird and mysterious glamour than you can recapture the sound of the violin you heard at night, faintly played and wandering, as you were sinking into sleep.

Thus I went out to my car, in the cool of the evening, with all Paris stirring to wakefulness around me, and set out for the villa at Versailles. It was all a vast shimmer, a ghostly halo round white monuments, alive with honking horns and darting auto lights that swept past and were lost; fleeting conversation, fleeting faces. And this presently faded as I crossed the bridge towards the Avenue de Versailles. . . . Down into a pale glimmering city, skimming over rises and dropping into a tunnel of wind that blurred the eyes, with a sensation as of wings—out across cobbles, wild bumping, with a jolt of springs settling now to a steady roar in the open country. I ripped open the cut-out, and over that pulsing drum I sent the call of the horn screaming like a battle cry.

When I reached my destination, just on the other side of Versailles, the shutting off of the motor was a sudden stillness, so that one by one the small night noises crept back again. There was the villa, a low white house where shaded lights burned, set down behind a rustic gate in a sunken garden, and surrounded by poplars along the garden's edge. Moonrise was trembling in ghostly brightness through the poplars, and spreading out across foamlike blossom in the shadow of the house. As I walked through the rustic gate the scent of those blossoms rose up in a wave on the still warm air, moist with dew.—Then I saw shadows across the latticed window to the right of the door, and I heard a voice. It was low, tense, electric. It was the voice of Edouard Vautrelle.

" . . . I can't stand it. You ought to realize that."

Sharon Grey replied, in a tone so cold, so flat and devoid of all expression, that it was startling:

"Why argue the question? There's nothing more; there never was."

"So far as you were concerned."

"Put it that way if you like."

He said, in a high-pitched, straining voice, "My God! you're not even leaving me my vanity—"

"No." There came the cool scratching of a match.

"You can't . . . I—"

"I'm expecting a guest to dinner, Edouard."

"—I brought you out the second act of my play," he said, rather wildly. "It's good. I know it's good. You—I—Now I'll throw the damned thing in the fire . . . !"

There was a little quiet, amused laugh.

"Melodrama, Edouard. You see, there isn't any fire. . . ."

I turned abruptly and walked out of earshot. The sound of that flat voice, not youthful, endowed with a quiet competence at doing these things, and, in contrast, the strained voice of this man who last night had put aside a murder with the same incurious detachment with which he would have picked a bit of lint off his lapel. Her laugh rang in the air, unemotional, rather pagan: tinny against the tense atmosphere of the room, like a laugh of common sense ridiculing a jack-o'-lantern ghost. I walked out to the steps leading up to the gate. I was angry, and I felt a gust of sympathy for Vautrelle. It was a revelation both ways; yet I felt that it was a revelation I had dimly suspected at the back of my mind. Now—why? Shouldn't I have been glad she was giving him the go-by? Instead, it came to me with hard elation, "She plays the game; all right, so shall I." When convenient, she, who was the essence of dramatics, could laugh heartily at her own household gods. It was a form of blasphemy, as though Duse, in the midst of a heart-sweeping scene from some play of youthful romance, had suddenly turned to the audience and said, mockingly: "You poor fools! Can't you even see what tripe this is . . . ?"

So I lit a cigarette and walked back to the villa, scuffling my feet as much as possible.

When I knocked on the door, there was a little flutter inside, and then a dead silence of aching and vital words which can now never be said. An old woman in cap and apron opened the door; then she vanished altogether. The tension was still apparent in that low-raftered room, where candles burned in silver holders over deep blue-cushioned chairs. Sharon, in a silver gown, rose coolly from a divan; she gave the impression of being interested in the long ash of her cigarette.

"Oh!" she said. "Do come in! You know M. Vautrelle—of course?" The faintest flicker of her eyelashes, the faintest way she accentuated that 'of course.' . . . She came over to greet me, stepping softly through a ruin. Vautrelle, his face a blank, was standing under the candles on the mantelpiece; he held some sheets of manuscript poised, dumbly, looking about like a man caught in a theft.

"Put them on the mantel, please, Edouard," she urged, smiling. "I'll look them over at my leisure. . . . My dear, fancy! M. Vautrelle has written the most *marvellous* play! *Hein, mon vieux?*"

I said something polite; I put my hat on a table beside the door, and wondered vaguely which way the ruin would topple. Vautrelle seemed to be fighting himself, so that the surcharged air quivered, and Sharon's queer little laugh only tightened the tension. I have heard that same laugh over sudden silence, in the ring at Madrid, when the bull raises his head slowly and seems to seek something with small bloodshot eyes—as Vautrelle did then. He stuffed the manuscript in his pocket. He straightened his shoulders and walked slowly across towards me. I remember thinking: "He's big; a hundred and eighty, probably. Straight up for the jaw if he moves his hand. Keep clear of the furniture. . . ." For an instant the seamed face looked at me. The wideset teeth appeared in a crooked grin; the eyes were pained and reckless. I felt a heavy pulse throbbing inside me, a quivering sensation, a mist. He took a step forward, and the quivering cleared as at the clang of a bell. I shifted, on my toes, and waited— Then his face swelled out in that grin. He bowed sardonically. With a cool and impersonal air he went over to the divan, where he took up hat, stick, and cloak.

"I do not intend making a scene," he said, calmly. "That would be foolish. It is not worth it. I trust you will not mind, mademoiselle, if I go out by the rear door? My car is in the lane behind."

When he had gone I felt rather shaken, and the whole thing had an unreal air. That tall swaggerer could have cleaned up the room with me, very likely— but he hesitated, as at some inner bitterness, some futility which seemed to make his entire life a series of encounters wherein he was alway beaten. Dimly I felt Sharon's hand on my arm, and heard again her light, low laugh.

We did not speak of the matter again. It was gone, blown into the summer night as though it had never existed, but when we sat on the blue-cushioned divan under the candles I still seemed to see Vautrelle's sneer behind the flames. And once, when I looked past her face out of the diamond-paned window behind the divan, I thought I saw him standing in the moonlight, arms upraised in curious pantomime. That window gave on a grey garden where Chinese lanterns glowed, but he stood apart, in a clearing by the gate in the grey wall. Except for that weird lost gesture of his arms, he was as motionless as the trees around him. Then, for one instant, I fancied that the gate behind him was being slowly opened. . . .

"*Do* have an *apéritif*!" I heard Sharon urging, and turned back.

A snugness and intimacy drooped down into the room. Candles and flowers, a scented wind from the garden rustling, the blue of the furniture, and Sharon's faint masklike smile under the wings of dark-gold hair—(*Was that a faint cry from the garden, then?* Nerves! You've got nerves! nothing else.)

High trees rustled away over the house. White shoulders in a silver gown, eyes moist and bright, with a sideways quirk, and a little strand of hair that trailed her flushed cheek when she moved her head—something breathless descended from the high emptiness of the night, from the Mona Lisa smile of the candles. The old woman brought in a tray of glasses. I drank a cocktail, then another, seeing Sharon's impish eyes over the rim of the glass, and feeling the light touch of her fingers when I took her glass to set it down.

A warm laziness stole over the divan, whose velvet under the fingers felt oddly like the brush of the girl's hand. We drank a third cocktail, and both of us laughed—and simultaneously both pointed out, as people will, that we had had nothing to eat since morning. We lit cigarettes (I had never felt more cosily at home in my life), and the very idea of being a calm, analytic detective seemed to me now the most fantastic nonsense. I must have mentioned the fact, for she said:

"Ooo, detectives, yes! You're not really, are you? I like to read about them. I can never go past a Chinese laundry without suspecting that the proprietor will chase me with the *wah-ha'-hoonglung*, or deadly whistling worm, of lower Burma—"

"And then," I said, "there's the equally poisonous pretzel adder from the Swiss Congo. It is so called because it curls up like a pretzel and is a convenient salty yellow color; it can be sent to your victim in a box of harmless pretzels. Sax Rohmer says there is only one way to detect the presence of this viper. You should always drink beer with your pretzels, for at the sight of beer this adder emits a faint but audible smacking of the lips, whereat you can seize it with a tongs and throw it out the window. Sax says he got the tip from an old Scotland Yard man who finds 'em in his bed every night."

"Yes! And master criminals—I love master criminals. They're called The Orange Octopus, or the Clutching Beetle, or something. I know. Edouard has one of them in his play. They control an organization resembling a glorified conception of the Benevolent and Protective Order of Elks—and at the end they turn out to be the invalid in the wheel-chair. Beware of wheel-chairs. Full of crooks—"

"Edouard has one of them in his play"; through this nonsense the sentence drifted grimly, and I stopped. The laugh in her eyes died; again into my brain came that knocking at closed gates, that sense of stealthy footfalls along a dark corridor, "Out, damned spot, out, I say! Why, then, 'tis time to . . ." "Edouard has one of them in his play."

"Oh," I said, casually, "was it a mystery play then?"
"Was what a mystery play?"
"This thing Vautrelle wrote."
She was very lovely, with her lips parted thus; she said in a small voice, "It was about—about a man who committed a murder and had a perfect alibi. I don't know how it ends."
For one breathless instant, while the candleshine dawned in her eyes and the black lashes began slowly to droop, I leaned towards her. You could sense her trembling motion, a deep breath—bright, bright burning flames! they contracted now in this draught of horror. Vautrelle who loved her, who must have killed her lover Saligny; yes! who came upstairs to put the blood on her hand and taunt her, and whom she did not dare betray even though she suspected. . . . My fingers touched her arm; she shivered, and put down the cocktail glass.
"Oh, can't we forget this! You—you know what I think now," she murmured. "I stood him off tonight, even though I was afraid of him. Didn't I tell you I was afraid? I felt—if you were here—he mightn't dare . . ."
Suddenly she looked up. And somehow her words sent through me a queer wrench of pride to straighten my shoulders, a surging pride that had behind it almost a sting of tears. . . .
"We're dining in the garden," she said, rousing herself decisively. "I think Thérèse must be ready now."
The Chinese lanterns, orange and red, were hidden among the trees, and through the darker branches above the sky was tinged in pearl. We walked into the secrecy of the garden through a low door, over thick soft grass to a space closed in by a wall of hedge, where

no sounds came. On the cloth of a table set for two the flames of two thin candles rose unwinking in the still air. . . . Out beyond, the grey garden wall murmured in pale blossom, the gate creaked faintly. There were rustic benches in the shadow of cypresses, and into the wall was set a dim drinking-fountain shaped like a lion's head, with water tinkling from its snout. . . . Here, sitting opposite each other in deep chairs, with the subdued candle-light falling on cloth and silver and glassware, we looked at each other in silence. . . . Silently the old woman was moving about the table, with a tender hand for dishes and wine. Oysters, accompanied by Roederer champagne, and without unpleasant "seasoning"; turtle soup and dry sherry; American sole; partridge, with Romanée Conti—thus we progressed, and in the deep red sparkle of that Burgundy thought was drowned. . . . Haunted Versailles, filled with the sound of wind in willows, with gilt and glass and the white finery of kings! This girl was as subtle a blend into the pageant of flower-beds as a Grueze head, as Antoinette at the Trianon, with laugh and harpsichord. Across the table she glowed in defiant gaiety, lips wine-moist, eyes bright and wandering, as the candles drew down their flames with the shortening night.

We talked of books. She was clever, but she did not force you to notice that. Neither of us seemed to pay the slightest attention to what the other was saying; it was not necessary, in a deep hush of uncertainty that came upon us. A voice faltered now and then, but that was all—we spoke only the more rapidly. She smiled and nodded, and I drained a glass of Madeira with the last course, and felt an uneasy tension thumping against my ribs. Books: Verlaine, Lamartine—her favourite was *La Crucifixe*. We disputed over the Rossetti and Swinburne translations of Villon, and she was passionate in her defence of all Rossetti's work. And then, listening to her from afar, I heard her say, "Lewis Carroll . . ."

"—fancy! I'd never read *Alice*! Raoul"—she hesitated, but rushed on—"a friend of mine was going to bring me a copy, but he put it off; and I got one. Don't you love the Mad Hatter's tea party? And the way they carried around flamingoes, and said, '*Off with his head*!'—?"

A dead silence. Her glass rattled against her plate. Like a malignant ghost, the wooden-faced woman's shadow fell across the table as she moved in to clear away the last course.

We sat back for a long time, motionless. "Off with his head!"—weren't we ever to be free of that? Struggle bitterly against it, thrust it from the mind, and at every turn of speech the cold satyr-face of murder leered into the garden. There was a wan little smile on her face, suddenly changed to a defiant curl of her lip.

"Oh, who cares?" she said in a hard voice. "Let's not run from it; it's no concern of ours." She laughed, very flushed of face. " 'Nor heed the rumble of a distant drum,' you know. People die, and it's no good bothering about them, is it?"

"No," I answered, "no—" and met her glance.

"Well, then! I want to be happy. I don't want things to prey on me. Thérèse! You may go now. Don't bother about the dishes. If you need money, take it out of my purse in the bedroom."

The wine swam a little in my head. It seemed a time

when every emotion pierced with sharp points into flesh and heart, one and the same, and aching. Laughter or tears, either would have been appropriate, for each was a part of this hurt of heightened senses. And yet—wine did not make the hands tremble. One by one the lights were dying from the Chinese lanterns. Dragons, gold and scarlet, pagodas and black letters, gave a last flicker before they faded among the leaves—here, there, within a few seconds of each other—and in their places moonlight settled slowly down through dark trees. Now only the two candles burned low on the littered table, in broad, nervous sheets of fire.

"A—a cigarette," she said, and made half a motion to rise.

I passed her my case. Its silver shone, motionless; then I heard the click of the clasp. She was rising, the cigarette hanging from her lips and her eyes fixed with a strained, intent look. Taking up the candle nearest me, I passed it to her for a light; when she breathed a cloud of smoke hesitantly, I lifted the candle again and blew it out.

There was a stillness. We had both risen. She made a queer little gesture, expelling the smoke hard; the amber eyes were fierce and glazed. Very slowly, without moving her gaze, she took up the candle nearest her and with a small breath extinguished it in a lingering flutter.

We walked in the garden, dark now except for the moon, past the grey wall of the blossoms, and into the cypresses' shade. A moth fluttered against my face. The tinkle of the fountain ran thin and clear and cool. No word had been spoken; the warmth and fragrance of that garden drew one into a dream. Now the fountain's plash sang more loudly, for at the rustic bench she hesitated, and, as I touched her arm, she sat down. Through pale rifts in the shadowing cypress I could see the dead white of her face staring up at the moon. It was like a dead face, except for the eyes; and she was like one dead except for the faint movement of the silver gown. And suddenly she said in a low, plaintive voice:

"How cold your hand is—on my shoulder!"

A faint movement of the lips . . . the words sank into my mind, repeated themselves with insistence, yet I could not understand. It grew on me, horribly, that my hands were clenched together, before me.

Clenched together, before me. I looked down at them stupidly.

The words clanged in my mind with sudden terrible suspicion.

"Get up!" I said, hardly hearing my own voice—it sounded strained and soft and ghastly. "Please get up—from there—a second—"

The thin song of the fountain shrilled mockingly. She turned her head. "Why—what's the matter? You look—"

"Get up from there!"

She started to rise. I swept her to her feet, out from the bench and behind me, and whirled towards the empty bench again. A chatter of repulsion went over me, a freezing agony that crept up to the brain and beat there with horrible hammer-blows. The moonlight, sifting down through the cypress, showed a man's hand protruding motionless from the back supports of the bench.

I ripped out the bench, flung it over in a thud, and

from a little screen of bushes a man's body pitched out into the clearing. It gave an almost lifelike twitch as it landed, but afterwards it lay still. Something wet splashed against my ankle. . . .

Nausea! Steady, now, steady! Get yourself together! It won't hurt you; it's dead, God knows! I gripped the rough bark of the bench, and bent in a sick coolness. The fountain shrilled steadily, as though it laughed. Come, now, turn him over! Your head's in the way of the moonlight. Get to one side, so you can see his face! *His* head's been nearly severed from his body. Never mind *that* stuff; you can wash it off. Damn that fountain!

Now the face, white and streaked with dirt, was turned full up to the moon. It was Edouard Vautrelle. His lips were drawn back from his teeth, derisively, and his monocle was still gripped in one sightless eye.

XIII. Death at Versailles

The killer had walked again!—he was here, in the garden somewhere, lurking about in these trees; he must be. But there surged inside me only a savage despair through a ruin of thought. The reaction was too great. My mind would not work. Do something! What is there to do?—I wish I could smash that fountain! *Who is it?* Who is this crazy murderer, in the name of . . . No, where is Sharon?

Something pulled me together then, in a cold rush of sanity and calmness. It was the sound of her voice, laughing hysterically. She was standing outside the cypress, in the moonlight, shaking with laughter, her hair partly fallen on her shoulder. Shaking off a daze, I walked out and seized her by the arm.

"Stop it! Stop it! Do you hear? Please!"

She pointed at the tree and said: "I saw him! I know who it is! He comes between us even when he's dead—he would!" And she laughed again.

"Will you stop that laughing?"

"All—right; I—I'll stop. Oh, he would! He's killed himself in my house—he would—!"

"You fool, his head's nearly cut off! Come to yourself!"

She glared at me through a mist. "You—you mean," she said in a choked whisper, "he didn't—*he* isn't really the one who—"

"That's what I mean. Go and see for yourself, if you want to."

"But—then who—?"

"How do I know? It's somebody. He may be here in the garden now, for all I know."

She seized my shoulder, and we stood there in that moonlit emptiness, looking at the trees. They seemed to be filled with suggestive motions, with leaves being parted softly, and crackling twigs. There was the grey wall, the gate; there was the hedge inside which we had eaten, and beyond it the darkened villa whose diamond panes glittered in the moonlight.

She murmured in a pleading voice: "Thérèse! I want Thérèse! Where—" and her head stirred faintly against my shoulder. Then she looked up and said, "You know I . . ."

I did not hear her. The chill of dread was back; a sense of being alone and without weapons in this whispering place of death, a sense of having to stand and fight a host of creeping things with hideous faces. Well, damn them!—so I could. A pounding sensation inside. I shuddered clammily, and shook my fist at the trees. . . . Then I saw, moving along the path from the hedge, the glow of a cigar. It moved up, it pulsed red, and ash was knocked from it as a shadowy figure came closer. Footsteps sauntered on the walk.

"My dear young man," said the voice of Bencolin, suddenly and lazily, "You seem to make no more efficient preventer of crime than I."

There appeared now the black loom of his opera hat,

the shapeless line of his cloak flung over one shoulder, and as he put the cigar in his mouth again I saw the gleam of his sunken eyes.

"Bencolin," I said, wildly—"Bencolin—I—Did *you* do—that?"

He shook his head, and looked up at the moon in a bitter grimace.

"No," he answered sombrely, "no."

And I burst out, still more wildly: "A hell of a detective you are! Letting things happen like this—!"

I had spoken in English. His head snapped down. He said in a low voice:

"That will be enough of such talk, please." After a tense pause he touched Sharon with his stick and added: "Pardon me. I think the young lady has fainted. You had better take her into the house. I'll explain how I got here, presently."

Yes, she had fainted, a dead weight sagging against my side. I picked her up—how light she seemed!—and started towards the house. "A moment," Bencolin said, hesitating. "I'll go in with you. The dead can wait."

We blundered into the house and Bencolin found the lights; no pretty candles, but electrics this time. Across the blue drawing-room I carried her, and into a bedroom of odd Egyptian lines and angles—grotesque place for a figure that now looked oddly childlike! Thérèse had gone. I laid Sharon on the silken counterpane. Wet towels and smelling-salts brought her round; she fought and muttered and squirmed, coming out, and then she lay quietly, looking up at the ceiling with glazed eyes.

"She's had a shock, that one," said the detective. "It looks bad. I think we'd better phone for a doctor. In the meantime I mustn't neglect my business. Is there a servant here?"

"There was, but she's gone; I don't know where she lives. Yes, call a doctor. I don't like the way she's breathing."

"No!" Sharon cried, suddenly and vacantly. "No doctor. I'm all right. I don't *want* a doctor—"

Bencolin had gone. She lay in the midst of that bizarre jumble of colours, breathing heavily on the huge bed. I went round softly and turned out all the lights except a shaded yellow lamp by the bed, so that she was entirely in shadow; but the whites of her eyes looked out of it, fixed and bewildered. I sat down beside her, feeling empty and wretched and helpless; occasionally I would reach out with a foolish motion and stroke her forehead. Once she smiled, trying to speak, but I shook my head fiercely and raised a warning finger. Then she took my hand, smiled, and curled up like a kitten, and her eyes closed. . . . Thus we stayed, motionless, and a savage, piercing tenderness rose inside me, until the clock ticked away half an hour and the doctor came.

I left him with her, a sympathetic whiskered person shaking a clinical thermometer, and went out to find Bencolin. The beam of a flashlight was moving along the garden wall. Bencolin flashed it in my face and came over slowly.

"Be comforted," he said, and his voice shook with vindictive triumph. "Be comforted. Call me as few hard names as possible. I was a fool, I grant you. I was guarding the wrong person—and I can't claim to be omniscient. But I knew who the murderer was before I came here, and"—he shrugged, and said harshly—"I swear to you that before tomorrow night we shall have our killer. Come with me."

"Did you find anything?"

"Yes. First tell me everything that happened this evening."

Trying to collect my thoughts in a drumming head, I slowly recounted every event of the evening. Several times he nodded.

"It fits," he said, finally. "Let me show you. . . ."

We went to the cypress and bent under it. He flashed the light down on the motionless figure lying with face twisted up.

"Don't track into it, now, but look carefully. No sword was used this time. He was first stabbed twice; once directly through the back, and once under the lowest rib on the left side. Then the murderer set to work to dismember his head—look! cutting through the cartilage of the vertebrae from the back. It isn't an easy thing to do for one unskilled in surgery, and the murderer desisted. I don't see any weapon. It was apparently a knife about an inch wide, and rather heavy; something, I should say, on the pattern of an American bowie."

The light flashed into the space behind the bench's original position, where was a thin sumach hedge, and beyond it a path a foot wide, following the garden wall under the drinking fountain. The beam played over this for a second, then swung to the left a few feet towards the rear gate.

"It's bloody," the detective said, shrugging. "There is the gate, you see. Vautrelle was standing near it when you saw him from the window. The murderer entered by that gate, behind him, and stabbed him in the back.

He was then apparently dragged over here and thrown into the sumach hedge against the bench while the murderer attempted to cut off his head."

A grisly scene for the moon! You could fancy that shapeless person bending with the knife, while the fountain sang and the dim light came through the cypress. A wind stirred vaguely. I shuddered.

"If I had looked out a few seconds more," I said, bitterly, "I would have seen—"

"Oh, never mind the recriminations. It can't be helped now." Bencolin shook himself and drew a deep breath. "And I am not sure," he added, slowly, "that this wasn't the best way. . . . *Tiens!* it's rather amusing, in a fashion! It has its points of drama." Again I heard his dry chuckle.

"There's the poor devil's play, in his pocket," he pointed out, after a pause. "Here, I'll disturb him for that. Take care of it. . . . Now let us look at the gate."

We came out into the garden again, around the tree to the tall wooden gate. Bencolin pushed it open with his foot. With the light going ahead, we emerged into a lane following the wall through open fields. A hedge, fragrant and spectral with blossom, enclosed the lane on the other side. For a while we stood there looking about, a cool wind from the fields blowing across our faces, a breeze that smelt of lilac and running water. Far up over a slight hill beyond and in front of the villa, we could see the dim wall of Versailles palace, and towards the town a few scattered lights. Bencolin was walking up and down, a luminous circle of light bobbing along the dirt road beside him.

"Here's Vautrelle's car," he called out of the dark. "The lane is rarely travelled; he turned out his lights and parked in the middle of the road. . . . Ah! Come here!"

The light had gone farther away. I followed it up, around a darkened Fiat car, and joined Bencolin at a point where the lane turned towards the main highway, at the end of the garden wall. Bencolin was down on his knees holding the light close against the road.

"Tire tracks," he said. "Michelins. Look"—the beam swept about—"a car came up this part of the lane from the main road, and parked here for some time: the impress is deeper over by the edge of the lane. Then it backed down and went into the highway again. Michelins—probably a taxi; the La Savoie company uses nothing else. Zut! Our murderer is getting outrageously careless! We can trace that cab in six hours or less. There will be very few taxis making that journey from Paris at this time of the night. It argues . . ."

"What?"

"As I thought. For once, our adversary's calm has gone. Put yourself in his place. You go to kill Vautrelle, and you think so little of the consequences that you take a taxi to within a few hundred yards of the scene of your crime. Certainly you are overwrought. *Hein?*"

"He might not have come to kill Vautrelle, remember that."

"And still bearing such a murderous weapon as that which he used? Which reminds me: the weapon should be somewhere near here. Let me see. The killer, coming back from his crime, realizes that he is still holding the knife only when he sees the taxi in front of him, and that the knife must be disposed of. He throws it—probably into the hedge, for if it were sent flying over that high garden wall it would in all likelihood be called to the attention of the taxi-driver. We can estimate it exactly; the murderer has not yet come into range of the cab lights, which face this way still—"

"The driver might have turned the taxi around while his fare went down the lane, mightn't he? In that case he wouldn't have seen—"

"Zut! Wake up! There are only two lines of tracks. This lane is too narrow to turn around in. Had the driver backed out to the highway, turned his car, and backed into the lane again, there would have been four lines. So the driver and the car lights are facing this way. The murderer has not come within range of the lights, which would be thrown"—he paced off a number of feet—"by light regulations, here, at the shortest. I go a little beyond and use my flashlight. . . ." He stopped and bent towards the hedge. "There's the knife, caught in the branches. See it shine? Don't touch it. We can go back to the villa now."

When we were returning along the road, he threw the light on his watch and whistled softly. "Name of a name! it's half past one. I had no idea the hour was so late. . . . Well! Do you feel sober now?"

"Oh, don't rub it in! Yes—too sober."

"Then do you recall what time it was when you saw Vautrelle standing by the gate?"

"I don't know; nine-thirty, possibly—Bencolin, what's it all about? For the love of God tell me what it means! There's no sense to it; it's crazy; it's . . . Look, the blood's still on me where I touched him. *He* didn't deserve to die! He—"

"Have you forgotten," asked Bencolin, softly, "that he, too, was a suitor of Madame Louise—like Saligny?"

"Golton intimated it, if that's what you mean; but does this madman intend to kill everyone who knew her? I thought Vautrelle was guilty; I could have sworn he was guilty. And then this thing creeps in through the back gate and Vautrelle dies. Who's next?"

We had gone back through the gate. Bencolin stopped and stared up at the moon. "You don't understand," he replied, shaking his head. "There's going to be rain before morning. I must phone the cohorts to get out here immediately, or any traces will be washed away. There ought to be a choice footprint or two in that mess. . . ."

Inside the villa again, I found the doctor waiting in the drawing-room. He had assumed a mournful air, and upturned his eyes.

"Madame your wife," he told me," I discover in a condition not pleasing, monsieur. She has been smoking and drinking far too much, and her nerves—ah, they are bad. She suffers from nervous shock. Frankly, her cure will be fewer cigarettes, fewer drinks, and absolutely no excitement of any kind. No, it is not at all serious; she will be on her feet tomorrow if she is allowed to rest. I have given her a triple bromide, thirty grains, which should quiet her. However, watch her, and if her condition does not improve, phone me. . . . Ah, monsieur, *merci; mais vous êtes trop gentil, alors! Cinq cent francs, vous voyez!—mais, si vous insistez—*" He shrugged. "Good night, monsieur!"

And now, in response to Bencolin's phone calls, cars were beginning to stop before the villa; we heard the eager baying of their horns, and the no less eager voices of their occupants. It would probably be the *commissaire* in charge of the district of Versailles, though

I couldn't tell by the insignia on his uniform when he entered the house. He was awed by Bencolin, and so his questioning of me was very deferential. When Bencolin suggested that mademoiselle was indisposed and had better not be disturbed that night, he murmured, "Ah, the poor mademoiselle! of course!" and shut up his notebook. The garden was invaded with lanterns, and I heard many exclamations and the sound of poking about among the bushes.

Presently I went into the bedroom and closed the door. The yellow lamp still burned by the bedside, from whose shadow I could hear Sharon's deep, regular breathing; her slippers lay on the floor, and the doctor had thrown over her a light silk coverlet. Here the clamour came faintly, but through a back window you could see the lanterns moving in the garden, and so I pulled down the shade.

Long hours before dawn! It was marked in phases, growing more cold and drowsy on the eyelids, more a stimulus and distortion of the brain, with each passing hour. First the noise in the garden died, the motor gears ground and faded up the road one by one. I was sitting in an easy-chair, stupidly, when Bencolin opened the door; his lips moved inaudibly in question. He pointed towards the road and raised his eyebrows. I shook my head—you couldn't leave her here alone. He nodded, and his lips framed, "Tomorrow." For a time he stood in the doorway, outlined against the glow from the drawing-room, a figure of wire and iron; the eyes, sunken and deeply lighted, moved inscrutably from Sharon to me, so that I fancied a faint smile in the pointed beard, a faint lift of his shoulders as he slowly closed the door. Afterwards I heard his car roaring up the road towards Versailles.

So I was left alone with speculations, with doubts and harassments, with the ticking of the clock and the dim night noises stirring round the house. To ward off drowsiness I prowled through the house in the dark, but always drawn back to the room of the yellow lamp. Over the soft carpets, endlessly, and then watching the face of the sleeper in its childlike, ineffable peace. The hair was tumbled about the pillow, the eyelashes wet, the whole countenance pale and shadowed, but a dim smile hovered over the red lips in slumber, and one out-thrown hand lay across the table of the lamp. . . . I rearranged the coverlet and returned to the easy-chair. Vautrelle's play! I felt the manuscript in my pocket when I searched after cigarettes. I pulled the table over gently, so as not to disturb her hand, tilted the lamp shade towards me, and spread out the typewritten sheets. They were crumpled, and stained a little along the side. . . .

I do not know whether it was a good play; calmly considered, no doubt, the thing was claptrap in the extreme. The characters spoke in a dialogue like nothing of heaven or earth, but behind it was an imperially purple imagination, the "tiger's blood and honey" of Barbey D'Aurevilly, and a kind of grotesque smiling detachment, like a gargoyle on a tower. There were two acts written, much interlined in bold script, and some comments had been noted on the margin by a feminine hand, such as "Too much stage mechanism here," or "Cut this down, Edouard; a little religious rant will make any play succeed, but too much talk about God is the surest sign of adolescence." The hero, a man named Vernoy, was a glorified Vautrelle, and in trying to give him good lines the author overstepped badly—but it was revealing. I quote from Act I:

VERNOY: The art of the murderer, my dear Maurot, is the same as the art of the magician. And the art of the magician does not lie in any such nonsense as "the hand is quicker than the eye," but consists simply in directing your attention to the wrong place. He will cause you to be watching one hand, while with the other hand, unseen though in full view, he produces his effect. That is the principle I have applied to crime.

MAUROT (*laughing*): You talk like a professor.

VERNOY: Exactly; and so I am. You would do well to study the subject. On the matter I was telling you about, Professor Münsterberg of Harvard has an interesting chapter in *On the Witness Stand*. I shall apply that principle when I kill—

MAUROT: Hush, man! Don't be ridiculous!

VERNOY: Oh, but I'm serious. I am going to kill this masquerader, and I defy any policeman in the world to tell how I did it. You see, the masquerader intends to kill somebody; and I feel justified in protecting my—best friend.

As the curtain falls, Vernoy *is standing against the black draperies, back centre, under a silver death-mask of Cesare Borgia; his fingers open and close slowly, and he smiles.*

Under this was scrawled, in the same feminine handwriting, *"Oh, Edouard, je t'aime! je t'aime!"* It brought me up with a start; it was so alive and moving in that pale procession of terrors. I looked towards the bed. . . . She had played the game, this æsthete who was sleeping so tranquilly, with her cool writing on the margin and her own act-endings in such a beautiful simulation of emotion! But, leaving her out of it, could any meaning be read into the play? Was Vautrelle writing his own version of the truth? That is, he must have known, or thought he knew, the "masquerader" who was planning to kill Saligny; in which case, his death stood explained in words written when he had no idea of dying. The masquerader knew that he knew, and was in danger of being exposed. . . .

The typewritten pages blurred in a wave of drowsiness; I struggled to get a sense of proportion, and to fight off this light-headed fogginess which was making the furniture of the room bob about like kegs in water. Rising, I walked about the bed, and saw again from the shadow Sharon's mysterious smile. How I hated her then! *"Edouard, je t'aime, je t'aime!"*—and then the memory of her flat voice saying, "There is nothing between us; there never was," saying it to the still figure with the monocle gripped in one eye, gaping up at the moon from under the black cypress, with a derisive smile also.

Up and down the room, pacing; then shall we think that Vautrelle really knew the outer shape which held Laurent? Mere supposition, but think of his air all through these events! Aloof, slightly knowing, from the very time he picked up the trowel in Kilard's house, and put it—incongruous act—in the medicine-chest. I thought of the old lawyer, nodding his bald head and showing the whites of his eyes. So Vautrelle, in this unfinished play, thought he had discovered a way for a murder to be committed in perfect safety; suppose—

suppose he had told that idea to the killer, without then knowing who the killer was? Did Vautrelle outline his plan to some person, and then, when that plan was put into execution, see naturally whose handiwork it was? Fantastic! . . . I switched out the lamp, and moved round in the dark, trying to straighten the tangle. Moonlight fell across the bed hazily, but the corners of the room were peopled with the faces of those we had seen, all grimacing and whispering with the clock-tick. Sharon stirred; and mumbled inaudible words.

Returning to the chair, I huddled into it. The night noises became a part of that babble in the brain—the clock, the murmur from the trees, the slow drip of a faucet in the bath. Through the side windows peered the dying moon from haunted Versailles, low-shining on the place of the kings. Drugged brain that would not work, sliding now into a gulf. . . . I was startled vaguely by a shrill cock-crow from over the hills . . . and then, as the light rain of dawn began to patter on the roof, I slept.

XIV. "The Silver Mask"— And Another

Theatre-goers will no doubt recognize this play from the single excerpt I have given—the freak drama called "The Silver Mask," which closed such an amazingly successful run only two months ago. It was thought inadvisable to do anything with the manuscript in France, but at Bencolin's suggestion a copy was sent to his friend, Mr. John Galsworthy, in England, who revised and bettered it though for obvious reasons he did not care to appear as author. "The Silver Mask" opened at the Haymarket Theatre in London in October, 1928. In the rôle of Vernoy, Mr. George Arliss endowed his characterization with a perfection of suave and deadly charm; but the remarkable thing was that the play had no ending. It was a hoax that stopped in mid-air at the end of the second act, with no explanations whatever, leaving the audience outraged, cheated, and intrigued. Out of sheer exasperation they flocked to see it. The critics were amused and approving; I remember that Mr. St. John Ervine wrote, "There, my dears, is a play! After carefully building up the suspense, the author has found absolutely the only convincing way to end it." In that form, the whole thing bore only a dim resemblance to the events at Paris—so much so that when Bencolin and I witnessed the *première* we could see no connection except in the one passage I have quoted. It was all veiled, hazy, and you could make no sense of any of it. References were thrown out and never explained, characters you couldn't place made speeches you couldn't understand, and who the "masquerader" was or what he was trying to do the audience had not the remotest idea. The authorship was anonymous, but nine out of ten critics swore it was the work of Eugene O'Neill.

When we were watching that tremendous and irrational second act, I recall thinking what a sensation Bencolin could have created had he risen from his seat and remarked, "Pardon me but I believe I can finish the play for you and show you how the murder was committed." Few people knew the truth of the matter, even though the play was widely billed as a "reconstruction of the famous Saligny murder." No, there were not many clues to the truth in "The Silver Mask," but it brought back again the atmosphere of over a year before, when the actual events had happened. The smell of powder and the vague rustling which haunt a theatre, the darkness, the draperies of sable velvet, the tall candles, the drawling voice of Mr. Arliss, and in the background the silver mask smiling like a satyr . . . again I was thinking of that spring in Paris, and of the night when I had sat by Sharon's bedside, reading this play; memories that recreated for me every detail in its hideousness, and its deep intangible pain.

For thus I fell asleep to the sound of the rain on the roof, and slept the little while until dawn. It was

Thérèse who roused me then. I explained what had happened, taking her out into the drawing-room so as not to arouse the sleeper. I felt cold and befuddled. I have some recollection of her brewing me coffee, but her excited voice seemed to come from a great distance, and it was not until I was driving along the road towards Paris that I collected my thoughts. Whirling sheets of rain flickered over Versailles. . . . Bencolin! I must see him about this play. Somebody had put up the top of my car; Bencolin, probably—it was a piece of thoughtfulness which fitted into the strange nature of the man. I drove almost by instinct, back along the familiar road. No dawn, but blowing fog and rain, with Paris growing up again about me out of the night, its lamps burning pale. Grotesque night figures were coming out of doorways and blinking, as you will see lizards crawl from under stones. Bleary men in blouses trudging against the downpour, women behind dingy windows mopping bar counters under gaslight. An early tram lumbered down the cobbles from Versailles; it bumped and screeched thinly on uneven tracks, and then its lights merged with the mist. Presently the vista of the river emerged through dripping trees; the wheels sang on smooth asphalt again. . . . But what had Bencolin been doing out there last night? He had not told me; he was playing his own dark game, and playing—as they say—a lone hand. It occurred to me that Sharon and I were now plunged into the matter as more than mere spectators. We might find ourselves undergoing a cross-examination as suspects in the murder of Vautrelle. Why not? It was the triangle again: Vautrelle, the outraged protector; Sharon, his innocent mistress, who had been swayed by me, the crafty moustache-twisting villain. Thus the French might very conceivably regard it. I could almost hear the hollow laughter of the prosecuting attorney as he pointed a cold finger at me and thundered, "Look upon this monster!"

At any rate, Bencolin's uncanny habit of turning up just in time to make a few gracious comments on the latest murder should give me some sort of alibi, even though alibis in this business never seemed to preclude suspicion. I realized how futile Vautrelle must have felt when everybody knew he couldn't have committed the crime, yet everybody persisted in murmuring a knowing "Ah-ha!" at the mention of his name. Everybody, that is, except Bencolin. It was time for this man to vindicate his colossal reputation.

There was no use in rousing him at this hour—it was six o'clock—and so I went home. Pinned to the pillow of my bed I found a note in Thomas's precise handwriting: "M. Bencolin phoned at three o'clock this morning, sir, requesting you to go for him in your car at ten tomorrow. It is urgent."

No let-down! I took a hot shower, and lay down for a little sleep before the appointment. He must have called shortly after he had left me at the villa in Versailles. Again troubled dreams came to fill my bedroom with gargoyles in the grey, ghostly light. It was nearly ten when Thomas roused me, and I hastened to dress. The rain still fell steadily, but I felt wonderfully refreshed. . . . When I drove round into the Avenue George V. Bencolin was waiting in the lobby of his apartment-house. With him stood a woman, flustered and red faced, dressed in Sunday black and with a most ungodly hat perched on top of her banged hair.

"This is *madame la concierge* at Fenelli's establishment," Bencolin explained. "She has been telling me how Fenelli has followed my advice. I have been intending to ask Fenelli some questions about our late friend Vautrelle, and I think we had better go there now. *A' 'voir*, madame; that will be all, thank you. . . ."

"*A' 'voir*, monsieur," she answered in that high monotonous voice peculiar to *concierges*, shrill and utterly without expression. She made a kind of curtsy, grasped her umbrella, and her small black eyes darted nervously. "You will not tell M. Fenelli, of course? I shall not return there now. I go," she explained dramatically, "to buy groceries. *A' 'voir*, messieurs."

When we crossed the Place de l'Alma and turned down the Avenue de Tokyo, the rain had nearly ceased. Up the hill Passy lay among its narrow streets; the rumble of a métro train swelled out of its tunnel and passed on the trestle over the rue Beethoven. And Bencolin said:

"*Madame la concierge* does not like Fenelli. She says, however, that he has now disposed of his drugs. . . ."

There was the house at the corner of the rue des Eaux, three storeys, with the grilled windows on the second floor, set behind its wall. The gate in the wall was open, and nobody in the *concierge*'s lodge challenged us when we went through. At the front door Bencolin hesitated, with his hand on the bell. Then he tried the door, and found that it was open.

The huge foyer was very gloomy, smelling stale. There curved the staircase with the red carpet, up to the gaming-rooms on the second floor. There to the right was the door into the empty dance-casino, where the orchestra had played. Bencolin stood awhile and looked round the dusky lobby. After a few moments he motioned me towards the stairs. We mounted soundlessly, seeing on the landing the big grandfather clock, and above it a grilled window through which some small light penetrated. As we turned at the landing, I saw a man moving down the steps, just as quietly.

He had on a tall hat which seemed even more enormously tall, and gave length to his set smiling face. Nothing about him moved except his head, which turned slowly, and his eyebrows raised as he walked past. It was Gersault, the valet at the Saligny home. The man appeared to float down those stairs; his masklike smile did not alter, and his *toupet* was set slightly awry under the tall hat.

"Good morning," he said.

"Good morning," said Bencolin. For once the detective was taken aback, and Gersault was nearly down the stairs to the lobby before he called:

"Odd place to find *you*, Gersault."

"Alas!" the other replied, not turning his head—"alas! I hope monsieur will not think I am neglecting my duties. I must find employment, now that monseigneur is dead. I had hoped that M. Fenelli might employ me. Alas! I could not rouse him."

He sighed, and continued his stately march out the door. Suddenly the voice of the great clock chimed ten-thirty.

"I have been in many places," remarked Bencolin, quietly, "but I do not think I have ever felt such an atmosphere of evil as appears to be in this house. It is an evil of the soul. Let us go upstairs."

It was even more gloomy when we reached the

second floor. Palm garden, door to the card-room standing partly open, door to the bar and to the *salon*, red carpet on the marble floor—all exactly as it had been on the night of the murder. This was a place which bloomed only at night. We moved up that next staircase, holding to its bronze rail with a kind of dread. The door at the top was locked. A stillness, poisonous and damned, lay through all the house. Bencolin's voice blasted against it.

"Open this door!" he cried, and struck the panel. It was a command in the name of the law.

For a time there was no reply. Again the echoes tumbled into silence, and I thought that I could hear from beyond the door a kind of excited sobbing. . . .

It was opened, hesitantly. In the semi-darkness I saw Fenelli's flabby face at the aperture, moustache draggling and overspread with a thin sweat; he worked his mouth stammeringly, and his eyes were filmed. With one hand he held a dressing-gown about his flabby body. Bencolin pushed the door open, and he lumbered back against the wall of the numbered doors, crying, "This is an outrage—!"

"Be still! What are you up to now?"

"I won't stand for this!" Fenelli shrilled. "What right—"

"More of your drug-dealings, I suppose?"

"No, no! You do not see. It is not that!—A girl—a woman of the streets—I find pleasure in—"

"Oh—so simple a matter as that? Where is she?"

"Over there; room two. She is not hurt, I tell you; I will not hurt anybody!"

Bencolin walked over to the door he indicated, and entered. His voice sounded harshly. There was a faint smell of powder in the hallway; I felt slightly nauseated. Fenelli, face a huge blank lump of clay, suddenly pointed his finger at me and said:

"*You* were the one who brought him here! I saw you come up the night before last, when the Englishwoman was here. You are marked—"

He checked himself, worked his big mouth, and wailed: "What have I done to deserve this? They try to ruin my business. God! I am not breaking the law—"

Bencolin rejoined us. "There is no reason for this hysteria," he said, calmly. "As you say, you are not breaking the law. It is merely another good business transaction. I shall send her out now, because I wish to ask you some questions. After a pause he added: "Take us to your office. I will give you time to dress." Fenelli disappeared through a door on the staircase side, after first pointing out a small cubbyhole at the end of the hall as his office. Bencolin said swiftly: "Come on with me, to the office. I don't want him to know that *I* know."

"Know what?"

"The villainy gets deeper as we proceed. He wanted me to think it was a prostitute he had in that room. The light was very dim, but I saw. The woman in there was Louise de Saligny."

He passed a hand over his eyes. "No sign to him, now! You see how it was done? They have made that woman a drug addict. She must have drugs, and she will suffer any humiliation at the hands of our greasy friend in order to get them. Very probably she has no more money, and Fenelli's business instinct immediately suggested a proposition—" He shrugged.

"Bencolin," I said, "let's strangle him. Let's go back

and—"

He gripped my arm savagely. "Lower your voice. There will be no trouble started here now. For the present everything depends on our working unknown. *She* does not know that I saw her there—and that, I fancy, would be her greatest humiliation."

We entered a very small room, equipped only with a desk, a chair, and a large safe. A lamp burned on top of the desk. There were no windows.

"No, she didn't recognize me. She was in a kind of stupor," explained Bencolin. "Close the door. Let her get down the back stairs without our notice."

As if there were not enough horrors that this woman had been through, another must be added by the effusive and artistic Fenelli! It seemed as though Louise de Saligny were pursued by an inexorable irony, a mocking circle of doom, so that wherever she turned she met the edge of steel at her throat. She, who had fled from a husband who attacked her, was now forced to receive sniggling lascivious digs from the hand of this bland clay-lump. . . . After a time he entered, impeccably dressed, with a gardenia in his buttonhole. . . . I fancied her in a crazy stupor, driven to laughter, going down those back stairs.

"Ah," said Fenelli, who had recovered his calm, "you wished to see me, messieurs, I think. I give you my word, M. Bencolin, that I have disposed of any narcotics I might have had on the premises."

"Vautrelle has been murdered," said Bencolin.

The other stared at him.

"He was stabbed last night, in Versailles," the detective went on.

"Why—why, this is terrible, monsieur! M. Vautrelle.

Yes, I knew him, of course." He paused, and uttered a little enquiring laugh. "I trust you have found his murderer, monsieur."

"It is known, naturally, that he was your agent, and procured for you people who might be interested in your drugs."

Fenelli, having lost his dignity once, was now at ease. With a plump hand he straightened his Ascot tie, patted his waistcoat, and shrugged.

"Monsieur was good enough once to look over my indiscretions. Let me assure him that any doubtful quantities are not on my premises at this time. My accounts, moreover, are open to inspection. I am within the law."

Smiling, he began to inspect his finger nails.

"We were discussing Vautrelle," said Bencolin.

"Dear monsieur, do you intimate that *I* know something about his death?"

"He claimed to be a Russian officer. A lie. He was a self-educated wharf rat from Marseilles, where you picked him up some years ago."

"Well—what if that were so?"

"I have here a number of cancelled cheques, obtained from the Crédit Lyonnais, to the amount of two hundred thousand francs. They are made out to Edouard Vautrelle, and signed by Louise Laurent, whose present name is Louise de Saligny. Are these the proceeds of your trade, Fenelli? She is in deep, isn't she, Fenelli?"

Fenelli's eyes distended, rumpling the rolls of fat. He looked at the handful of cheques which Bencolin held up.

"Cheques! . . . I know of none. So! He was dishonest, that Vautrelle! Let me see them. Yes. I suspected that he was dishonest."

"And you made her pay twice for what she got. Is that it?" asked Bencolin, leaning across the roll-top desk and speaking very softly.

"Dishonest!" cried Fenelli, tragically.

"Or"—still that gentle voice—"was it blackmail, Fenelli? Did you bleed her thus on the threat of exposing her to her future husband?"

"No!"

"Ah, that is all I wanted to know," said Bencolin with a polite smile. "Come, my friend, we have finished." He replaced his hat. At the door he turned suddenly, and the white flash of his teeth showed through his beard as he observed:

"One more word, Fenelli. Lest you be tempted to try again making certain bargains with Madame Louise, let me warn you earnestly against it. That's all."

We walked down the stairs in silence, Bencolin knocking his stick thoughtfully against the balustrades. When we were again in the doorway of the house, he said:

"You understand now the tragedy of the man called Edouard Vautrelle. Here was a boy, suckled on water from the gutter, who grew up creating for himself a world wherein he moved in glittering colours. He nearly reached his dream world, but never quite completely; something would always shake him out of it. Other than seeing himself as he wished to be, he did not care. He was willing to have you think him a rotter, if only did not doubt he was an aristocrat. You might think him a murderer; he did not care, so long as you did not doubt he was a Russian officer."

"And he wrote a play," I said. "I have it at home—I intended to show it to you, and forgot—"

"Ah yes; his play. He wanted to be a ruler of destinies, I fancy. And he had the usual tendency to *embroider*; he wanted not only to make his life and his work a story, but a very fancy story, with garish trimmings. Mark that; it is very important. I fancy that being accused of murder even pleased him, when he knew that he was safe. He is dead. But keep his ghost before you, for that image tells us much of the truth."

In line with my theory of the night before, that Vautrelle had unwittingly communicated his elaborate fictional plan for committing a murder to somebody else, and from the dead paper had risen its actuality!

"Bencolin," I said, "both of us were rattled last night—or at least I was—and we came to the conclusion—or at least I did—that both these crimes had been committed by the same person. I'm not trying to pump you, if you want to keep your secret. But tell me that much—did the same hand kill both of them?"

"Yes. Yes, it was the same person. We face a murderer who is utterly cold-blooded and cynical, and who firmly believes that these acts are done justifiably, to avenge wrongs. The crimes are the means of venting on the world a spite too deep for ordinary expression."

"A diseased brain?"

He pondered, looking out through the gates in the wall to the rue des Eaux. "In a sense, yes; but not diseased in a way that Grafenstein would have you believe. I am not too much a believer in all the tenets of abnormal psychology. The streak of Cain is too pronounced to confine it to a separate category; these men are the successors to Lombroso's nonsense, and I am tempted to doubt whether they are an improvement."

"And this murderer is here—we have seen him, talked to him, known him as a figure in this case?"

"Oh, very much so!" he returned, looking at me queerly.

"Thank you. Let's go back to my apartment now and look at that play—unless you have something else to do?"

"Why, I shall have to take you down to the prefecture sometime today and have you go over your testimony about last night; but there will be no trouble—I can provide you with a perfectly straight story. I think, too, that we should pay another visit to Versailles. But let it wait."

"No new information about last night?"

"My men are at present tracing the taxicab and the knife. *Allons!*"

We exchanged no more words on the return drive to my rooms. I think that I had become a bit sneering in regard to Bencolin as more than a little of the charlatan; he intimated that he knew so much, yet in demonstration he appeared to know nothing at all.

When we reached my apartment I found Mr. Sid Golton waiting for me in the drawing-room.

XV. When the Wall Fell

Sitting in an easy-chair by the window, Golton was smoking a cigarette and devouring the contents of the *New York Herald*. The other Paris papers published in English, the *Chicago Tribune* and the *London Daily Mail*, were spread out on the floor. I was astonished and annoyed to find him there—I later learned that he had come in tossing Thomas a fifty-franc note, and I have never seen Thomas more insulted in his life—but his presence seemed to interest Bencolin.

"Say!" Golton cried, flourishing the paper, "you're gettin' to be some celebrity. Look here! Go out for a quiet evening with this mamma and Eddie Vautrelle gets bumped off right in the back yard! Sit down. . . . Hello, monsoor! What's your name? You're the district attorney or something, aren'tya?"

"Good morning, Mr. Golton," said Bencolin in his careful, precise English. "I am pleased to see you."

Taking my cue, I welcomed him and told him to make himself comfortable. As was natural, he wore knickers, and hooked one plump leg over the chair-arm while he blew smoke approvingly at the ceiling.

"Johnson of the *Tribune* will be up here to seeya—don't mind, doya?—we looked up your address in the directory. I'm thinkin' about going out and seein' if Sharon Grey's all right. Siddown, siddown! You make me nervous! Got anything to drink on the premises? I got myself ungodly oiled last night—woof!"

Bencolin seated himself in a chair on the other side of the window while I went out to get drinkables; after all, Golton was my guest and should be shown courtesy. When a freezing Thomas with a shaker of Martinis marched into the room, the two were discussing art. Bencolin was explaining that Morland was not the name of the person shoeing the horse in the picture above the piano, and Golton observed critically that those boys were all right, if you liked them, but on the whole he much preferred some gentleman named Brown who drew illustrations in the *Saturday Evening Post*, for which you had to pay seven francs to those low-down gyps who ran the newsstands. After the conversation had dealt awhile with art, Bencolin said:

"You knew Vautrelle, I think, Mr. Golton?"

"Well, in a kind of way I did. I heard a lot about him—you know how talk travels—and once he had a drink with a friend of mine up at Payne's. I met him there; told him I knew his friend Raoul, and Raoul spoke better English'n any Frenchman I knew. Say, *you* handle the lingo pretty good, monsoor. Yeah, and once before that I nearly got photographed with him at

Nice, and got my picture in the paper; but I couldn't get close enough—I was too far over; you could only see the edge of my ear. I sent the newspaper picture back home, and it was printed in the paper there." He took a reflective sip of his cocktail. "Yeah, that reminds me. I gotta leave here in a couple of days. Good times are over; gotta go home."

"Indeed?"

"Gotta get married," said the other, gloomily. "You see, it's like this: my old man wants me to get on in the world. My old man makes the best near-beer in the United States; he's a smart boy, my old man is!—he took my mother's family's coat-of-arms and made it the trade-mark on the bottle, 'Castle Skelvings Ale, the Aristocrat of Brew, None Genuine Without Coat-of-Arms.' Well, he wants to get me a wife—he's been touring, too—with, you know, nice people; and now he cables me he's got one. We-el, 'sall right with me! Pour me another cocktail, willya? By God! he's got thirty million, if he's got a cent; I *oughta* get a good wife!" With this consoling thought, Mr. Golton settled back. "I kinda hate leavin' all the good friends I've got here," he mused. "But there's nothin' like gettin' back home when you get right down to it. And I'd kinda like to have a good home, with a wife to bring my slippers in. . . ."

Bencolin sat regarding him with quizzical politeness, one finger against his lip, and nodding his head while Golton dwelt at length on the theme of mother, home, and heaven. Finally he rose to go.

When he had eventually completed his farewells and descended to the street Bencolin stood at the window, watching him swing off down the Avenue Montaigne. With eyes narrowed, the detective was tapping his fingers against the pane. At last he turned, and said, "Well—!"

"Now that it's over," I remarked, "I'll get that play. You might as well stay to lunch. Thomas is no mean cook."

"No," said Bencolin. "I have much to do, and so have you. Let me see the play. Tonight, as I promised," he added, quietly, "I am going to explain the murder."

I do not know whether the reader has ever been entangled in any such gruesome mess as this, or even peeped into the events surrounding any death mysterious and violent, not seeing them through the medium of the newspapers—where the worst tragedy seems unreal, incomprehensible, and often absurd—but terribly close in the company of the people who produced them. Even the lengthy accounts of trials are clogged with that self-consciousness which man exhibits before a camera. Crime, in written outline, is as far off and unconvincing as the account of a battle in a history book, full of unreal sound and fury, of generals striking heroic attitudes and dying in the moment of victory; so that you find difficulty in imagining that it ever happened at all. If, then, you who read this have never experienced the hopeless and caged uncertainty, the bewilderment and black suspicion of everybody, that comes with such things in your own life, I cannot make it clear. Can it be, you think, this or that person? *How* can it be? Do such things really happen? Are there emotions, crazes, strong enough to drive such people as myself, in my own placid life, to this meaningless brutality? Yet here it is. It is like looking in a mirror and seeing hideous things reflected in one's own face.

In preparing this record I have tried to show how these men and women felt and acted, precisely as they were, without gloss or change. I have tried to stick to facts, even where I should have preferred to tone down a bit—to give a complete account of every detail, even where I should have preferred to omit altogether—for undeniably the general atmosphere was that of a slaughter-house. And the purpose is this: to make the reader understand fully what I believe to be one of the great masterpieces of analytical reasoning, Bencolin's solution of the case.

A climax was coming, we all knew, but that it should become a series of climaxes, each worse than the preceding one, I am glad not even Bencolin suspected. What had gone was quite bad enough. When I looked in the papers that morning—or noon, rather—while Bencolin was running through the script of Vautrelle's play, I got a start: impossible to realize that these people they talked about were ourselves! They seemed to move about in a glorified world, almost heroic in their trappings, and not to partake at all of the characteristics of the bewildered, ordinary humans we were. Familiar apartment, familiar things. . . . I wandered about, and remembered my correspondence; I had not glanced at it for two days. Thomas had piled it neatly on the salver in the hall. A couple of invitations, a letter from home (Ho! ho! Wasn't the *pater familias* going to get on his jolly old ear when he heard of this?), a tailor bill—and a *pneumatique*. Must have come in the last half hour or so, while I was out; handwriting unfamiliar. Who the devil was writing me *pneumatiques* at this . . . ?

> DEAR JEFF: I'm in a most dreadful mess! Got a cable from my Dad this morning. Jeff, he *can't* have heard so early. He's taking the first plane from London, and I can't imagine what's the matter, but I'm scared. They've been talking about me, and I haven't done anything; *you* know that. Jeff, you come out tonight, won't you? He hates the French; maybe you can get round him. It's beastly here—they're trying to make me stay in bed—but I want to thank you for being there last night. *Please!*
>
> SHARON.

Well, I could understand that. Things were coming down on everybody, all at once; the dance and the suspense whirled faster, and suddenly they smashed, together. Go out there? I would go out there sooner than tonight: if I could do anything—I couldn't—but something, you had to do something. Thus I stood reading the letter over and over, until Bencolin's voice roused me. I said nothing to him about the letter. There was nothing especially private in it, nothing very personal; yet I simply didn't want to talk about it. I wanted to see Sharon. . . .

We snatched a cup of coffee for lunch, and then he took me to the prefecture. Several times on the way I caught him glancing at me speculatively. Once he seemed about to speak, but didn't, so that I was on the point of saying, "What is it? What's bothering you?" and there jingled foolishly in my mind, " 'What makes you look so white, so white?' asked Files-on-parade." Back came insistently the answer, " 'I'm dreadin' what I've got to watch—' " Bosh! Bencolin was overwrought, the result of no sleep for two nights. It seemed to strip him to the raw nerves and put new wrinkles around his long, narrowed eyes, watching me brightly from their corners. But certainly he was a man without nerves, if one ever existed. I was imagining things. Still, the atmosphere persisted, " 'I'm dreadin' what I've got to watch,' the color-sergeant said."

At the prefecture the ceremonies seemed to be endless. We must have talked to a dozen people, and over and over again I told my story, so that I came to repeat it mechanically. Several times I was required to produce my identity card, which was scrutinized with great care, after which everybody nodded profoundly and said "Ah!" and passed me on to some one else. My chief recollection of the place is that everybody appeared to wear a moustache. The rooms were dusky, some with barred windows; we passed through many of them before I met the chief of the department, a solemn, courteous gentleman with soft white hands and a beard like an Assyrian bull. He asked me a few blunt and disconcerting questions, among them being, Was I in love with mademoiselle? He didn't attempt to browbeat; he was so polite and sympathetic that I went right ahead and explained everything at great length, almost oratorically. I poured out matters I had never even intended to mention. At the end he too said,

"Ah!" and smiled—a great lump of wisdom in the dusky light—and everybody else smiled, too. We shook hands all around in such a companionable fashion that I was tempted to invite them all out to have a glass of beer. He sat quietly stroking his beard, this guardian of the law, when Bencolin and I went out.

It was late. We had consumed an enormous amount of time. I voiced an inclination to go out to Versailles, but for some reason Bencolin had changed his mind.

"No," he said. "No, I prefer that you do not go. Tonight—perhaps, if we finish. You may disregard me, of course. But I am showing you the world of death with which I deal every day"—as he said this he stared ahead with a face curiously pinched—"and I think you will follow my advice."

Yes, so I would. Instead, we bethought ourselves of Grafenstein, and went up to find him at his hotel. He was in the midst of packing to return to Vienna, but he hailed with blinking suspicion Bencolin's invitation to be in at the death. Together we started for the *grands boulevards*. "Off our minds for the present! There is another person I want along with us, if he cares to come," Bencolin explained, "and that is M. Kilard. Until then, we speak of other matters."

How far away that seemed in the hot night's quietness! Four of us stood in a hush of filmed moonlight on the lawn before the Saligny house. It stood up black above the trees, showing only one light. At my elbow was M. Kilard, vulture face looking out from under a soft hat, leaning on a heavy cane. The moonlight gleamed on Grafenstein's spectacles. Bencolin said, softly:

"Gersault, I think, is at home."

Then he led us up the lawn. Gersault answered the bell. He smiled, adjusted his *toupet*, and remarked, "I have been sitting beside my master. It is only just. The funeral is tomorrow."

"Take us there," said Bencolin.

That was all. From the dull lamps of the hall we passed into the even more dim atmosphere of the drawing-room. Gersault had banked the flowers with good taste; they filled the room with a sickish-sweet odour, and shone faintly by the wall-lights burning far up towards the ceiling, around gleams on the white metal of Saligny's everlasting house. I caught sight of my image in a long mirror over the fireplace; it was rather pale. Kilard took one glance at the coffin, after which he sat down with his hands folded over his cane, and his mouth seemed to twitch. Bencolin placed a briefcase on the table.

"Gersault," Bencolin asked, "is there a pick or a crowbar in the house?"

"A what, monsieur?"

"A pick or a crowbar. . . ."

Kilard's dry voice rasped with sudden harshness: "My God! what are we going to do? Rob a grave?"

Retreating towards the white casket, Gersault passed his hand over the glass above the dead face. "I know," he said. "*I* know, monsieur! You are going to investigate the dead things that walk in the cellar. I have heard the dead things scrape their feet down there."

He clicked his fingers against the glass in the coffin.

"But *he* does not walk, monsieur. I sat here all last night, waiting for him to walk." Gersault's long face smiled. "I will get the pick, monsieur. The men who dug the drains left one here. . . . Do not disturb him while I am gone, please."

"Disturb—whom?" Grafenstein asked, after a pause. Then the big Austrian took off his spectacles and began to wipe them carefully. Bencolin, his chin sunk on his breast, was standing motionless in the middle of the room. . . .

Gersault presently entered with a heavy pick and handed it daintily to the detective.

"Take it," Bencolin said to me. "It is for you. Now come with me."

The tap of Kilard's cane sounded on the parquetry as we went out. Gersault, folding his hands, sat down in a chair beside the casket; I caught a glimpse of him sitting there bolt upright in the dim light, before the portières fell. . . . We moved out into the hall, through dark music-room, dining-room, and into the kitchen. Somebody was breathing heavily. Bencolin switched on the lights in the kitchen and opened the cellar door. From behind a pile of mops he took an oil lantern, which he lighted and trimmed. He held it up, and his eyes moved from face to face.

"Now," he said.

Kilard pulled his hat down a little more tightly. Grafenstein was regarding the pick in my hand. In single file we went down the stairs to the cellar, Bencolin's lantern shining ahead on whitewashed walls. The stairs creaked underfoot, a strand of cobweb brushed my face with repulsive clinging, the smell of damp earth and mould rose as our monotonous *clump-clump* took us down. I grew to counting the beat of the footfalls; "what . . . makes . . . you . . . look . . . so . . . white, so . . . white?" became a refrain. Still the lantern moved, now on the earthen floor, flickering over white furnace-pipes, farther into the depths of the cellar. Our shadows were gnomelike. It occurred to me, "Is the murderer here? Who's behind me now . . . ?" Only the whites of Kilard's eyes shone from under his hat-brim when I turned, his cane grasped now like a club. The cold damp soaked into one's skin, for we had stopped. Bencolin stood before a low door with a padlock.

"The wine-cellar," he said, and produced a key.

Into that small room the four of us came. Tiers of bottles were on the walls, over the heads of great casks. But as Bencolin held up his lantern I saw that there was one wall where there were no bottles, and the bricks were uneven in ragged outline. At the foot of the wall was a little heap of mortar, and suddenly Kilard's foot kicked something which rolled over with a clatter. It was a trowel.

Through his beard Bencolin's teeth gleamed as he smiled, and his eyes lighted up; the lantern-shine did not move.

"Smash in that wall!" he said.

Pushing past Grafenstein, I lifted the pick and whirled it against the ragged outline of the bricks. Dust and mortar flew as I yanked it out; two of the bricks tottered. Again I swung, and the wall buckled.

Once again, and with a sudden sliding crash it fell in a choking cloud of dust. The light was obscured for an instant, while nobody moved . . . then its rays fell into the hollow that wall disclosed.

I was looking into an eye, glazed and staring and motionless, from the hollow, and at part of a rotting face. The thing must have been propped in there against the bricks, for its decayed hand popped out almost in my face.

Vaguely I was conscious that I had dropped the pick, and that unless I got a grip on myself I was going to be sick. . . . Somebody uttered an unearthly gasp, a horrible groan, and somebody croaked, "What is it?"

"M. Kilard," said Bencolin, "I wanted you to see the last of the Saligny line. There is Raoul, the real Raoul, before you. . . . The man who for the past three weeks has been impersonating him, the man who was murdered the night before last, and who now lies upstairs in the coffin, is Laurent himself."

There was a silence. I turned round abruptly to shut out that sight. Kilard, in a vague, complaining voice, was muttering:

"One of those bricks hit me on the leg—one of those bricks hit me on the leg—"

XVI. How a Man Spoke from a Coffin

Bencolin, looking inscrutably from one of us to the other, held aloft the light, round which the dust-particles were still settling. In an absent voice I heard Grafenstein mumbling. "But it's not *possible*! — it's not *possible*!" he repeated, doggedly; and Kilard cried, "Are you mad?"

"No," the detective returned, curtly. "Come upstairs. I will show you."

We got back to the drawing-room somehow, and it was a bit of a shock to see again those tiers of flowers, the white casket, and Gersault sitting there telling his beads. Kilard looked at the flowers; then he took off his hat and with a spasmodic gesture flung it against them. The high bald skull seemed almost luminous. He cracked the joints of his fingers and asked, shrilly, "You seriously maintain that over in that casket there" — he pointed with a long finger — "is Laurent? You mean to say he killed Raoul and them impersonated him? Is that it?"

"I see you still don't believe me," said Bencolin with a

shrug. "Well! I didn't expect you to, at first. So I came prepared to give you details. I intend to show you everything you should have seen yourself, and back it up with such proof that even a lawyer will not presume to doubt me. Sit down, messieurs."

"But—but somebody killed Laurent and Vautrelle, then!" said Grafenstein. "Some *other* person—"

"Precisely. The murderer we seek killed Laurent and Vautrelle, just as Laurent killed Saligny and put him into that wall downstairs. *That* is the person we seek. In other words, we have discovered the imposture, and we are still at the beginning of the riddle! . . . Wait a minute, Gersault; don't go. Give us some light here at the table." He began to open his briefcase.

No other word was spoken. Whatever the others felt, I was stunned, and rather more skeptical than they could possibly have been. We all sat down, while a lamp went on at the table, and we heard nothing except the sound of Bencolin sorting papers. He stood up straight and regarded us, with the casket and the flowers behind him, his face hanging over the light of the lamp.

"Messieurs," he said, "you were all handicapped from the start, because you did not have the faintest idea what it was you were investigating. Thus blocked at the start, I am afraid you did not see straight through so plain a series of events that, once given the connecting fact, your minds will run ahead faster than I can talk.

"Here in France, in my position it is necessary to be a most versatile person. It is not demanded, of course, even if it were possible, that I should be an expert with all the tools of the detective—chemistry, ballistics, psychoanalysis, medicine, microphotography; with all the uses of the spectroscope, the chromoscope, the camera, and the ultra-violet ray, or any of the devices of the specialist. But I must know enough about these things to tell the experts what to look for, and to understand their findings afterwards. I must control the vast resources of the prefecture so that by my direction there shall be no wasted effort, no groping in the dark, no tests at random. My brain must work out the only logical combination of events, which it is their business to prove.

"To begin with, before any murder in the gaming-rooms had occurred, I was teased by a curious fact—which is why I wanted Doctor Grafenstein's opinions—involving a point of psychoanalysis. Here were the two husbands of Madame Louise—two men utterly different in character, with not a single trait or interest common to either. Madame loved Laurent, the scholar, until he turned insane, after which she professed to abhor him. It made a deep scar on her nature. But not long afterwards she loved just as intensely Saligny, the athlete. Out of many, Saligny was the one who drew her from the still present terrors of that first marriage. It struck me that in the back of her mind was still that subconscious crushed love for Laurent—and *voilá*! there appeared the strange *physical* resemblance of Saligny to Laurent. In essentials, this was so pronounced that she herself commented on it. Do you remember, messieurs? She said that she fancied sometimes seeing Laurent in Saligny, and it terrified her. So it did, but it was the secret of her attraction to Saligny in the first place; for this resemblance was coupled with the idea that she was turning from one type of man to a type entirely different. She thought that she was doing so—in reality, she was being reminded of Laurent, after forcing him from her thoughts in the terrible shock of knowing him a madman. Here were these two men: both tall, both with peculiarly luminous brown eyes, in facial contour bearing a resemblance. Laurent's nose was convex, Saligny's straight; Laurent had brown hair and a beard, Saligny's hair was blond and he was clean-shaven. Alter the shape of a nose, bleach the hair, shave off the beard, and you have not an exact similarity, but a passable one. It would *not* deceive any friend of Saligny if that friend knew him well. But the point is, as you know, Doctor, that we know our friends rather by their mannerisms than by their exact appearance; for if their mannerisms are not always the same, that is the thing which surprises us, and we say, 'Why, you don't seem like the same person.' The physical appearance, unless it bears to us a psychic significance, is vague. A casual acquaintance whom we pass in the street could make a hundred small changes in his appearance, but if his outstanding characteristics, the things by which we place him—colour of hair, shape of nose, way of wearing a hat—are unchanged, we should see no difference. An impostor who aped outstanding things and kept himself aloof from everyone could pass muster. Paradoxically, the only one who might have found him out was the only one who could not possibly do so—Madame Louise. She saw Laurent, not Saligny, even when the real Saligny stood before her.

"This, as I have said, was only an idle speculation in my mind at first; it had not even assumed definite shape when I spoke to you, Doctor. I was plagued by the reason why this woman had fallen in love with the last person one should have expected; for I am not one of those romantics who dismiss an extraordinary attachment with some tender sentimentality about the impossibility of explaining random arrows from the bow of Eros. There was another reason, too. I am not prepared to maintain that she really loved either of them, and that also was in my mind when I spoke.

"I looked, then, at some of the things which have come under our observation as the case progressed. We knew that a month or more ago Saligny received an injury to his spine and his left hand—the *left*, please remember, as the Viennese doctor's telegram said—and that he went to Vienna to have it dealt with. When he left Paris, he was the gallant sportsman: the tennis-player who had nearly beaten Lacoste, the swordsman, the fearless gentleman who had attacked a mountain lion with a hunting-knife. He moved in a sporting circle, from which most of his friends were drawn. He was an expert on horses and rifles, but a not overbright individual who rarely read a printed line and spoke no language but his own. He cared nothing for social affairs and little more for the social register. He was a sort of thoughtless idealist, who worshipped his promised wife, paying no attention to the advances of any other woman. He was a healthy, hearty swash-buckler, always entertaining his friends, but caring little for the pleasures of the table or the drawing-room. A man, in short, bred of good solid red earth, who would look with astonishment on a person who recited Swinburne to a young lady, read *Alice in Wonderland*, or discussed famous criminals at a bachelor dinner."

Bencolin paused, checking off the points slowly.

"Is that clear? You remember these instances, I take

it?—Now we have Saligny returning from Austria three weeks ago. In the space of time he has been away what an astonishing change! One week in the city of Vienna has given him, magically, the precise opposite of each of these qualities.

"He dreads his marriage; he is terribly afraid of Laurent, this man who attacked a mountain lion with a hunting-knife. He trembles at the very idea of some one threatening to kill him. Shutting himself up here in the house, he sees nobody. He drops his former sporting companions altogether. Then he hires Gersault to be his confidential servant, and nobody else is in attendance on him; Gersault shall write his correspondence, because he has hurt his hand and cannot use it even to sign letters." Mockingly Bencolin held up a bundle of photographs. "Look at these, messieurs; you have seen them before. They are pictures of Saligny indulging in almost every sport, and I dare say you have noticed that in every case he uses his right hand—tennis-racquet—foil—always the right. Now, when he returns, he cannot write; he cannot fence, he cannot play tennis, because his hand is hurt. Astonishing! The injury was to his left.

"One week in Vienna has given him a knowledge of the English language so complete that an American named Golton swears he speaks it better than any man alive. He drops all pretence to homely virtue and falls passionately into the embrace"—Bencolin looked politely at me—"of a young lady he has previously scorned. He begins to quote to her Poe and Swinburne and Baudelaire—"

I cried, suddenly, "He was the one who was bringing her the copy of *Alice*; she told me so!"

"Ah, yes. Refusing all offers to indulge in sports, he has not gone in for book-collecting. We will come to that presently. But our versatile gentleman has other habits, too, which nobody would have suspected. He is discovered to have gone in for opium-smoking on a somewhat elaborate scale, and we note with surprise that he has been indulging in the habit for over a year. In other words, we have him sucking at the soothing poppy at a time, a year ago, when he was eliminating the world's foremost tennis-players at Wimbledon. After a strenuous fencing-bout, we are asked to believe that he found relaxation in an opium pipe, and the next morning boxed ten rounds to a draw with M. Carpentier."

Bencolin raised his eyebrows deprecatingly.

"Human life, messieurs, and human character, also, show many inconsistencies, but I am inclined to believe that Munchausen himself would shriek with agony at such a tale. I therefore set about looking more closely at the cause of these changes. I glanced not only at the new circle of friends with whom he had surrounded himself—inviting here to dinner, for example, people he had never seen before, and suddenly taking up friendly relations with his lawyer, whom he knows very slightly—but I glanced also at certain visual evidences lying about. Laurent, he says, has written him a letter; he brings it to me in nervous supplication, this man who with one heavy blow could have knocked Laurent into a lengthy sleep. Good! It is in Laurent's handwriting. We had in our files specimens of this handwriting from a former occasion. We compared them. We took this new note, completing the up-and-down-strokes with ruled lines several inches long. We then enlarged it, and compared the slopes with the authentic specimen; likewise we measured the angles. They were the same. Any forgery would immediately have been apparent.

"The microscope disclosed, however, a slight wavering; not the unsteadiness of the forger, but the precise symptoms of nervous instability caused on the system by drugs. Comparison with specimens of writing from addicts demonstrates to us beyond question, my laboratory chief tells me, that the drug was opium."

Kilard broke the silence.

"You can tell all that from a man's writing?" he demanded, shrilly.

"A mere commonplace. Doctor Bayle does it every day. . . . The letter, then, had been written by Laurent; but Laurent had taken to drugs. Now look at the letter itself; I have it here, just as we marked it in seeking for any forgery. Analysis of the paper fibres shows that it is a very fine linen pulp, made by the Tradell factory in Paris. Out went our nets!—two quires of this paper were ordered eight days ago by M. de Saligny. Still, it might mean nothing, so we must look at the pencil-marks, for the letter is written in pencil. Pencils are divided into four classes: those made of a mixture of carbon, silicate, and iron—writing grey-black; graphite, silicate, and iron—writing a soft deep black; colored pencils made of pigments; and the copying pencils, generally composed of aniline colors, graphite, and kaolin. We apply to *these* marks a solution of acetic acid and of ferro-cyanide, by which we get a colour reaction. Under a microscope we see that this reaction is unusual, and yet it falls within our classifications of the different pencil-marks. This letter was written by a copying pencil, and comparison will show us the particular make; it is a Zodiac No. 4, an unusual pencil. Good! Upstairs in this house, in Saligny's desk, I found yesterday a Zodiac No. 4. It was compared by microscope and spectroscope with the marks on this letter, exactly as fingerprints are compared. The letter was written with that pencil."

Bencolin dropped the sheets and smiled, his eyes very brilliant.

"Another commonplace! We now find that the note was written by Laurent, on a type of paper ordered by 'Saligny,' and with a pencil in 'Saligny's' desk upstairs. The net tightens! Here," he tossed a book on the table, "is a volume of *Alice in Wonderland.* We have reason to believe that 'Saligny' was going to bring a copy of this book to Miss Sharon Grey; this particular copy is found in the booth where 'Saligny' has been sitting. A name has been erased from the flyleaf—a fatal error, as forgers discover when they try to bleach out or erase lines from their work. This was merely a clumsy erasure. We photograph this flyleaf with orthochromatic plates; a negative is developed, then reduced and intensified with mercury perchloride. When dry, it is placed in a frame, and a second plate is exposed by contact. This process we continue half a dozen times. Look, messieurs. Here are the negatives!" He spread them out under the lamp. "At the seventh, the effaced writing stands out clearly."

He stood motionless, his finger pointing downwards. "The name written on the flyleaf, in the same hand as the letter, is 'Alexandre Laurent.'

"I say to you now that there can be no doubt that 'Saligny' is Laurent. But we must proceed! We must tighten the coils about this impostor until he cannot even wriggle a finger. I have made my deductions, and the mighty brain of science has verified them. Now we must ask ourselves, where is the real Saligny? Laurent has done away with him; so much is obvious. And if anybody doubts this"—Bencolin leaned across the table—"I will offer the final, the obvious, and absolutely infallible test. This test has not yet been made, because when I had the body for the autopsy I was not certain—photography and chemistry had not come to my aid."

"Get on with it, man!" Kilard said, hoarsely, "about—downstairs."

"Again I seek a lead. I ask myself, if Laurent killed Saligny, and is impersonating him, where did he kill him? Saligny was himself before he left for Vienna. It was, then, either in Vienna or after Saligny had come back to Paris. Well! Our ubiquitous friend, Mr. Golton, has met Saligny on the train coming to Paris from Vienna, and there 'Saligny' speaks his excellent English—therefore, the killing was done in Vienna. What has the murderer done with the body? Remember, he has not a world of time. He must get rid of the body utterly, for to have it discovered was to run the worst risk of discovery. He would not even dare throw it in the Danube, or mutilate it and trust to luck. There must be *no* suspicious corpse anywhere that might in any fashion tend to betray his plan; and what a devilish cumbersome thing a human body is! Put yourself in the place of this man whose nerves are steel, planning an imposture of incredible daring: he must have conceived of the cleverest possible plan. He would take the corpse back to Paris, in one of Saligny's trunks, and he would conceal it in the man's own house—of who would think of looking for the corpse of Saligny in Saligny's house when he was to all accounts alive?"

"Sheer theorizing, you say. Ah, but it was not! What have we learned about 'Saligny'? That after his return from Vienna he has suddenly and unaccountably taken an interest in his wine-cellar; he allows nobody to go there, and discharges a butler for presuming to enter. The key he keeps himself, always. Never has he done so before. Cellars! We have an association there, surely. 'Saligny' gives a bachelor dinner, and afterwards when Vautrelle and you, M. Kilard, sit about the table discussing murderers, Vautrelle speaks of Poe. He tells of a man being walled up in a cellar. Can't you hear his words, M. Kilard—'You're *very* familiar with that story, aren't you, Raoul?' And for once 'Saligny's' steel nerve breaks; Vautrelle *knows*. He starts up from the table, the false Saligny does, realizing that another person has learned his secret; and thus we see him momentarily, naked and at bay, among the candle-flames and the roses."

Bencolin's eyes were vacant, his fingers crooked towards us, and his voice tense. I stared at the lamp-light before his face; and now all the irrelevancies, all the weird suggestion of that house, were gathered up as he continued:

"The details we have yet to learn. How he killed Saligny, probably at the latter's hotel in Vienna; how he shipped the body here; how he gained his knowledge of Saligny's ways and friends, probably from Saligny's correspondence and the endless material published about him. There were books and articles about Saligny's exploits. The journals were always chronicling him or publishing his picture.

"But conceive of his madman's dexterity: 'silky brown beard and mild eyes behind spectacles, and a perpetual smile'—gone now. Conceive how he plotted in this stealthy way, having the surgeon shape his nose, cutting him like a garment to resemble those pictures of Saligny. He died with the photos of Saligny on his person, studying them endlessly as once he studied the languages of the earth! Conceive how his wily and devilish imagination pictured a revenge which should satisfy every dictate of poetic justice. That was his nature. He would come back to Paris as Saligny, he would keep himself under cover until his marriage, he would marry this woman a second time, and when he had brought her here to the bridal-room he would reveal himself at last in the monstrousness of his revenge! He would take her down to the cellar and show her the body of her lover . . . a joke, wasn't it? A mad, wild joke! Do not his words to Miss Sharon Grey come back with terrible suggestion, 'I want to tell you something tonight; you'll appreciate the joke' . . . ?

"I can fancy him pacing these halls at night, reflecting the plan he had evolved, chuckling at an irony which was in line with the tales of the mediæval writers he loved. Nobody in the Renaissance conceived of a vengeance quite so delicious. He had deceived everybody, he had written a note to himself warning himself of danger, he had acted to perfection before the stupid police. He had won."

Chimes rang from the clock on the mantel in that haunted room. The flowers looming behind Bencolin, the shine of the casket, the play of the lamp on the detective's face . . . there he was, that madman, in his narrow house. . . .

"And shall I show you now the final proof that I am not romancing?" Bencolin asked, softly. "Gersault, open the lid of the casket!"

Hunched and ghostlike, hardly seeming to understand, Gersault rose from his chair. He did not reply, but he waited a time to let the order penetrate his consciousness. Then his clumsy fingers fumbled at the white lid. Bencolin had taken an ink-pad and paper from his brief-case; he walked over and watched while Gersault strained to lift. I was straining forward, half expecting the dead man to sit up, seeing in a daze the white cushions gleam as the lid was raised against the weird light. . . . Bencolin bent into the coffin. Gersault uttered a kind of screech and put his hands over his face. The lid banged, and I saw Kilard start up. . . . Its hollow crash had not ceased echoing when Bencolin walked back and threw two sheets of paper under the lamp.

"Look at it! There are Laurent's fingerprints from our files. I have just fingerprinted the dead man. Compare them! They are the same."

His finger still on the sheets, he looked up after a long pause.

"He drew a million francs from M. Kilard. He ordered the servants not to come back to the house for many days. You remember? He ordered them not to come back on the morning after the wedding-night. For after he had shown madame the body of her lover in the cellar he intended to kill her, and then he would go away with this money, leaving her here on the marriage-bed, and it would be days before they discovered her. . . ."

Kilard sat down suddenly and buried his face in his arms.

"But there was another person more clever than he, another person who knew it besides Vautrelle," Bencolin murmured. "Another plotter for this house." The detective paused, and said, softly, "His murderer."

XVII. We Hear the Name of the Killer

Bencolin went, in silence, over to the coffin, where e stood staring down at the face inside.

"You know," said Kilard, raising his head and speak-ıg in a strained voice, "something is off my mind at ıst. For one thing I am very glad. It is nonsensical—it ; unimportant, I suppose—but I did not like to see the pectacle of a Saligny in such cringing fear of death as ıe false Raoul was when he came to me." He made a esture, looking slowly round the walls. "The Salignys vere soldiers! . . ."

That was all—"The Salignys were soldiers!"—but ıe way he drew himself up when he said it, the way he lenched his hand, showed a proud triumph. . . . At ıst he said, in a more even tone:

"How did he die?"

"The body is greatly decomposed, as you saw," ;encolin replied, "but I think we shall establish that his kull was fractured by a heavy blow from behind."

Here Grafenstein, who had been studying the mat-:r with his ponderous bulk spread out on a gilt chair, uddenly raised his hand.

"Wait! *wait! Donnerwetter!* You go too fast for me.

Some of these points you have made fairly clear," he admitted, turning the thing over in his mind, "but on others you appear to have supernatural knowledge. I protest. I want police work, not magician's tricks. How did you know his skull was fractured? You didn't look at him down there."

"Why, no! As a matter of fact, I examined him yesterday. I took out a few of the top bricks and replaced them."

"Yesterday? You said nothing about it. *I* was here."

"No. I hoped to trap somebody, with that body as bait. I will explain why presently. By the way, M. Marle here saw me coming up from the cellar, but with his usual discretion he forbore to question me—"

I mumbled: "It slipped my mind. Damn!"

"Hold on a minute," Grafenstein continued, tenaciously. He muttered, nodding and running over something on his fingers. "Yes! You tell us that Laurent decided to ship the body back here. Well, that seems to be right; so he did. But you said Laurent killed Saligny 'in a hotel room' and shipped him back 'in a trunk.' Why," argued the doctor, "a hotel room? And why a trunk?"

"My dear Doctor," said Bencolin, a trifle impatiently, "I said only that this was his probable course of conduct; but please use your common sense. I find in a cellar a corpse with a fractured skull, in such a state of decomposition that death must have come over three weeks before. I have already indicated to you a few of the reasons why Laurent could not have killed Saligny in a place in Vienna very far removed from where Saligny was staying: he couldn't go through the streets lugging a corpse, and why should he? Wouldn't th simplest course be for him to go to Saligny's hotel? In his guise as Saligny, he could walk right into the hotel and up to Saligny's room without anybody suspecting him—one would naturally think he *was* Saligny. If anybody in the hotel saw them both, it wouldn't matter so long as they were not seen together. To kill him in Vienna was better than to do it in Paris where he was constantly surrounded by friends, and it would be difficult to find him alone. To send the body to Paris was better than to have it lying around Vienna to provoke a police investigation . . . *Eh bien!* You are stranded with a corpse in a hotel room; you can't burn or destroy it here, and if you send it to a false address in a trunk, or dismembered in parcels, you are going to provoke police investigation with a vengeance. Further, you are going to have them discover the head of Saligny, a man who isn't supposed to be dead, and who will be identified immediately—worse and worse! So you ship it to Paris in your luggage. Say you sent it in a hatbox, a paper parcel, or anything you like, but I submit that the simplest and most logical thing would be the dead man's trunk. Furthermore, Saligny was one of the few people in Europe with whom this would be possible; as I pointed out to you, *he enjoyed royal immunity from having his luggage searched*. I defy you to tell me any other way by which it could have been sent through the customs undetected. But the main reason, I think, why Laurent wanted to ship the body here—"

"Ah," interrupted Grafenstein, triumphantly, "now I have a poser for you! You made an outlandish statement that Laurent wished to have a joke about showing the corpse to Madame Louise when he brought her here on the wedding-night. It's a fanciful idea, and it fits with Laurent's type of mind, but what reason have you for supposing that?"

Bencolin adopted a patient air, not unmixed with mischief.

"Doctor, your thoroughness delights my heart. Look at it this way: Laurent has run terrific risks in bring the body back. His whole intent, we have reason to think, is to destroy utterly this evidence of an impersonation. He now has it back here, where he can safely dispose of it. A fire in the furnace, a vat of lye or sulphuric acid, would remove every trace by which he might be caught; here he could make preparations without suspicion, as he could not do in Vienna. Instead, he takes this corpse down to the wine-cellar and clumsily, almost negligently, secretes it in a hollow of the wall. When he walls it up he makes no attempt to hide the new brickwork. He puts in mortar so flimsily that I, with a trowel, could without exerting myself pull out the bricks; and, when M. Marle attacked it with a pick, three blows alone were enough to bring down the whole edifice. Clearly the arrangement was not permanent. Clearly, also, it was not a hasty move to get the body out of the way, for he had three weeks' time in which to destroy it. Then he had a purpose in keeping it there where he could get at it easily, had he not?—I cannot conceive any hypothesis to fit the facts except that he was using it as a character in his play of renaissance vengeance, the 'joke' he mentioned to Miss Grey. And that, I have reason to think, is the main reason why he brought it back to begin with."

Bencolin lit a cigar. He took a turn around the room and paused again before Grafenstein. "Right there, Doctor, is the essential difference between the mind of

Laurent and the mind of Laurent's murderer. You should have realized that this 'note' which Laurent sent to warn the false Saligny, sent to himself, was out of character. Laurent worked in the dark; his last wish would have been to advertise himself. He did not want to let Saligny know he planned to kill him. His only chance, and the only thing that gave him pleasure, was to steal up and strike without warning. . . . Whereas the *other* brain, the brain that planned Laurent's murder, was intent on advertising his cleverness to the world. He wanted to let the world see the pyrotechnic display without knowing the hand that sent up the rockets."

Grafenstein studied the assertion.

"But all this," he pointed out, waggling his hands, "proves nothing. It doesn't show how Laurent was killed. We saw an impossible thing happen up in the gaming-rooms. Don't ask me to believe in ghouls and werewolves and vampires; somebody killed Laurent—and they tell me—Vautrelle. I don't see how."

Bencolin stood at the table, head bowed, absently pulling the chain of the lamp off and on, so that the light flickered jumpily. He seemed to recollect that he was smoking in a room of death, and threw away his cigar. With a decisive motion Kilard rose from his chair in the dimness, and limped on his cane over to the coffin.

"I ought to forget," he said, "but I don't. Damn you!" he added, bitterly, and shook his fist at the dead face. "You didn't dare to face him, did you? You hit him from behind, like a common thug. . . . *He* wasn't afraid to die; you were the one who pretended. . . . I'd have killed you myself, if I'd known." The lawyer raised his skinny arms and let them fall. Then he turned to Bencolin. "I am beginning to think, monsieur. I—I want to thank you, in the name of the house of Saligny." He was biting his lips, this old vulture, and he was moving his head from side to side. "Zut! No sense to this! I am a little unnerved—I do not ordinarily—it means a great deal to me, you understand. . . . And I see now—the trowel! The trowel was his symbol. It was his seal, his signature—"

"M. Kilard," said Bencolin, softly, "are you sure?"

"Am I sure of what?"

"Remember the question I asked you yesterday, monsieur—did you find any trowel in the medicine-chest of Madame Kilard's bathroom?"

Kilard's eyes filmed; again you noticed that rustling dart, as of a rattlesnake. He said, "What—do you mean?"

"Madame Louise said she believed she saw Laurent in that bathroom. At the time, Laurent, posing as Saligny, was in the other room with M. Vautrelle. It could not have been Laurent she saw. Who was it?"

Grafenstein uttered a shout of triumph.

"I told you! I told you it was an hallucination—!"

"The hallucination, Doctor," said Bencolin turning his head, "did not make *us* imagine we saw a murder, did it? You do not believe we merely imagined we saw that bloody business in the card-room, a thing which happened under precisely similar circumstances?"

As though drawn, we had all come up slowly to that table of the lamp. I felt my heart turning over queerly inside me; a sense of rushing force and tensity, as though a car were hurtling to crash against a tree. We all stood round the table, and I could see my companions' faces lighted by the glow shining up on them against the circling dark. There was no sound; you could not even hear the clock. . . . Bencolin, one shoulder hunched higher than the other, arm stiff and fingers on the table, was looking at us over that shoulders, sideways. The pointed face was shadowed and lined harshly, the jaw very tight under its Satanic beard; again the hooked brows were drawn down over long gleaming eyes, as though he heard the salute of mighty battle fleets steaming to sea. . . .

Far away I heard Grafenstein's voice: "She—she told us she saw a man in that bathroom, dropping a trowel on the floor. If it was not an hallucination, what was it?"

"A deliberate lie," said Bencolin. Suddenly he crashed his fist down on the table. "Because Madame Louise killed Laurent and Vautrelle!"

XVIII. The Last Battle

For a long time nobody moved. Bencolin's eyes travelled slowly about our group. The walls seemed to recede, to grow larger and waver; my companions' motionless figures were distorted like shapes in water. The shock of that assertion was a physical blow against the brain. It numbed us, it left us bewildered and uncomprehending, but never did it occur to us to doubt him.

Kilard was the first to move away. He made a vague little gesture.

"Oh," he muttered in an absent way, and continued haltingly, "you mean—Madame Louise. Yes." It would have been silly had it not been so terrible. "You mean—Madame Louise. Yes."

Bencolin nodded.

"Oh," said Kilard, nodding in comprehension. "Yes, I see whom you mean. Yes, of course. . . ." He took a few steps, suddenly turned with a twisted face, and cried, "*O my God!*"

For the first time Bencolin dropped his eyes. He drew a long breath and began to pick up the papers on the table; Kilard put a nervous hand on his arm. "But," persisted the lawyer, "do you really mean it?"

"It's hard to believe," Grafenstein said, gruffly.

Bencolin spoke in sudden irritation, almost as though he, too, were strung with nervousness:

"What's the matter with you? Are you fools? or children? Brace up!" Then he quieted. "Almost from the beginning there was never any doubt in my mind that she was the killer. That was why I went to Versailles on the night Vautrelle was murdered, but, like a fool, I failed to prevent *that* because I was guarding the wrong person; I thought she would attack Miss Grey instead of Vautrelle. You will see why presently.

"In there"—he pointed to his brief-case—"I have records of all the purely court evidence which will send her to the guillotine. The ashes of her hashish cigarette on the floor of the card-room; the cigarette itself outside the window, its end smeared with her brand of lipstick. The silk fibres which Laurent's finger nail scratched from her stocking when he fell. The testimony of the taxi-driver who took her to Versailles the night Vautrelle was killed; the blood-stained cloak that was found in her room; her fingerprints on the handle of the knife with which he was stabbed. . . . But these were not the things which told me she was our killer. The real evidence was there, for you all to see. . . ."

Bencolin leaned across the table, and said, very softly: "Oh, you blind men, do you understand now why we found the body of Laurent in that grotesque kneeling position? Do you see the only way it would have been possible to induce him to kneel before his murderer? He was attending to the fastening of a lady's slipper."

I saw her as vividly as though she were there, I heard

again that voice of one who did not care; I seemed to see her lip curl in a sneer, and her haunted eyes with their film of dried and bitter tears. . . . But there were the contorted faces of Kilard and Grafenstein, jabbering, and I heard the doctor cry:

"Impossible! She was with us when—"

"Come with me," said Bencolin, quietly, "and I will show you."

No other word was said. How we got out of that house I do not remember; but I felt the cool of the night wind on my face, and heard Bencolin say, "Fenelli's," before I awoke to the consciousness that I was at the wheel of my car. That drive was a stormy, roaring race. Beside me Kilard sat hunched up, his strained face poked ahead in the light of the dash-lamps, tapping his stick nervously against the floor. He did not protest when we tore past traffic orders and skidded through the press of cars in a din of yells and banged fenders, with people scuttling before us like chickens in the yellow glare of the headlights. Presently we stopped in the gloom and far lights of the Avenue de Tokyo, and Bencolin led the way up to Fenelli's. . . .

Shriek of cornet, wail of sax, banging on kettle-drums—this blast greeted us through a sudden blinding glare of light when we pushed into the foyer. Spatter of applause, whir of electric fans, jagged talk floating up from a moving mass of people. The roof rocked to the echo of the noise; nothing is stable, but everyone runs about like the lights on the marble and gilt and red plush of the foyer. Marble columns, crimson and gilt everywhere; people pluck you by the arm, hammer on tables, cry for waiters. . . . Bencolin opened a lane through them, and we followed, up the stairs to the sedate old clock on the landing.

Here on the second floor the marble seems to shake under your feet with the din below, but people walk quietly along the red carpet, enter into *salon* or smoking-room just as they did two nights ago. . . . The palms have all been set right, and under them, on the long doors to the veranda, a young man is earnestly talking to a firm young woman, as they do. . . .

"Where is M. Fenelli?" Bencolin asked an attendant. He showed his tricoloured badge, and afterwards there was no hesitation.

"Upstairs, monsieur; but I do not think—"

We circled the next landing, where another attendant stood before the door to the upper regions. Again the tricoloured badge appeared. The door opened before us; as it closed, the noise downstairs was blotted away so suddenly that one's ears rang.

As we hesitated in the dimness of the pale Venetian lantern on the greenish tapestries, it was so quiet that we could hear Fenelli's voice from behind the door of the office. A thread of light lay under the sill. . . . Bencolin strode down ahead and threw the door open.

Fenelli had not quite time to close his safe. He was bending over it as we burst in; and clutching the edge of the desk, one hand partly lifted, was Madame Louise de Saligny. She had taken up a bronze paperweight, and her rounded arm shone in the light, tensely. Her eyes turned towards us, blank, frightening, from the contemplation of Fenelli's back. . . . I am not sure precisely what happened, for there were too many of us in that small office. There was a clang of the safe door, and a whir as Fenelli spun the dial. A packet fell on the floor and broke, spilling white powder; then it was ground under Fenelli's heel. Madame leaped toward Fenelli. As she leaped, Bencolin caught her arm and the bronze weight fell with a crash. Whether Fenelli was starting for Bencolin or madame nobody knew—perhaps not himself. All I know is that he said something in Italian and lunged towards them, his fingers opening and shutting; as he thudded against me, I knocked his knees out from under him and smashed down across the back of his neck with the rabbit punch.

It was all over in a moment, but it left us panting and unsteady. I found that I was backing away against Kilard, who had caught me by the arm and was peering over my shoulder. Fenelli lay in a sodden lump at our feet, his face against the carpet. Bencolin, still holding madame's arm, was looking down quietly at him; but madame had ceased to be interested. She was cool and exquisite. The teeth showed through her pink mouth in a smile. Quietly disengaging her hand from Bencolin's grasp, she smoothed the black hair, and in her dark eyes was mockery.

"What brawling!" she said.

"True," agreed Bencolin. He kicked Fenelli, and said: "Get up! You're not hurt. . . . May we have a few words with you, madame?"

No further reference was made to what had been going on in the room. Fenelli, breathing stertorously, still refused to raise his head from the floor; he shook his head with stubbornness, and his fingers dug in fury at the floor. . . . So Bencolin shrugged, bowed madame politely out the door, and motioned us to go. When we left the room he took the key and locked Fenelli in.

"I have a headache," said madame, touching her temple. "You—you wished to see me, you said?"

"We shall not trouble you long. Perhaps you wouldn't mind going to one of these rooms—?"

Did she suspect something? She gave Bencolin a sudden sideways look and murmured: "I do not care. All the gentlemen—?"

I was agitated, for I began to apologize profusely to her for what I had done in there, so that she and Bencolin exchanged a smile. If she suspected our errand, she was magnificently sporting; you saw no aftermath or reaction from the tigress cunning of the woman who was about to swing that bronze weight in the office, except a faint spot of red in her cheeks. . . . Whether by accident or design, Bencolin chose room number two, and again madame glanced at him. It was the same veiled look of suspicion she had directed at us two nights before.

Another of the orchid lamps—were all the rooms equipped with them, as at an hotel?—burned by a divan. Bencolin indicated it politely, and just as politely madame indicated a place for him to sit down beside her. . . . The rest of us stood in the outer shadow, watching those two in the circle of light, precisely as one might watch a vaudeville act. Kilard was nervously twisting his fingers.

"A cigarette, madame?" said Bencolin. When he proffered a case, I saw that in it were some of the hashish cigarettes such as we had seen that other night. . . .

A pause. Bencolin was still holding out the case. Abruptly there were tears in her eyes, trapped and hunted.

"We have discovered, madame," added Bencolin conversationally, "that you were being victimized in many ways. For instance, you were going to marry the wrong man—"

"I had better take one of them, hadn't I, then?" she asked, smiling wanly. She had taken that blow with no paling. "May I have a light?" By the line of her lips, by that wandering fierceness in her eyes, I knew that if he delayed long in lighting that cigarette we should have to deal with a madwoman.

"Madame may spill ashes, if she desires, on *this* rug," said Bencolin.

He said it with just the faintest deprecation. Her hand jerked. It was the most devilish kind of baiting; but she only opened her eyes a trifle wider, and suggested,

"I think you said—victimized? That is nice. I am glad you see it."

"Why, yes, victimized. For all the money you gave M. Vautrelle—two hundred thousand francs, was it not?—he scarcely played fair in using it to give tokens of his esteem to Miss Sharon Grey."

She closed her eyes.

"The handwriting on your cheques," explained Bencolin, "is—you will pardon me?—the same as this handwriting on the manuscript of M. Vautrelle's play, whereon you inscribed some discerning comments. I regret that one of the comments, '*Edouard, je t'aime, je t'aime!*' was not inspired by quite so much discernment. It naturally aroused your wrath when you learned from Mr. Golton that Miss Grey was his mis—"

Kilard cried, "Bencolin, for God's sake—!"

The detective turned his head and regarded Kilard

coolly, terribly.

"M. Kilard, let me remind you that I have my duty to perform. I hope I shall not have to order you out of this room. . . . Now, madame, as we were saying, you have been victimized by everybody. Even, I may add, by Fenelli; it must not have been pleasant to have to suffer his attentions for such a physically modest person as yourself—on this divan, was it not—?"

This inhuman stroke nearly smashed her. Still Bencolin had not changed his voice from its sympathetic calm, his smiling tenderness, but his eyebrows were raised a little over pendulous lids.

"Madame is naturally an optimist. Still, it is enough to change almost anyone's optimism to have all her ideals fall. For instance, she believed in M. Vautrelle and cherished him as her own dazzling gentleman. I do not know whether she had this confidence dispelled before he showed himself too cowardly to put through a plan which he devised—namely, the plan of killing the impostor downstairs—or afterwards, say, when he demonstrated that he did not care for madame. Possibly, when M. Vautrelle was urging madame to kill the impostor—in order, let us say, that you two might inherit the fortune and fly, as they have it in the cinema, to some tropic isle—I do not know whether M. Vautrelle artistically cited another play . . . 'Salomé.' "

She had let the cigarette go out. Her nerves were being unstrung, one by one. She sat back against the pillows under the orchid lamp, and the white bosom rose over the black lace bodice, and the pearls gleamed no whiter than her face. Thin black arch of eyebrows, cold black stones for eyes . . . yet you sensed that all the human sympathy, all the desire to be loved and to love, which had frozen inside her, was coming back now at the very moment she was being indicted. I think the mere fact that some one *knew* loosed this warm torrent, and that Bencolin had known it would. He sat smoothing his moustache, watching her; and suddenly he said:

"Would madame prefer that I tell her how it happened?"

Even then she drew herself up. "M. Vautrelle—was not cowardly!" (A frantic cry, that; a defiance against the gods, a stubborn refusal to have the last idol go.) "He—may have been—not faithful. Why, you know," she made a pathetic gesture, and tried to smile, "most any woman will forgive—that. But he was a genius! If he planned something, I know that *nobody*," proudly, "could beat him. For God's sake let me know that!"

"His plan for the murder," said Bencolin, "was sheer flimsy paper. I saw through it in half an hour."

Still he maintained that courteous surprise, as though he observed, "Could you think for one moment that Vautrelle would deceive anybody at all?" "Vautrelle was almost always mistaken." added Bencolin. "For example, you must have known he was mistaken when he affectionately advised you to take up drugs. How tender he was! It would soothe your nerves. In reality, madame"—his fingers closed on her wrist, but he still smiled—"it would stimulate you to murder."

I should not have liked to have those eyes of the detective watching me as they watched her.

"Very well, then. I will tell madame's story, if it be only to show her how stupid and theatrical was her friend M. Vautrelle.

"Here was she, wooed by the swashbuckling Saligny—drawn to him by a strange fascination she did not understand, in reality the image of her other husband—yet the one she actually loved was M. Vautrelle. Can she not understand? M. Vautrelle, the histrionic, half a poet, like Laurent; half an athlete, like Saligny—all a thoughtful and dignified person who was always tender, always advising her for her own good. She would read his plays and flatter his vanity: with her he could preen, for she worshipped him—"

A strange light, a sleepy reminiscence that was almost happiness, came into madame's eyes.

"She gave him much money. He was interested in selling her drugs, or seeing that she bought them here; but this money was—amorous profit."

The light vanished. She made a spasmodic movement.

"Vautrelle has discovered, as soon as the false Saligny returns, that this man is in reality Laurent. Laurent, too, has fed on drugs, but of a different kind. He has eaten the soothing opium, which gives him dreams. He fancies that he can deceive one of Raoul's friends, which, you will admit, is a ridiculous idea. I think he never deceived Vautrelle for one day. As to the rest—they would be fooled, because they did not know Saligny. . . . And now there rise the crosscurrents, the vanities and stupidities of man. Vautrelle, afflicted with another kind of dream, has *his* plan. The false Saligny shall die. If he dies after the wedding ceremony, madame, inheriting his fortune, will be most excellent prey for Vautrelle's aims to wealth. No, he must not die until after the ceremony. Similarly, it must never become known to the world that this false Saligny is an impostor, for then Vautrelle's chief aim, the money"—he glanced casually at her—"would not be forthcoming. So Vautrelle takes from a play he is writing the idea for a crime by which he fancies he can deceive—the police of Paris."

Bencolin looked over at us and pursed his lips in amusement. "Do I need to do more than call your attention to those lines from his play: 'I intend to kill this masquerader, and I defy any policeman in the world to tell how I did it. You see, the masquerader intends to kill somebody; and I feel justified in protecting—my best friend.' Ah, deft, that touch! He had told madame, and he was playing on madame. The masquerader intended to kill *her.* So Vautrelle, with his heroic gesture, has the character say, with emotion, 'My best friend.' And it was under that line, you remember, that madame, writing out in protest, put 'Edouard, I love you!'

"This, of course, has no place in our analysis except as a sidelight on the character of Vautrelle. Remember what I told you all, messieurs—his tendency to embroider. He could not help it. He could not help these gestures, even when they led him to outlandish statements and outlandish acts. He must have his grotesqueries, his curtain lines.

"Picture him fancying the way he is going to outwit both Laurent and the police, no less than the evil fortune which has made him the hanger-on of Fenelli's house. He is going to beat the world!—and he has to sway only this woman who loves him. But he must take few chances, too, he believes; if any blame falls, it must be on her."

I hated his deliberation, I ached—not, at that moment, with either pity for madame or interest in her as she sat blankly, wetting her lips—but with the recurring, "*How? How did it happen? How? . . .*" But Bencolin was fighting his battle with her, he was going to make her confess.

"Our groping through character becomes the night of the wedding. Here they are all downstairs, in this house. They enter, each behind his separate mask. Laurent is trying to play his part as Saligny; the others are trying to play their parts as his dutiful wife and his best friend. All so loving, these three! They come here at ten-fifteen—shall I invite you, madame, to go over the time-sheet we have prepared? Something here, madame, surely strikes your innocent mind as curious. Your husband stayed in the smoking-room until nearly eleven o'clock. Then he left the smoking-room, saying that he was going to play roulette. But he never went to the roulette-room, our time-sheet tells us! Between ten fifty-five, when he left the smoking-room, and eleven-thirty when he supposedly entered the card-room, *there is a gap of thirty-five minutes when he was not seen by anybody.* We know from our witnesses that he was not in the roulette-room, not downstairs, not in the lounging-rooms, not in the hall, not upstairs. There is only one place he could have been after he left the smoking-room—the card-room."

He spoke slowly, carefully, as though explaining something obvious to a dull-witted child. At last a change, an icy stare, was coming into madame's look; she fought it, she tried to get up, but, as she seemed about to let out a cry, Bencolin suddenly twisted her round to face his smile.

"And of course, madame, we know by our timesheets that you left Fenelli's room up on this floor at some time closely after ten-fifty. It is clear, then, that you must have met your husband in the hall. . . ."

She broke his grip. She leaped to her feet, and stood there, tottering, with her eyes fixed on us in a terrible appeal. . . . Then a slow sinking, a sneer, a quiet laugh, metamorphosed her from a wretched woman to a woman of proud and pitying calm.

"Oh, does it matter?" she asked, and shrugged and laughed. "Yes, I killed him. I admit it." Then she threw back her head, still laughing. "it's comical—you all look so funny! Won't somebody please open a window here? It's awfully hot. . . . Yes, I did it. I killed him. *I!*"

With a last defiant gesture, she sank down on the divan and faced us with a brimming smile.

XIX. THE HOUR OF TRIUMPH

Bencolin bowed, rising. As he turned, I could see sweat on his forehead; he gave no sign of it, but the end of the battle left a reaction on him. He went over into the shadows, and I heard a creak as he lowered one of the panes in the skylight. A cooler wind came in. Faintly you could hear from downstairs the sound of the orchestra playing a waltz.

"You had better talk," he suggested, gently, when he returned to the divan; "it will make you feel better."

She raised her head, and cried, dully, "Are you going to take me away?"

"I am afraid it will be necessary."

"Then I won't confess!—My God! I was crazy! I didn't know what I was saying! I don't care if you kill me, but I won't be shut up!"

"I should have been forced to arrest you whether you confessed or not, madame. It is possible, if you tell all about it, that the court may be inclined to leniency. That, of course, I cannot say."

"Don't you understand? It isn't—death. No. It's being an instant inside that hole!—They put you in with rats—!"

"I assure you, madame, that such an idea is pure fiction."

She seemed to meditate. Her beauty took on a defiance; with an effort she mustered all her self-command, and her panting breath came shorter. But she was still running her fingers along her throat, thoughtfully, with eyes fixed on some dim vision of the future.

Suddenly she said, "Very well. I am going to tell you. I still think you don't know how it happened, so understand this: I'm telling you of my own free will, and you'll understand I don't care, anyway. . . . Care? I was going to kill myself, anyway.

"Do you think I could feel any remorse for killing Laurent? Remorse? When I learned who he was," her finger tips touched her throat and grew tense, "why, I could have seen him torn into bits . . . !

"We came here that night, as you say. Edouard had given me his plan. I was only worried about one thing—I was afraid Laurent would touch me, and I would shiver, or give myself away, somehow. I had to endure him looking at me all that day; I had to stand up to the altar and marry him, swear to love him again—and see him watch me. And once I remembered when I had first married him, and I loved him—I was a simple little innocent!—but . . . I remembered that, and I thought, why—maybe I could stand that all over again. But then I saw Edouard, and I got courage again; I remembered how much he'd hurt me. And while I was looking at Laurent, I could imagine I saw the brown beard on his face again, and the spectacles—he was laughing like Raoul, too. I thought to myself, I thought—God! which is which? They are so alike; they change, one into the other, like horrible things you see in dreams. . . .

"So we came here that night. I hated Laurent even more, but I had to have something to nerve me to what I was going to do. I was afraid I might fail. There was all the noise, and the orchestra, and the sound in the gaming-room; and some of my friends came round to congratulate me, too. . . . Well, at a little before eleven o'clock I came upstairs here to get some of that stuff I smoke." She made a gesture of repulsion. "I was just as though I had been set on fire when I got it. It made me wild. I saw Laurent's face before me all the time: I mean, I saw Laurent looking like Raoul. I felt very cool and very strong. Every wrong multiplied; no, they didn't need to multiply, but I saw every wrong stand out, and I heard voices talking to me. The voices told me again just how to go on, just the way Edouard had said. Edouard was very careful.

" 'I am taking him to the smoking-room,' Edouard said. 'You wait on the stairs for him. When he comes out of there, meet him; but be sure there's nobody in the hall.'

"He left the smoking-room at eleven o'clock. . . . I can see it down there now, just as it was. The red carpet on the floor, nobody in the hall, the orchestra playing downstairs, and the clock striking eleven. Then Laurent walked out of the smoking-room. I said to myself, 'Be cool, now; don't let him suspect.' All the while I looked at him, when he laughed and walked to meet me, I could see Laurent's beard on his face.

" 'The card-room, Louise,' Edouard had said to me, and I was all prepared. When Edouard had first taken him to the smoking-room, I had gone to the card-room and taken down the big sword on the wall, and put it under the pillows. How I liked to feel its hilt, and run my hands along it! 'The card-room, Louise,' I could hear Edouard saying; 'nobody will be there tonight. And you must use the big sword, Louise—remember, the big sword!—and you must try to smash his head off, because, remember! if you don't disfigure his head, if you don't split his head wide open, they may examine him carefully, and see that he is not Saligny, Louise.' "

It was only then that I realized the significance of the murder being committed with that great blade. She was going to try to slash his face wide open, that the deception might never be discovered!—now the proud voice, sunk to a monotone, was talking faster and faster:

"As I told you, I heard the clock strike eleven when I saw him there in the hall. . . . I had smoked one of the cigarettes; it was eating my heart out, and I had lighted another. I heard a little buzzing in my head, but it was nothing. I was very cool and very strong.

"I led him into the card-room. I was all smiles and seductions, for I thought, 'I am doing this for Edouard, and I am going to avenge Raoul!' We went inside the card-room, and there was a red lamp burning there. He—ran his hand along my arm, slowly, and I looked right into his eyes; and—I could see that this man was burning—with passion—for me! And so we stood there, and I was almost fascinated by his look. I hated it, and yet I saw both of them there; both of these husbands of mine, the same flesh. He had no brown beard, but he had the brown, horrible eyes. Then he kissed me, standing in the card-room. It was a terrible thing, and I almost swooned from it; and in the middle of it I remembered that I had come to kill him, so that it gave me delight to be kissed thus, and return the kiss. I pressed him hard. I dropped my cigarette on the floor, and remembered it suddenly. 'Wait, Raoul,' I said, and smiled; 'I've dropped my cigarette.' When I picked it up I remembered that nothing like this must be left here. So I said, 'Raoul, will you open the window, so I can throw this out? There's no ash-tray.' He opened the window. . . ."

For a few moments she turned over the scene in her mind, and through the open skylight drifted the sound of the orchestra.

"We walked back to the divan, and he was drawing me down there where the sword was. I saw his hand go out. I heard the orchestra crashing into a song, I heard the croupier crying on the other side of the door, and people talking. . . . I was confused, and cold to the heart, and I felt such horrible strength in me that I could have strangled him—oh, terribly cold, and I saw his face through a mist. 'Raoul,' I said, 'the button on my slipper is unfastened. . . .' and I smiled at him, and put out my foot. I was leaning with my right hand touching the divan, and my foot out. As he bent over it, with his back to the divan, so that I was nearly sideways to him, I jumped aside. He was still kneeling there; I was blind, but I jerked out that sword and swung it as I would swing an ax. . . . I grew faint. It nearly threw me off my balance, and I almost stumbled, and I heard the orchestra crash into the final bars of 'Hallelujah.' And when I opened my eyes, his head was wabbling on the floor, and the blood had spurted almost across my stocking. . . .

"O God! I had thought to swing the sword right in his face, when he looked up at me, and split it in two. Instead I had chopped off his head—chopped it off clean, like an executioner. . . ."

The ivory face and the slow lips moving, the dark-clouded hair and eyes fixed . . . curiously enough, she had never seemed so alluring as in this moment of revelation; and I thought of those women of the renaissance, who derive a part of their very fascination from the poisoned cruelty of their beauty, and their moist lips whose charm blots out the dagger behind the back. 'I had thought to swing the sword right in his face and split it in two'—she said this with hypnotized explanation, without a tremor, looking at us in turn. And as she said it Kilard uttered a groan and put his face against the wall; and it seemed to me that Dr. Grafenstein was looking very pale. Madame contemplated them in wonder.

"Why—yes. But when it was over I grew very calm. I had to remember what Raoul had said; I had to remember how the plan was to go through. I had killed him. I had executed him, as he deserved, as he would have been executed at the guillotine. . . . But now I had to continue the plan. For, you see, messieurs, it would provide an alibi for both Edouard and me—both! They could not possibly accuse either of us. Once

I had killed him, Edouard said, *he* would take care of everything else.

"It was a little past eleven-fifteen. I looked out into the hall from the card-room door; there was nobody in sight. I came out. Nobody had seen us go in. . . . There was Edouard waiting for me. He was unstrung, but he said, 'Have you done it?' and I said, 'Don't look so pale, *chérie*; I have done it. . . .' " She began to laugh hysterically. " 'Isn't that a step on the stair?' he said, and I said, 'No, it's only the orchestra. Don't be a ninny.' Oh, it was so deserted, there in the hall. 'His head's on the floor,' and for a moment I thought Edouard was going to faint when I said it. 'Listen,' he said to me. 'I told you that when we got here I would pick out somebody for you to practise our deception on—it might be anybody, but I know who it's going to be—it's going to be that detective, Bencolin! He's out there in the roulette-room, with some friends. Now do just as I told you before I came here—do it *at eleven-thirty*. See that clock on the landing? It's nearly eleven-twenty. Keep an eye on your watch; and remember what you're to say at eleven-thirty. Go in now to Bencolin. Don't be uneasy." He said this to me! when he was nearly fainting himself. 'Did you leave any fingerprints?' he asked. I said, 'I don't know. . . ."

"So I came in and joined you gentlemen in the gaming-room. You see, we didn't know whom we were going to select; it had to be somebody sitting in that alcove, which is so far away from the gaming-room door which leads into the card-room. I joined you, you remember? At eleven-thirty Vautrelle came in, and with his back turned, sixty feet away from you, he walked through the door of the card-room. There was where you were fooled!" she cried. "It was the very idea of Laurent's deception which put it into Edouard's head; he said, 'What a way to kill Laurent! We will kill Laurent and get away with it in the same way Laurent killed Saligny!'—

"That was how it struck him—as real justice. Don't forget that Edouard has yellow hair, too, and that he's tall. He didn't need to look like Raoul, you see? All you gentlemen had to notice was some tall man walking through the door, for you were too far away to tell who it was. *I* said, 'There goes Raoul, now, into the card-room.' You were clever, yes, but you believed me . . . but the man who went in was really Edouard.

"Wasn't Edouard clever? He just walked through the card-room, pulling the bell-cord as he went, walked out the door into the hall, and then turned again through the door in the projection of the smoking-room which conceals the card-room from view of anybody at either end of the hall. Don't you know how it's arranged downstairs? That projection![1]—well, he went into the smoking-room. He told me that walking through the card-room took just twelve seconds. Twelve seconds, you see. So, when he came into the smoking-room again through the projection door, the detective had been on duty just for five minutes. At eleven-thirty and twelve seconds he went up to the detective and asked him the time—eleven-thirty."

She inclined her head proudly, like Bernhardt waiting for applause.

[1]See plan.

There was a silence. She had forgotten everything in what she considered was the cleverness of the feat, and she explained, lest we should not appreciate it:

"So, you see, both of us had an unshakable alibi; that was what Edouard wanted. He could prove we were both in places where we could not have committed the crime; I with you, he asking the time of somebody—he picked on your detective, monsieur! He had rung the bell himself, you see. He invented a story about Raoul having an appointment, and told the boy to take a tray of cocktails to the room when the bell was rung. Good! He rang the bell himself. Then the boy could go and discover the crime, and Edouard could prove that when Raoul entered the room he was out asking the time of somebody. He knew you would question the boy about the time, and he knew the boy would testify that the bell was rung at eleven-thirty. Neither of us knew that you gentlemen would help by noticing the time at which Raoul apparently entered the room—for it was neither Raoul nor Laurent who entered then. Isn't it droll? That was what appealed to Edouard."

"Help, madame?" asked Bencolin, quietly. "That was the mistake, that we should notice at what time the man entered the card-room. It proved an impossible situation."

"But we had alibis!" she said, with some pride. "We had alibis!"

"Which of you stole the keys from the pocket of the dead man?"

"Ah, I forgot to tell you that! I did. I had them in my

wrist-bag when I was talking to you. . . . Edouard told me to take them." She paused, and asked, uncertainly: "You knew about that, too?"

"Yes. I fancy that Vautrelle took the keys and went to Saligny's house that night. He wanted to be absolutely certain that the rest of the world never knew 'Saligny' was an impostor. He went through Saligny's desk upstairs and destroyed all papers—knowing, of course, that the impostor would likely have left behind damaging evidence of his imposture. Letters, a diary in Laurent's handwriting, or other suspicious material would surely be found when the attorneys went over the house."

She nodded listlessly. "Yes. He said he found some bank notes, but he had to leave them behind. Fancy Edouard leaving—!" Sudden bitterness flared up.

"Oh, but he did, madame. He wanted everybody to think that Saligny had destroyed his own papers; that was why he left the keys in the door of the study. He wanted us to think Saligny had left them there himself. Naturally, then, he couldn't steal the dead man's money. Yes, he left it. Where he erred was in throwing away the key to the wine-cellar. He wanted nobody to go prying there, but in reality it had the helpful effect of calling our attention directly to the wine-cellar. . . ."

Bencolin stared ahead of him for a moment, and then demanded:

"No matter! We were talking about his going through the card-room. The plan, then, hinged on finding reputable witnesses to swear to your separate alibis. You took us. Vautrelle humorously chose the detective at the end of the hall; otherwise, I suppose, he would have asked the time of the smoking-room steward. I imagine he would have asked the time of this steward just as the boy was preparing to carry out the cocktails at eleven-thirty . . . proving he was in the smoking-room." Bencolin paused. "Twelve seconds! Did he tell you anything else he did in there, madame?"

"What do you mean?"

"He bent over the dead man an instant, I fancy. That was where he got a little of the blood on his hand."

"What of that?"

Bencolin said, harshly: "You may be interested to know how jealous he was of the fact that the false Saligny was carrying on an affair with Miss Grey, who was upstairs. Vautrelle went up to terrify her, and smeared this blood on her hand, with one of his usual melodramatic speeches. The fool!"

She looked at him uncomprehendingly. When the significance of it penetrated her mind, she asked in a queer voice that hovered on the edge of mad laughter:

"You mean—you mean that even—even the—my first husband was interested—?"

"Yes. While he was kissing you in the card-room he had made a plan to go up and see her. Vautrelle anticipated him. I suppose Vautrelle had overheard him making the appointment during the wedding-day."

It was now slowly coming over her again what her position meant. But she only said, hesitantly, "Even—*Laurent* . . . !" and she made a tiny, empty gesture, moving her head from side to side, and suddenly she laughed.

"Yes!" she cried, passionately, "and tonight I would

have killed that wretched fat thing who owns this house. Do you blame me? See." She suddenly ripped open the front of her gown. Against the white breast were deep scratches, which the tearing of the bodice caused to bleed afresh. She pressed her hands to them, and her eyes glittered with tears when she turned to Bencolin. "*You* know of it; I suppose you recognized me when I was here yesterday. Don't you think I've had enough of being shamed?—I, forced to grovel, forced to go down on my knees because I must have—those cigarettes! Down on my knees! Tonight, when he opened that safe, I was going to take all he had. . . . Do you blame me? Isn't there anybody in the world who can understand what I've been through?"

This was no plea for mercy. It was the despairing cry of a woman who cannot be self-sufficient, yet finds nobody with whom the smallest confidence will not lead to disaster. She was proud; she sat there looking at us levelly . . . arrogant damnation that pierces the heart with pity.

Kilard said: "Bencolin, let her go . . . let her go! We're the only ones who know. Can't you—"

"Please," snapped the detective, "be quiet, everybody! Do you think I like to do what I'm doing?"

"I don't want your sympathy," madame cried, fighting those sobs, "and I don't want your damned sermons, either. Do you hear? I wouldn't take your sympathy. I'd know it was another trap of some kind."

Through the tensity, as she stared from one to the other of us, Bencolin's inexorable voice continued:

"I must ask you to tell us about Vautrelle."

She looked at him blankly, passing her hand over her

forehead.

"Oh . . . Edouard. Yes. I can't seem to recapture the mood I was in. No, it just doesn't seem to matter to me now . . . But it did then. That woman, that Sharon Grey, came up to see me the morning after Laurent had been killed. I had done all this—for Edouard, you see, because Edouard said he loved me. . . . But while Sharon was there, that horrible fat American came up, and he said—she was Edouard's mistress."

Abruptly the ferocity came back. "Well, why shouldn't I do what I did? I'd given Edouard all the money I had in the world. I'd done everything for him. Oh, he made such nice pretty love speeches—how he cared for me alone and how I was his inspiration to write his play, and how it would help me so much to take those drugs! . . . When the American said that, about Sharon's being Edouard's mistress, she was there. I didn't need to look at her. I knew it was true. So this American was babbling, and Sharon was getting pale and nervous—damned little prig! *I* was the one who gave!—and she was ashamed of herself. I was the one who gave, with all I had in heart and soul! So I was giving Edouard money, and Edouard was giving that money to support her. And at Edouard's order I had killed a man. I—I don't know how you can do more. . . .

"But did he care for me? No, he was in love with this nice white simpering creature, who liked to be so virtuous! Oh yes, she did. What does she know about how much a woman can love?—a woman like me. Look at me! Quiet, you say; quiet, and repressed, and dignified, and—O God, I turned to fire whenever

Edouard came near me—!"

She had stretched out her arms towards the dusky skylight. She was unearthly, terrifying, with her teeth fastened in her lower lip, and her eyes brimming over.

"Do you blame me? Do you? I can see straight through it now; I know what he was doing; but then—when I first heard that—it nearly broke me in pieces. I couldn't stand it. . . . When all of you came in to talk to me, that afternoon, I thought I'd given myself away because I burst out against Edouard; I couldn't help it. Did you know?"

Bencolin, staring at the orchid lamp, said in a low voice:

"I was warned, madame. But I made a mistake. I thought your—your anger would be directed against Miss Grey."

"I deceived you all I could," she went on, ramblingly, "but I didn't care. I didn't care what you knew. All I could think of was Edouard kissing this nice pale Englishwoman. . . .

"I phoned to him. I wanted to hear him deny it. If he'd denied it, I think I would have believed him. But, no, he couldn't come to see me, 'dearest,' 'heart of his heart'—it sickened me when I heard him say all that. He had an important business engagement that night. Business engagement!—*I* knew where he was going."

She leaned forward; she partly rose from the couch, with a hypnotized stare that took her back to that night, and her voice sank to a crooning. Behind her, shoulder humped, bearded chin in hand, I could see Bencolin watching with tense and glittering eyes . . .

". . . I had a knife there in the house—a big one.

Raoul had given it to me as a souvenir of a hunting-trip. I didn't care who saw me. All I wanted to do was repay Edouard for what he'd done. I smoked, you see—here's one of the cigarettes—and when I smoke one of those—I don't know why—I am capable of anything. I took a taxi. I came up to the villa by the back gate, and when I came in by the back gate, he was standing there." Her arm flashed up and over. "I struck him. I hacked him—I was bathed in his blood; I liked that!"

She stood there in triumph, ecstatic with head thrown back, while the sound of the orchestra floated through the skylight, and Bencolin sat motionless on the divan, staring at the lamp. She had kept her appointments with three men; she would have murdered them all.

MYSTERIES
By Mary Roberts Rinehart

THE CIRCULAR STAIRCASE (1723, $3.50)
Rachel Innes became convinced that her summer house was haunted, and the explosion of a revolver along with a body at the bottom of the circular staircase ensured she would have many sleepless nights. She had acquired a taste for sleuthing and her niece and nephew were prime suspects in the murder.

THE HAUNTED LADY (1685, $3.50)
When wealthy Eliza Fairbanks claimed to have found bats in her bedroom and arsenic on her strawberries, Miss Pinkerton was promptly assigned the case. But apparently someone else was watching too. For the old lady's worries were over, but so was her life.

THE SWIMMING POOL (1686, $3.50)
With a deadline to meet on her detective story, Lois had no patience with her sister's strange behavior. Except the mystery Lois was writing was not nearly as deadly as the mystery about to unfold. For ravishing, willful Judith was about to disappear from her locked bedroom, and a woman's body would be found in the crystal blue depths of the Swimming Pool.

LOST ECSTASY (1791, $3.50)
When Tom was arrested for a not-so-ordinary murder, Kay's life turned upside down. She was willing to put her own life in danger to help Tom prove himself, and to save him from those out to silence him or those after revenge.

MISS PINKERTON (1847, $3.50)
Old Miss Juliet had endured quite a shock when her nephew committed suicide and her nurse, Hilda Adams, was determined to keep an eye on her. But the old lady wasn't as frail as she looked, and Hilda wasn't sure if she had murder or suicide on her hands.